# The Cottage Industry

by

Edward McSweegan

**The Cottage Industry**

Cover Art by *The Wild Rose Press, Inc.*

The Wild Rose Press, Inc.
PO Box 708
Adams Basin, NY 14410-0708
Visit us at www.thewildrosepress.com

Publishing History
First Edition, 2024
Trade Paperback ISBN 978-1-5092-5431-6
Digital ISBN 978-1-5092-5432-3


Published in the United States of America

## Dedication

To my editor, Nan Swanson, who helped me gain a foothold in the publishing world, and to my mentor and fellow writer, Susan Moger, and to the many early readers of this story in the Monday Night Critique Group and the creative writing classes at Anne Arundel Community College in Maryland. Thank you all.

The time is not far off when the last remaining open area on Connecticut's shoreline is usurped for some private purpose."

*~Governor John Dempsey, 1961*

"In the Infantry a man breaks down through an explosion or otherwise and develops the thing suddenly, but in the Flying Corps they get more and more nervous until somebody sends them on leave or until they crash."

*~F.A. Hampton, RAF Medical Officer, 1922*

Chapter 1

He came in low, skimming the tops of tree branches dappled with early spring buds. Farther below, the ground was a blur of leafy brown debris and green mossy rock. He pulled up as he approached the riverbank. The sun warmed his stubbled face, and the rush of the wind pulled at his brown hair. Downstream, small sailboats tacked back and forth along the course of the still-chilly river. He pulled the stick back and rolled to the left, upriver from the bridge. An expensive powerboat turned in tight circles, churning the green surface and sending rooster tails of cold water into the morning air. He dropped back toward the ground, straightened the rudder bar, and roared through a tight gauntlet of bare-armed trees and glacial boulders. The narrow band of riverbank forest gave way to plowed farm fields and unpaved roads. He felt the engine revs drop; he lurched forward in his seat. Jerking to the right, he hit his head on the windowsill. He opened his eyes.

*Dammit. Dreaming again. Anyone watching?*

He relaxed his hands and glanced around the compartment as the train's engine continued to slow. Diagonally across from his window seat, a young woman in a long blue motoring coat and a velvety black cloche hat stared at him. She gave him an apologetic smile and turned back to the young child sitting beside her.

David Enders rubbed his chin and mouth, hoping he

1

had made no odd sounds to annoy the other passengers. The woman across from him did not seem alarmed, so hopefully he had not been a sleeping spectacle of wild gestures or animal noises.

The train crept toward the Milford rail station. Enders looked across the car to the opposite windows. Lauralton Hall, the girl's Catholic prep school, rolled past the cracked windowpane. Then he saw the station's southbound platform slide by and felt the sudden friction of steel wheels biting steel rails. The train lurched to a stop. The air brakes hissed as a uniformed conductor belatedly announced, "Milford Station. Milford, Connecticut."

Beyond the platform, Enders could see a row of trees, a barren field, and across an oiled road, the white outlines of a large wooden building.

*Home again, home again.* He sighed and stood.

He pulled a small leather-strapped trunk off the overhead luggage rack and swung a canvas-and-leather rucksack over his right shoulder. Two passengers squeezed past him as they hurried to the exit. Enders turned to follow them but stopped to let the woman and her child get up and make their way to the car's exit. With the child clutched in one arm and a large suitcase and purse in the other, she moved to the end of the car and stopped before a monstrous wicker-and-steel stroller in the luggage alcove. She stood for a second, contemplating the bulky contraption.

"Need some help?" Enders came up behind her.

She smiled at him. "Oh, I'm afraid I do. I can't wait until he's old enough to walk."

"Well, then you'll be chasing after him, wishing you could toss him back in a stroller." He inclined his head toward the door. "Go ahead. I'll pull this out behind you."

He followed her out, banging the stroller across the gap between the train and the wooden platform. He pulled it beside her and she settled the child in the stroller. The tiny boy smiled at Enders.

"Thank you." She stared at Enders' sheepskin jacket, the smooth diagonal scar on his neck, the alpine pack, and the French stenciling on his trunk. She seemed like she wanted to say something more, but then Enders said, "You're quite welcome," and turned away.

He got two steps across the platform before she asked his back, "You were over there? In the war?"

Enders hesitated. "Yes. Not in the trenches."

He wanted to keep walking, but she stopped him again. "Do you…dream about it?" In a gush of words meant to hold him still, she said, "My husband. He has terrible dreams. All the time. It's been three years; I don't think he's had a restful night's sleep since he came home. Nightmares… He won't tell me any of it."

He wanted to put her off. Tell her to find a doctor. Or a priest. But the look of pain and desperation on her face held him. He searched the platform. The passengers had dispersed. He glanced toward the graveled parking lot, once full of horses and carriages and delivery wagons, and wondered where her troubled husband might be. Was he meeting her at the station?

Enders took a step in her direction.

"Do you have nightmares too? You were dreaming on the train. I thought you were."

"It was just a daydream." Enders put his trunk down and ran his fingers through his hair. He let out a loud exhalation of air and frustration. He wanted to be on his way. Other confrontations and difficult discussions awaited him. Enders stared at the woman again. She was young. Pretty. Looking as stylish as a new mother could manage in a small Connecticut town. He put out his hand as if to begin some public declaration, but then let his arm flop back to his side. There were no passengers or interlopers on hand to rescue him from this woman's private anguish.

Finally, he said, "Listen. Your husband...he can't tell you what he saw over there. Or what he might have had to do there. He doesn't want you to have nightmares too. Or maybe think less of him for what he did or didn't do." He paused, remembering his own damaged, drunken self and the clinic in Lyon.

"I wish he'd talk. For both our sakes."

He stared at the platform planks. "Does your husband have a friend or neighbor in town who was in the war too? Someone he might talk to?"

"Yes, perhaps. But he doesn't talk about any of it. Not with anyone, as far as I know."

Enders waved a dismissive hand at her. "Get him, your husband, and someone else who was there. He won't feel like he's on the spot if there's someone else there too. Get them in a room with someone they know. Someone they trust. An old teacher, a former coach, a priest, if nothing better. Someone older. Wiser. With some authority. Someone who can ask them questions. Get them talking. And keep them talking. That's key—keep them talking. Keep them moving forward. With luck, something'll come out. There may be some crying. Recriminations. Guilt. Maybe screaming. Like lancing a boil, it'll hurt. And then it might be over. Some of it, anyway."

They stared at each other for several seconds. The woman asked, "Did you do that too? This talking? A kind of cure?"

*Who is she to be asking me these things?* But he said, "Yes. A version of it, back in France."

"And did it work?" she asked with a hopeful look in her wide, gray eyes.

Enders smiled, remembering the woman in Lyon. "Yeah." He nodded more to himself. "It did help. I sleep through the night. And sometimes on the train."

"Well, thank you. I'm so sorry if you think me rude for asking such personal…"

"It's fine. I understand your wanting to ask. It's hard on everyone. The fellas who were there and the people who weren't but want to help."

He stepped away and dropped down the wide staircase to the parking lot. A taxi pulled away. A Ford touring car with a crumpled front right fender and its canvas top set back rolled into the lot and stopped near the stairs. The driver honked the horn and Enders turned to see him wave at the woman on the platform. The driver, a thin man in a loose suit and striped tie, jumped out, waved again, and hurried up the stairs. Enders noticed a slight limp on his left leg. He turned away and cut across the lot and into the line of trees.

*Ah, shelter among the trees.*

He let a hand slap against the rough bark of a giant oak. He stopped and stared up its length to a distant rib-works of massive limbs and arching branches. Zigzagging through the trees, he stepped among small green ferns and inhaled the dampness of the springtime woods.

At the edge of the woods, he confronted a muddy

brown field. No Man's Land.

He hesitated, as much from the open, muddy field as from his destination on the opposite side of it. He picked his way along the edge of the churned-up land, skipping over puddles of clay-colored water until he reached the road. Then he hiked back along the length of the field and crossed the road to a hard-packed lot. Before him stood the white building with a red-and-black sign: Enders Hardware & Lumber.

He stopped before the open, double-wide doors and the broad porch decorated with rakes and brooms and other implements of daily labor. A saddled horse was tied under the maple to the right. A dirty Ford truck with a stack of lumber hanging off its bed was parked to the left. He heard the whine of the lumberyard's circular saw spinning behind the building. Muffled voices emerged from the store's interior. He took a deep breath and filed up the two broad steps and set his luggage beside the open doorways.

The interior was dim. The dusty front windows diffused the April light. He smelled oil and wax, and fresh sawdust. A man in tweeds and a canvas hunting jacket nodded at him as he left the store clutching a bag of nails and a new pair of work gloves. Deeper in the store, an old man in a white shirt and a black bib apron stood rearranging tins of turpentine. He saw Enders standing in the main aisle.

"Well, well, well. Look what the cat drug in."

"Hello, Mr. Sullivan. How are you?"

Sullivan stepped to him and put his hands on Enders' shoulders. "You're lookin' fit. Better'n most. Where you been now? The war's over, you know."

"Yeah, I heard. The Huns left a helluva mess. I stuck

around to help clean up."

"That so? Broom and dustpan work, huh? Well, your ma, she's been worried about you. Worried for years."

"She does worry. If worrying was a paying job, she'd be a millionaire. So, how's the business?" Enders glanced around at the stocked shelves and the pallets of seed and fertilizer.

Mr. Sullivan dropped his hands and said, "We're busy. Can't complain. People are buying and building. Economy's chugging along like the New Haven Rail. Handsome Harding's doing a fine job of it."

"I'm sure the boss will have found something to complain about. Where is he?"

Sullivan inclined his head. "Back office."

"Guess I'd better start there. Thanks." He stepped past the old man, but stopped again to ask, "Still got all your fingers?"

"All eight of them." Snorting, Mr. Sullivan held up his hands to show off ten dirty fingers. "I keep my glasses on and my hands off that saw. The sawmill business is for agile men. Like you."

Enders flashed his own ten fingers in reply and walked to the back of the store. Behind the broad customer counter was a small office closed off by a Dutch door and brightened from the back of the building by pebbled-glass windows. He pushed the door open.

Inside, a gray-haired man in suspenders and a checkered flannel shirt sat hunched before a rolltop desk, making notations on a blotter calendar. He looked up. Long seconds crept by. The man said, "Your brother telephoned. Said you'd be on the morning train."

"Hello, Dad."

Enders' father tilted back in the wooden office chair and said, "War's been over a long time now."

"Yeah, everyone keeps reminding me."

"Here you show up three years afterwards looking like a fella in need of a shave, a haircut, and a job. Your mother's been expecting some polished-up, Frenchified officer. She'll be disappointed."

"No, she won't. Where is she?"

His father pointed toward the ceiling. "Your sister's there too. What part of her's still awake and aware, that is."

Enders flinched inwardly. "Well, I guess I'll go and tell Mom I'm back." He turned on his heels, closing the office door behind him. The impulse to slam the door had passed before he was aware of it. He walked back through the storefront and stopped by Mr. Sullivan. "Well, it's about what I expected. Same old man."

Sullivan looked at him and touched Enders lightly on the shoulder. "People don't change much, son."

Enders worked on a smile. "And I'm glad some of them don't. I'll see you tomorrow, Mr. Sullivan." He waved and walked back out to the porch to retrieve his luggage.

Outside, he picked up his gear and stood for a moment, looking past the field and the treeline to the train station.

It was where he had left from, years before. Eagerly left from. Leaving behind a father who could never be satisfied with his eldest son's efforts or interests. Leaving behind a business and a life he did not want to be a part of. Leaving behind a town, which had grown smaller as he had grown larger, and needing a larger space in which to stretch and explore.

Now he was home again, from a world war, a pandemic, a bitter and tenuous peace, and a personal crisis that had eaten away years of his young life. The station was there, waiting for passengers. Waiting for him. But where would he go? His purpose had ended with the war. Wasn't he home again to find a new purpose? Maybe he was home again simply because it was home.

He hopped down the steps and marched around the building. In the back lot were two roofed, open sheds for stacking cut lumber and a long open-air building that housed a gasoline-powered circular saw. A line of trees divided the back lot from another field and a cluster of houses in the distance. Enders climbed onto the back porch and mounted a set of wooden stairs leading to a second-floor porch and the kitchen door.

He slipped through the doorway. Inside, he caught the aroma of freshly baked bread. *I'm gonna miss France with every passing meal. Every passing day.*

He called out. "Mom. Mom. I'm back." He lowered his luggage to the floor.

A tall woman with salt-and-pepper hair appeared from a connecting hallway. She dropped the small white towel she had been holding. "Oh, my God. Finally." She ran to him and threw her arms around his neck. She buried her face in his jacket and clung to him.

Enders hugged her. "It's okay, Mom. I'm home. A bit late, but I'm here."

She lifted her head. Her eyes were watery and rivulets of salty tears crept down her uneven cheeks. Meredith Enders looked at her son's unshaven face and his tired brown eyes. "You're taller…"

"No," he said, smiling and shaking his head.

"And heavier. All that French food," she said. "Look at you." She saw the scar on the left side of his neck. "Oh, dear God, what's this? You were shot? Burned? You never said anything in your letters."

"There was a war on, Mom. People got hurt. This is nothing." He touched the shiny, smooth reminder with his fingertips and blinked away the memory of his razor-thin luck.

She wiped her eyes with the backs of her hands. "Yes. So many men came home… Well, you're home. And safe. You're staying here? Not running back to the city with Donald? In that awful village neighborhood?"

"I'm staying, Mom. My room still available, or is there some day-boarder picking through my stuff?"

"It's as you left it. Though your brother comes out often enough to rattle the place."

"Carole? How's she doing?"

His mother looked like she might start to cry again. Instead, she glanced down the hall toward the bedrooms. "It's as if God hates her. She got the influenza in 1919. I wrote you. Just for five days. Then she was fine. Up and around and as busy as ever. She got the flu again this February. She seemed fine again. But in March, late March, she got tired one day. Went to bed. She's been there ever since. Like one of those cartoon zombies."

Enders nodded. "I got your telegram just before I left."

"We're gonna take her to Yale-New Haven in a few days. There's a specialist." She took his hand. "Well, come see her. She might wake long enough to recognize you."

He let her guide him down the hallway, watching the blue-and-white checkered pattern of her house dress and listening to the light tapping of her heeled shoes on the hardwood flooring.

At the doorway to his sister's bedroom, he hesitated. His mother's hand slipped away.

He had a flash memory of a young nurse with an Alsace accent who had led him through a temporary ward of heavily bandaged men who smelled of burned meat and iodine, their individual agonies silenced by morphine drips. She led him outside, under a covered walkway, to a second ward of men with stumps and shot-away faces, most of whom were silent and wide-eyed with the fear of having to go on living. In the third connecting ward, he found his Belgian mechanic among a gaggle of influenza cases, shell-shocked trenchers, and lightly wounded soldiers.

A stray shell had landed near the aerodrome, igniting a stack of methanol tins. The nurse told Enders the man had first-degree burns from the alcohol flashover and a concussion from the exploding shell. Enders pulled him off the cot and said, "We're leaving," and forced his way through a barred side door with the grateful mechanic in tow.

He wanted to escape again, but his mother beckoned him to his sister's bedside.

"She's so thin," said Enders, standing near the campaign bed. Her face had a blank, slack look as if her facial muscles all had been anesthetized. Her hair was combed and pinned back. She wore a familiar tartan nightgown.

"It's a chore to feed her. And to get her to the toilet. And to rotate her against bedsores."

"Yeah." He crept closer, finally sitting on the edge of the bed. He took hold of his sister's bony hand.

"Carole. It's me. David. I'm home from the war."

Carole's head moved on the pillow. He could see her eyes moving behind shuttered eyelids. They fluttered to a sudden stop. Her fingers twitched.

He placed his sister's hand on top of the bedspread. *This isn't the giggling little girl on the backyard swing I remember. Christ.*

"They say it's like a kind of sleeping sickness," his mother said. She placed her palm on the pale forehead of her daughter.

"What are they calling it? You mentioned it in the cable. Lethargy…"

Meredith stepped to a bookshelf and picked up a thick file folder. She slowly read the words scrawled on the file face. "Encephalitis lethargica. Sounds like church Latin." She handed him the file and Enders opened it and flipped through a stack of newspaper clippings, doctors' notes, and a 1919 issue of *The Journal of the American Medical Association.*

He looked at his mother. She said, "I got the *Journal* magazine from Dr. Fairfield. It talks about a dozen different cases of this influenza sleeping thing. Maybe you can make more sense of that article than I can."

"Not likely." He looked back at his sister. *What the hell? I got the old man downstairs, a comatose sister upstairs. Donny running wild in the Village. Mom.* He turned to look at his mother.

She said, "I know. It's a lot to take in. Come along. Unpack. I'll fix lunch shortly. We'll see what tomorrow brings. Okay?" She took his hand. "It's good to have you home."

****

There was little to unpack. Enders dumped the

contents of his alpine pack on his brother's bed. In less than a minute, he put away a change of clothes, some toiletries, a small bundle of letters, and three books. He tossed the empty pack into the room's shallow closet. His small trunk sat on his own bed, and he unbuckled the two leather straps and opened it. He took out another book, some maps, a stack of photographs, and a square, glass-fronted case of stained wood. He left everything else in the trunk and slid it under his bed.

His mother breezed in and hugged him from behind. "I'm going to feed your sister some soup and get her cleaned up. Then we'll eat."

Her son turned to look at her. "Do you need help? I can…"

"No. I have it worked out now. It's no trouble. Just slow." She saw the case on top of the dresser and picked it up. "What's all this? Medals and ribbons."

"My lieutenant's bars, my *Armée de l'Air* wings, Air Service patch, the French roundel, *la croix de guerre, la médaille militaire,* and *la médaille des blessés de guerre* for not getting killed."

"It's nice. Your French sounds so good."

"Mom, I dream in French. It's all I spoke for years."

"Well, I suppose you'll stop with everyone speaking English here." She placed the case carefully on the dresser but seemed reluctant to let go of it. "You'll have to tell me sometime about the flying over there. It must have been frightening with the Germans trying to shoot you all the time."

"It was worse being on the ground. In the trenches."

She said, "It's over now. There's peace again." She looked at her son, who, in some indefinable way, may have seemed almost a stranger. Here and now, his quiet solidity maybe obscured her older, familiar image of a hyperactive high school boy wanting to catch a ride on a flying machine. "Well, lunch soon. You can set the table if you're done unpacking." She looked around the room. "Three years. You didn't bring much home."

"I was traveling light. You got my gifts?"

"Yes, thank you. There's nothing like receiving things from overseas. The Swiss clock is in the parlor. Did you see it? Have you even walked around the house yet?"

****

David set the table. Done with that familiar task, he sat at the far end of the polished trestle table, watching his mother fuss about the kitchen and laying out a covered kettle of vegetable soup, cold sliced ham, and still-warm bread. Coffee percolated on the stovetop. A cherry pie had appeared magically at the end of the counter.

He was leafing through his mother's file of medical reports and newspaper clippings when he heard the dining room pocket door slide open and shut. His father appeared in the doorway and glanced at the wall clock.

Meredith Enders looked up from the sink. "Right on time, Fred."

Fred Enders brushed his hands across his pant legs and sat at the opposite end of the table. He looked at David looking through the file of encephalitis lethargica articles. He asked, "You become a doctor over there in France? Been away long enough to have done medical school."

"Nope." David leaned back in his chair ignoring the jab about his long absence. "Just curious about what's happened to Carole and a million other people. Flu one minute and coma the next. Doctors can cure diabetes, but they can't wake up Carole. It's a mystery. And a tragedy."

Meredith sat. "Let's eat now. David, do you need anything?"

He chuckled. "A chilled glass of Petit Chablis?"

"You're years too late for that too. Unless you're ready to break the law," his father said.

Slicing a piece of ham, David said, "Already broke the law with Donny in Greenwich Village this weekend. They must have more back-alley bars and speakeasies than apartments or legit businesses. Nice of the government to give everyone time to prep. He told me some private New York clubs stockpiled enough liquor and champagne to last for years."

"Well, there's no sense in getting arrested. You've only been back in the country a few days," said his mother.

Fred Enders said, "Little chance of gettin' arrested anyhow. Harding let Debs out of prison. He's been freeing all kinds of Reds and radicals. Meanwhile, bombs are going off on Wall Street. Hundreds injured and no one's been arrested. Police don't seem so inclined to arrest kids for having a beer. Or doin' much else."

"You can't lock up people just because their opinions conflict with the Espionage or Sedition Acts. Seems like Wilson was trying to make the world safe *for* democracy and the U.S. of A. safe *from* democracy. Harding's a relief in that regard," said David.

"I think that's enough politics for the table," said Meredith.

His father grunted, smiled, and said, "Your mother's just got the vote. Now she's making speeches. Be running for office soon enough." He looked at David. "So, you wantin' a job or you got something lined up yet?"

*Hell, no. You've been my boss for too long.* In response, David pulled a folded newspaper advertisement from his shirt pocket. "Yeah, I might have something." He unfolded the *New York Times* ad and said, "There's a real estate company in Saybrook. They're buying up shoreline farms and building summer cottages. Might just be seasonal work, but I thought I'd take the train over and see what's what. I still know my way around a hammer and saw."

"Wouldn't you prefer a pleasant office or indoor job like your brother?" asked his mother. "He says he's making lots of money."

"Let's hope it's real money," said his father. "He quit the bank—where the money is real—to sell bonds, which, as far as I can see, is just the promise of money somewhere down the road. A bird in the hand, you know?" Fred Enders looked at his open palm propped above the dining table.

"David, you know how to fly. You might want to look at the government's new Postal Air Service," said his mother. "They need pilots."

"Yeah Mom, I heard about it. Flying decommissioned Jennys and De Havillands. Problem is most of their pilots are dead from crashes. I didn't survive the *Boche* just to get killed delivering postcards and packages to Boston. I'm grounded."

****

In the afternoon, Enders strolled into his hometown to see what might have changed and who might still be around after the Great War, and the influenza pandemic.

The town had grown with wartime spending but still felt small and insignificant compared to the cities and towns he knew in Europe—even after some of them had been blasted to rubble. He stood on a street corner looking at the shops and their overhead apartments and wondered if any army would bother to train its artillery on the town of Milford.

He waved to familiar faces, stopped to talk to people who knew his parents, and dodged a sudden flood of grammar school kids released from their school. Pressed against a shop window by the tide of energized children, he stared at a display of two-dollar crystal radio sets for sale. A poster beside the sets declared, "Listen to music and news at home. For free!"

"Then why go out?" he asked the sales poster.

He followed the wash of children up the street. At another street corner, he ran into a fellow high schooler who had survived the war by staying far behind the trenches fixing damaged army trucks and staff cars. Now he made a quiet living as a mechanic and gasoline station attendant. He directed Enders two streets over to another acquaintance who had converted the family's garage into a beer hall. Curious, and thirsty, he headed toward this convenient small-town speakeasy.

The old garage, once a carriage house, had not been painted since before the war. The two windows facing the street were papered over. An old sliding door was shut but a brass peephole had been added to its wrapped face. A shadow on the other side of the peephole slid the door open in response to Ender's fist.

Inside, a dozen people stood or sat drinking beer and what looked like gin-and-soda. Two men played checkers. At the back of the room, a poorly built bar supported a beer keg, a collection of mismatched glasses, and two bottles.

The bartender looked up from an ongoing conversation and shouted, "Dave Enders. Back from the dead! Hey, you know the war ended in '18?"

Enders reached the bar and said, "Really, Bobby? Guess that's why it's been so quiet lately."

"Always the funny egg."

The man with whom Bobby had been talking turned to Enders. "Hey, stranger."

"Brian Lonergan. How's tricks?"

The two men hugged. Enders stepped back to look Lonergan up and down. "Haven't changed. Mom said you went to San Fran. Out there hiding from the war in some Chinaman's opium den?"

"Yeah, but they found me. Spent the war typing Wilson's propaganda at Fort Dix."

"Well, you said you wanted to be a writer."

"Not what I had…"

Bobby interjected to say, "Hey, this is a bar…" He put a finger to his lips and glanced around the garage as if fearing eavesdroppers. "You want to gossip over tea and cookies? Go in the house and talk to my ma."

"Pretty crappy bar," said Brian, looking around.

"Pretty crappy barkeep," said Enders. He looked to his left. "What's in the keg?"

"Beer, of course."

Enders held up two fingers.

Bobby poured out two glasses and set them on the bar. "Oh, did I mention we're collecting money for the church? They're in need of new hymnals and me sainted Ma is organizing the fund drive. There's a jar set on the wall there for *voluntary* donations." He held onto the two glasses of beer.

Enders saw the jar and said, "Ah, of course. Happy to donate to a worthy cause." He dropped some coins in a slot cut in the top of the tin-capped jar. Bobby waved his hand to encourage another donation and Enders dropped in another nickel.

"May the saints bless you for supportin' the church so charitably," said Bobby.

"So, I can't *buy* a beer, but I can donate to the church?" he asked.

"'Tis a messed-up country with a messed-up set of moralizing laws, which we'll have to foxtrot around," said Brian. He picked up one of the beer glasses and said, "To Prohibition."

Enders swallowed a mouthful of his beer. "Not bad. A bit yeasty. Kinda flat."

****

Bobby's covert bar got busier. Enders and Brian Lonergan moved to a table to drink gin and tonics chilled with icehouse chunks of ice.

Lonergan asked, "Hey, you read anything by this guy Scott Fitzgerald? Short story writer. Kind of become the beat reporter for the Jazz Age.

"Oh, good. It's not over. The Jazz Age, that is. I'd like to meet a few more flappers before everyone comes to their senses."

"That's the kind of stuff I'd like to write. Interesting scenes, interesting people. Not local baseball scores and filler pieces for the *New Haven Register*."

"If he wasn't writing in French, I missed him. Was he in France? In the war?

Lonergan shrugged. "Remember Miss Michener, the French teacher? Quite the Sheba back in the day.

She'd be impressed with you now, Davey-boy. Practically a Parisian. Show her your French kiss homework." Lonergan stuck out his tongue.

"Yeah, Miss Michener. Maybe she's gone flapper too." Enders finished his gin and set the glass on the battered tabletop. "Hey, you seen Jim D'Arcy around?"

"You'll need a séance to talk to him."

"Oh…"

"Killed in May 1918. My mother wrote me."

"Too bad. He was a really great guy. The best."

"Well, you know, they were five brothers and two sisters. If no one told his parents, they may not have noticed he's missing."

Despite himself, he laughed. "Jesus, Lonergan, that's just awful. Even for you."

Lonergan held up his glass. "Another? Those hymnals won't pay for themselves."

"I should go. Gotta clean up and catch the train tomorrow. Looking for a job."

"Not with the old man?"

Enders shook his head. "Already been through one war. No need to start another."

Lonergan nodded, downed his drink, and looked at Enders. "You were a persistent guy."

"What…?"

"Taking the train to New Britain all those weekends. Badgering that aeronautical guy—Nelson—for a ride in his flying machine.

"Hamilton."

"Then you wind up a pilot with the French Army. From small things…"

"That the opening of something you're writing? From small things…?"

20

"You make poor story material. Unless you want to tell me about that scar on your neck."

"Plenty of time for war stories if Bobby's gonna keep this place going."

"No room for an orchestra or dance floor, but it might make for a local concern. You gonna be around this weekend?"

"Imagine so."

"Well, telephone the house or look for me here. I feel a sudden obligation to Bobby's career as a bootlegger."

Looking around, Enders said, "Yeah, it's nuts. You can't buy or sell booze, but you can make it and drink it."

"Well, I'm not just coming back for a drink. I want to see what kind of donation Bobby'll be collecting next time. Charm school tuition for his little sister?"

Walking home, he wondered how many more speakeasies were tucked away in the town. Did every small town have at least one? How many people were breaking the law on a daily basis and not giving a damn about it? New York City had seemed as wet as ever—as if every doorway led to a covert bar with a ready supply of whatever one could afford.

When his ship—more cargo carrier than passenger liner—docked in Brooklyn days ago, his brother Donald had been there to greet him. Dressed in a brown three-piece herringbone suit and smelling of oily aftershave, Donald had whisked his older brother back into Manhattan to a surprisingly spacious Greenwich Village flat he shared with three other bankers and bond traders. Calling themselves the Smarter Set—a jab at Menken's *Smart Set* magazine—they hurled Enders into a series of neighborhood parties, uptown speakeasies, and Lower East Side dance halls.

By Monday, Enders had had enough and had gladly, almost gleefully, pushed his little brother out the door to go back to work. Donald and his roommates were younger; they had missed the war and its endless variety of terrors. They knew only easy money in the boom economy, the wartime heroics delivered in censored films, and the small-time thrill of illegal gin. From the front window, he watched them disperse along the sidewalk as they headed to their offices. *Kids. If I could somehow make you understand what I saw and did in France, you'd be too scared to get out of bed.*

Alone and sober, he set out to explore the city again, tasting its post-war prosperity and sensing the government's heavy hand of paranoia about immigrants, Bolsheviks, and labor organizers. Times Square was awash in honking automobiles of every make, their drivers seemingly determined to run down as many quick-stepping pedestrians as possible. The subway was crowded, but free again of uniformed men headed to war in France. Elevated trains flanked Third Avenue as autos and a few horse-drawn carriages rolled up and down the avenue. He found refuge in the park, which was on the verge of a budding spring. He fed the squirrels and read the papers, thinking he should start searching the want ads for a job.

Early Tuesday morning, he knew it was time to say goodbye to the Smarter Set, go home, and start the life he had spent the last three years first avoiding and later struggling to reclaim. He caught the morning commuter line back to Milford.

Chapter 2

Wednesday morning, Enders sat on the right side of the train car watching the coastal scenery flicker past the windows. After the smoky bustle of downtown New Haven and its barge-filled harbor, the land had returned to pastoral greens and browns, dotted with small towns and large farms. Sheep and cattle meandered through salt hay fields, which stretched down to the rocky shoreline bordering Long Island Sound. Offshore, a few white sails luffed in the morning air.

He was not dreaming this time. Enders sat upright in an old suit that felt tight on him after five years in storage. He wandered through the business and employment sections of the *New York Times,* the *Hartford Courant,* and the *New Haven Register.* Mr. Sullivan was right; there was a boom underway. Two-and-a-half-million men had come home from Europe to displace the women and Negros who had taken their jobs during the Great War. Still, there were new businesses and new opportunities. He was confident he would find something interesting to do with the rest of his hard-earned life.

He had not finished scrutinizing the newspapers before a conductor entered the car to announce Saybrook Junction. After a minute, the train began to slow. Enders packed his newspapers into his brother's Gladstone bag and waited for the train to stop. The single-story station house rolled by. The train struggled to a tentative stop.

He jumped down the carriage steps and marched through the station to exit onto a gravel lot crowded with Model Ts and work trucks, and a shift-change of now idle conductors and engineers. Overhead hung a sagging black web of telephone and telegraph lines. Glancing left, he spotted the shuttered doors of the concrete trolley-car barn. He cut across the lot and passing the Coulter House restaurant was tempted to stop in for another cup of coffee.

*Time enough later.* He noticed rust on the trolley tracks curving into the Junction. He continued up Main Street, passing small shops and tall Victorian houses on narrow lots. Enders nodded to the grocery man standing in front of the market. He continued to the corner of Sheffield Street and a two-story brick building. At a set of double doors in the building's front, he saw a framed notice: James Joyce Johnson Realty. 2nd Floor. Enders opened one of the doors and started up a wooden staircase lit by a screened window in the back wall of the second floor.

Up you go, Lieutenant Enders. Don't forget to salute, he told himself.

At the top of the stairs were two opposing doors. To the right was a glass-fronted door with gold lettering that spelled Jas. J. Johnson, Esq. The door to the left was his destination, the realty company. He knocked and opened the door to find himself in a bright reception office with views of the main street and the rear fire escape. A woman of uncertain years sat at a large oak desk talking into a gray Grabaphone and scribbling on a message pad. A large sofa and matching easy chairs stood to one side. Between the chairs was an expensive-looking center table displaying company brochures and newspapers. A silver coffee and tea service stood in one corner. Two padded accent armchairs were angled in front of the desk. He stepped beside one of the chairs. She looked at him and held up an index finger. Enders waited, standing.

She ended the call, placing the phone's handset carefully in its cradle as if it might shatter. She looked at him again and smiled, waiting for him to say something.

Finally, he did. "I'm here about a building job. There's a Mr. Spencer I hope to see." Enders glanced at a closed door behind the woman.

"Oh, hon, he's gone off to Sound View. He's gonna be at the field office over there most of the day. You wanta go see him? I can telephone, if you like. Let him know." She smiled at Enders again. "I'm his assistant. He likes to call me a secretary, but he needs lots of assistance. There's eight or so sites he's trying to run from here or Sound View, or the apartment when he's done in." She cocked her head in the direction of the closed door.

"Sure he's not hiding in there now, miss?"

"Ann. Pleased to meet you. I'm sure he has from time to time, but right now he's in Old Lyme. You got an automobile?"

"I took the train." He lifted his arm to check the military watch strapped to his wrist. "Is the trolley running?"

"Not since 1919. Where you been?" She leaned forward to stare at his watch. "You got one of those soldier watches? A lot of men are wearing them these days. Were you in the war?"

"Ah, yes. Briefly. So, I'll take the next train to…"

"Sound View station. Shore Road. Walk up the hill. There's a tiny blue house with our sign out front. It's the field office for Old Lyme. I'll call Mr. Spencer to make sure he stays put."

"Thank you. Tell him I'm on my way." Enders swung around with his bag and hurried back to the train station.

****

Sitting on the right side of the carriage again, he watched a sea of yellow cattails wave by the open window. He caught the odor of low-tide mud as the train slowed to pass the shack-like Connecticut River station. Then the train was on the iron-and-stone drawbridge. In the distance, he saw the two lighthouses marking the narrow entrance to the river. The train pulled through Old Lyme, though most of the town's buildings were hidden on the other side of wide salt marshes and lumpy fields of rock and grass. There were few trees. Windmills turned slowly in the morning air as they pumped fresh water to houses and inns. The train rolled past the shuttered Black Hall station and its empty platform. Enders leaned around to look back.

*"Where you been?" she had asked. Where, indeed? So much has changed in the last six years. Stations closed. Trolley lines shut down. Everyone seems to have an auto to zip along paved roads. No beer or wine to be had without sneaking around. I wonder if this is how Rip Van Winkle felt.*

The train slowed. The Sound View sign slid by. Enders jumped up and exited the almost empty car to stand on its iron steps. The train stopped, and he lighted onto the hard ground. He followed a well-worn path to Shore Road. From the road, he looked down the sandy length of Hartford Avenue lined on both sides with two-story buildings and shops. At the far end of the street, he caught a glimpse of the Sound sparkling in the late morning light.

He threw his bag on his shoulder and marched up the slight hill to find a little blue house with a peaked corner on the side of the road. It looked like it had been dropped there by accident. A phone line and an electrical cable snaked from the utility pole to the back of the tiny house. A large window on the right and an arched door below the roof peak were painted white. Enders stepped to the screened door and peered inside.

In the miniature house, a man sat at an executive desk staring at a map and scribbling on a pad of blue-tinted paper.

Enders knocked on the white doorframe. The man looked up, leaned back in his wooden armchair, and waved him in.

"Ann called me." The man pointed at the battered candlestick telephone on the desk. "You the guy looking for work?"

Enders stepped forward, dropped his bag on the floor, and sat in the straight chair set before the desk. "Yes, sir. Dave Enders from Milford. I saw your ad in the *Times*."

The man nodded. "John Spencer. I'm the director for most of JJJ's development projects along the Connecticut shore. James Joyce Johnson. JJJ. Cute, huh?"

"I suppose it beats KKK."

"Ha. Yeah, probably does. So, what've you been doing for work? Know anything about building? Permits? Surveys? All that stuff? We're pretty busy

27

construction-wise in the warm weather months."

Spencer wore a tired fedora tilted far back on graying slicked-back hair, fancy suspenders, worn gray pants, and a wrinkled white shirt in need of bleach. A balled-up tie of uncertain color rested in a wire basket on the desk.

"Yes, I know the tools and techniques of construction. But more recently, well, I've been in France and Switzerland. Odd jobs here and there. And some translating for wire services out of New York and London." *I don't think this guy's gonna be impressed with 'odd jobs' and speaking French. But I need a job. I need to get out of the house and out of town.*

"You were in the war?"

"Yes, sir. For three years. Pilot and lieutenant with the French *Armée de l'Air*."

"Pilot." Spencer nodded then looked off into space. "I was in a war once. '98. Cuban jungle. Bullets everywhere. Scary as all hell. Lucky it only went on a week."

He focused his attention on David again. "You were an officer? You gave orders to people?"

"Ah, yes. Mechanics, armorers, admin, and mess staff."

"Can you take orders?"

Enders smiled at the question. "Yes. I can take orders."

"Great. Lotta generals in this company. Always wanting this or that yesterday. We're a national business with projects here, New York, Chicago. Trying to get into Florida. Got half a dozen projects just in this area alone. And now I'm short-handed."

Spencer looked at Enders as if he had had a sudden

thought. "You graduate high school?"

"I did."

"Good. Not many do. I read where it's only about seventeen percent."

"Yes. I read and write. French and English. I can read maps and handle a compass."

Spencer handed Enders a clipboard. "Write your name, address, birth date. Got a telephone number? Oh, can you drive a Ford?"

He wrote fast. "Yes, I've got a Milford phone number, and I can drive a car."

"Okay. My crew foreman decided to run off to Florida with the best-looking lunchtime waitress at the Pease House. So you're the new crew foreman. Try to stay out of the Pease House. The job pays fifty-two a week. It's not a suit-and-tie, sit-down kinda job."

Enders did the math in his head. He leaned across the desk to return the clipboard. "Okay…" *Yeah, when was the last time I gave anyone an order? 1918?*

Spencer glanced at what Enders had written. He stood up and reached across the desk to shake Enders' hand. "Welcome aboard. Listen. I'd show you around today, but I've got phone calls with the generals in New York and some potential buyers coming around this afternoon. What's today? Wednesday? Come back Monday morning. Eight o'clock. Two more days… Guess things will keep till then. I'll show you the works and the crews. You got time now, you might walk up to the Kloss farm. We're angling to buy the place for another beach association." Spencer jerked a thumb toward the back of the little office-house. "Or walk past Sound View to the White Sand development. You got an automobile?"

"No…"

"Maybe think about a bicycle for around here. We've got Black Point, Giant's Neck, White Sand, couple of places in Saybrook. All close by. And there's the train. Better find a place to live, too."

"Okay. Thanks again. I'll see you Monday." Enders pushed the screen door aside and was about to leave when Spencer asked him, "Hey, you ever get shot down in the war?"

He glanced back and said, "Three times."

\*\*\*\*

Enders hiked up the hill to a large white farmhouse with a cut-stone wall fronting the road and a signpost on the corner. On the post, two signs announced Kloss Dairy Farm and Manor House Rentals. He approached the house and knocked on the front door. A woman of his mother's age answered the knock.

"Afternoon, ma'am. I saw your rental sign. I was wondering if you might have a room for next week. I was just hired by the James Joyce Johnson Company…"

"Oh, yes. Mr. Spencer. He's spent a few nights here too. A busy, restless man. Hardly has the time to construct a complete sentence."

He smiled at her comment. "Yes. I expect I'll be pretty busy next week too. Too busy to look for permanent quarters for a while."

"Well, you're in luck. The season hasn't started yet. You want the whole of next week?"

"Monday to Friday should do."

She took him upstairs. His right hand traced the curved maple railing to the second floor, stopping at an open door across from the staircase. Mrs. Kloss showed him the single bed, the *en suite* water—a corner sink—

the closed fireplace, and the narrow closet. They agreed on a price that included breakfast but not the weekend. Enders got the time of the next westbound train from her. He checked his watch and left his bag on her front step.

He hiked down a rough sandy road toward the ocean. A barbed-wire fence held back several dairy cows nibbling at the salt hay and scrub. A dome-shaped rock had emerged in the center of the cow's paddock. At the end of the road, he stopped on a low dune sprinkled with beach rose and switchgrass. The beach was empty. The sun was warm. The tide was out, revealing a bottom of barnacled, weedy rock. Wading here would be painful. To his left was a massive sheet of rock extending a hundred yards into the Sound. He hiked across the loose ground to the firm wet sand of the high tide mark and then over to the protruding outcrop.

From there, he looked east to a line of tall mansions set on a bluff half a mile away. He peered back at the local beach with its dunes and rocks and rotting piles of seaweed.

*No mansions here. Just a whole lotta dairy farm. Looks about as hopeless as Bobby's speakeasy. And who's gonna clear all those rocks outta the water?*

****

The doctor was everything Carole was not: talkative, upright, roiling with energy, moving around the gurney as if it was his dance partner. Enders was exhausted watching him examine his sister as he fired off complex words and phrases at a nurse who acted more like a stenographer.

The family had driven Carole to Yale-New Haven Hospital in the back of an open-bed Ford truck to see this man. David had carried her from her bed to the truck parked behind the store and had ridden with her into New Haven. Now the doctor—minus the usual white lab coat and stethoscope—took off his glasses and slid them into the upper pocket of his buttoned brown vest. He sat in an office chair beside the gurney. He looked like he might spring out of it again at any moment.

"Well, this seems to be a common enough case. Which is not to say I can give you a very hopeful prognosis. It's just I've seen a number of cases similar to your daughter's and read of so many more."

"This isn't influenza?" asked Fred Enders. "Some different kinda flu?"

"No. These cases of *lethargica* often are coincident with influenza, but the etiology may not be identical. Perhaps influenza is a triggering event for something else. It might start with flu-like symptoms, such as headache, chills, pharyngitis, fever, vomiting, et cetera. There are hundreds of cases like this in the U.S. now."

"What's going to happen with her?" asked Meredith Enders.

The doctor glanced at Carole's mask-like face. She was dressed in a floral-patterned nightgown. Her hair was newly washed and combed into a long braid. Her hands, one atop the other, rested on a light wool blanket. She appeared to be asleep and unaware of the conversations around her or the prior, energized examination by the doctor.

"Well, a prognosis is... Well, to be blunt, it's guesswork. The overall mortality rate appears to be somewhere between 20 and 40 percent. Some patients make full recoveries and go on with their lives. But many others will develop neurological or psychiatric conditions. These post-encephalitic sequelae can occur suddenly, leading to serious disability or death. But sometimes they also occur slowly. Sometimes they remit and disappear. This phenomenon is new. And we're all in the dark trying to find a candle to light the way out of it."

David said, "She seems to be in a coma."

"It's not a true coma. There is some awareness—for a while—of the world around her."

"What about the rest of the world? Are there foreign cases?"

The doctor tipped forward in his chair. "Oh, yes. In fact, some of the first cases were described and studied in 1916 in Austria by a brilliant fellow named Constantin von Economo."

"The aviator?" asked a startled David Enders.

"Oddly enough, yes. One and the same."

His mother turned to him and asked, "David, do you know him?"

"No. Of him, yes. He flew on the Italian Front during the war." David sat back, wondering how a famous pilot had become a famous doctor, or how a famous doctor had become a famous pilot.

"So now what should we do for her? We're feeding her and keeping her company. Will this go on forever? Or is she gonna wake up again? Like normal?" asked Fred, a man who seemed to prefer yes or no answers and not the wishy-washy mysteries the doctor was relating.

"I'd like to keep her here for a while. We have a small ward of similar cases. She'll get proper care and stimulation while we do some testing and observations." He glanced from David to his mother to his father.

"If you think that would be a help..." said Fred Enders.

"Can we visit?" asked Meredith.

"Yes, of course. Visitors are probably the best therapy for those still...for those aware of their surroundings. Yes, please come as often as you like."

"Have you had success in treating these lethargy patients here? Do some of them leave eventually?" David Enders asked.

"Ah, well, so far, recovery is...rare. We do what we can, but as I said earlier, we're in the dark about this syndrome. We must hope for the best."

Enders glanced at his immobile sister. *How much does hope cost? And does it run out before the money does?*

\*\*\*\*

He sat against the cab in the bed of his father's Ford truck. There was room to stretch out now, without his sleeping sister and the spread-out bedding that had supported her. He twisted around to see his mother's hat in the back window of the cab and wondered what she might be thinking. She had just consigned Carole to the care of a man who didn't know how to care for her. Not that anyone seemed to know. He leaned back and looked up at the high clouds drifting through a quiet blue sky.

There also were scattered clouds and bright blue air at eleven thousand feet. His French squadron had flown north of Verdun, crossed the trench lines, and dropped to two hundred feet to attack German planes still on the ground and strafe nearby ground crews and fuel depots. They climbed back over the trenches, heading home and attracting furious bursts of archie—anti-aircraft fire. Enders had climbed back to eleven thousand feet, felt the cold thin air, and leveled his Nieuport 17 biplane. He looked right and left, seeing most of his colleagues. He wanted to relax, but he was cold, and he knew there was still time to die. His back teeth began to click together like a charged telegraph key. He listened to the thumping engine and the harp-like tremors of the wing wires. A tiny movement in the corner of his left eye made him look closer at the round mirror mounted above the gun sights.

A Fokker Eindecker followed him only a hundred feet back. Enders froze. The German pilot fired.

Enders rolled to the right and drove his machine toward the ground. But he was already hit. Black smoke seeped from the engine cowling. The engine choked once, sending a spasm through the fragile body of the plane. The smoke became denser. He remembered thinking, *Merde! Where's our superiority over the Fokker mono?! Now it's crash, burn, or jump. Merde!* He jerked around in his seat, looking for pursuers.

Flames appeared on the outer skin of the wood and canvas craft. The fire crept back toward the cockpit. Soon the biplane would be a torch. Then a bomb.

In the distance, just beyond the French line, he saw a small lake. More duck pond than lake, but Enders aimed his burning plane at it. His vision contracted to that dark oval of resurrecting water. As he got close to it, he killed the engine and pulled the plane up, shedding most of its speed. The tail skid sliced across the water's surface. The hardwood wheels hit the water and sank. The plane flipped over in the sudden deceleration.

He smacked his forehead as the plane somersaulted. Now he was underwater. Upside down. Still strapped in his seat. His goggles filled with water. He groped for the harass buckle.

He forced himself to move slowly and deliberately

and not waste air tearing at his harness, all the while repeating to himself: I'm not going to drown in a duck pond.

The leather harness gave way. Enders pulled himself out of the cramped cockpit. He kicked off from the muddy bottom and broke the surface. He yanked off his leather helmet and goggles. Overhead, planes roared by. He listened to the pop-pop-pop of machine guns and the whine of stressed engines. Enders climbed onto the tail section and tore at the buttons of his water-logged flight coat. He dropped the leather and sheepskin burden. Diving back into the water, he swam for the grassy shoreline, desperate to get clear of his wrecked machine.

On dry land, he looked around wild-eyed, his heart pounding through his wet shirt. Seeing an apple orchard ahead, he ran for the rows and columns of short, arthritic trees. Behind him, he heard the growl of a low-flying plane. There was a burst of gunfire; someone was shooting up the remains of his plane. He ran faster. He jumped to the right and curled up behind a tree trunk. The surrounding ground erupted with machine gun bullets and tracers as another Fokker passed over the treetops. Two French machines—arriving too late to prevent the strafing—gave chase.

Enders rolled onto his back and looked at a sky speckled with drifting clouds of oily smoke. Water ran out of his calf-high boots. He coughed up more water. He let the war continue without him until his wet clothes brought on a chill. Then he stood on wobbly legs.

He gave the tree behind him a thankful pat and tramped toward the football pitch, his temporary air base.

*Shot down. Almost drowned. Strafed for good measure. Hell of a day.*

A light tapping on the truck's back window brought him back to 1922 Connecticut. He turned and looked up to see his mother's palm pressed against the glass. He put his right hand up to cover her hand on the other side of the glass barrier.

****

On Monday morning, the train dropped him at Sound View station. He headed to the Manor House, passing the little JJJ office. Mrs. Kloss met him at the door. He went upstairs and tossed his bag on the bed. The back window offered a sunny view of the dairy farm and the Sound. Enders glanced in the oval mirror above an old dresser that rocked on the warped floorboards. A clean-shaven face stared back at him. He wore a chambray shirt, light wool pants, brown Wolverine work boots, and a brown fedora. He tilted the hat back on his head.

*Well, the man said it wasn't a sit-down office job. Good thing; I don't own many ties.*

He grabbed his old flannel jacket and headed back down the road to the little blue office.

There was a Ford truck parked beside the building. Inside, Spencer sat at his desk, glancing, alternately, at a street map and the telephone, which he seemed to think might ring at any second.

"Good morning," said Enders, stepping inside.

Spencer looked up. "Ah. Right on time. What time is it? Eight. Right. Okay, have a seat. Let's get started." He searched through his desk, finding a thin cigar. "*Cohiba Panetela* from Cuba. Wonderful. You smoke?" He struck a match and lit the skinny cigar.

"A pipe on rare occasion."

"Ah, too much work. The pipe. The pouch. Lighter.

Matches. Penknife. Stem cleaners. Tires me just thinking about it." He stood and put his hat on. He handed Enders a file folder and said, "Okay, let's go see some property and then get your hands dirty."

Spencer swerved around his desk, and pushed aside the screen door. Enders and a blue cloud of cigar smoke trailed behind him. Enders grinned through the smoke. Spencer reminded him of a Belgian mechanic from the war. The man talked fast, often in an abbreviated, staccato French. He was skilled at fixing engines, jammed machine guns, and sagging wings. Equally important, he had the mysterious power to lay his pilfering hands on whatever the squad needed: fuel, ammunition, flares, food, winter clothing; and the things they didn't need but wanted anyway: liquor, wine, sweets, weekend passes, and the names of friendly local girls. After he was killed in a bombing raid, he was mourned as much for his great heart as for his sticky fingers.

Outside, Spencer jumped into the driver's seat of the Ford truck. Enders hesitated. His new boss looked at him and said, "Get in. No need to strongarm the engine crank. Thanks for offering. You've been away too long."

Enders climbed into the cab. "Wasn't sure how this one started."

The engine came to life and Spencer turned the truck onto the paved Shore Road, drove a few feet east, and crunched back onto sand and gravel. "More people moving here for the summer. Well, the town or the state will have to finish paving this road." He chuckled to himself.

They drove by the Manor House, past another farm, down a steep hill, and followed the railroad track until they came to the South Lyme station. Just beyond the station, Spencer turned right and drove under a tight railroad bridge. Ahead, the land was flat and open, but off to the left stood a thicket of trees and a cemetery enclosed by a sloppy rectangle of stone walls. The trees thinned out, and Enders saw a long mound of layered brown rock that thrust a high, sharp point into Long Island Sound. They stopped beside a short wooden bridge that crossed a grass-lined tidal creek. They got out and Enders looked around to see dozens of small cottages and larger houses scattered about the open field of grass and sand. Surveyor stakes formed rectangular patterns among the standing houses. Other summer homes in various stages of construction perched along the shoulder of the rocky peninsula behind the two men.

"Nice, huh?" asked Spencer. "Can I see the folder?"

He surrendered the folder, and Spencer opened it to extract a map, which he unfolded on the warm slope of the truck's hood. "Here's the layout." His index finger stabbed at the map. "There's a general store. Properties all through this flat area. Easy to build stuff. Up on the mount there, it's trickier. All that rock. So, exposed water pipes and above-ground septic. But the views are great. That's what we're selling there: the views."

He pointed at the creek and the small pond it had formed farther inland. "See this? Dredge here and there, make a small-boat basin. Throw a bridge and boardwalk across the outlet so people on the point can get to the beach. Be great. Even got tennis courts here."

Enders nodded. "Yes, beautiful area." He pointed toward the water. "So, that's the main beach. And that line of cottages…"

"Yeah. Come on. Let's head over there. Meet the

crew. See what house building on sand is like."

They crossed the footbridge and hiked toward a row of wood-framed houses being erected on the edge of the smooth beach. Enders could hear the banging of multiple hammers and the steady growl of a crosscut saw in the hands of someone who knew how to use it. The beachfront cottages stood in a line of progressive evolution: from cleared lot to framed building to completed house awaiting its occupants. Spencer called to a man standing beside the cleared lot, a roll of blueprint papers tucked under his arm and a cigarette clamped between his front teeth. "Jesse. How's the job?"

The man waved and walked over. "Hey, boss."

"Jesse Martin, meet Dave Enders. He'll be playing your part at White Sand. Brought him here to see what we've been doing these last years."

Enders and Martin shook hands. "Welcome aboard," said Martin.

"Thanks." Enders looked around the beach and felt the cool of an onshore breeze. "Great location. Any closer, you'd be in the water."

"So, how are things?" asked Spencer.

"Need more hands. Some good day laborers."

"Workin' on it."

Martin turned to Enders. "You do any beach building before?"

"Not yet."

"Well, come over here. I'll show you how we start."

The three men strolled to a leveled lot of sand. Twelve holes had been dug in a pattern of four by four by four. Martin pointed into one of the holes. "Dig. Pour a two-by-two concrete foot so the pilings don't sink. Then stack blocks or pour a column—depends what's on hand. That big center hole is the chimney footprint. Brick is heavy, you know, so we pour a big foot and stack these new cinder blocks. Basic stuff."

They went to the next lot with twelve short pilings of cinder block sticking out of the ground. A narrow brick tower was beginning to take shape in the center. "Now we have a base for laying joists for the flooring and wall support. Good solid base," said Martin.

At the next lot, two men were laying down flooring on the joist frame. The upright outline of a back wall was already in place. The next house was framed and enclosed by beadboard walls and tarpaper. Martin pointed at the building. "Just awaiting doors and windows. And the shingles." He pointed to the front roof. "Bump out some dormer windows right there."

"For the view," said Spencer. He turned to the Sound and spread his arms. "Always for the view. Speaking of the view, we'll head up there for a quick look around, then get you to White Sand and to work."

*Okay. I can do this*. Enders said to Martin, "Thanks for the tour."

They shook hands again and Enders followed Spencer back to the truck. They backed the Ford around and drove past the cemetery and up a narrow road of rock and dirt until they could see water on either side of the high stone peninsula.

Enders pointed to three large houses near the tip of the point. "Almost mansion-sized."

"Yeah. If the owners want their own design, that's fine. It's their money. Mostly, we stick to the basic designs. Cheap. Easy to build. Most people don't want a lot of summer house to take care of; they'd rather be sitting at the beach. So, what d'ya think? Great view, huh?"

"No argument from me." The morning sun lit the surface of a calm ocean of green water. He looked south to the tip of Long Island, some nine miles away. A steamer ferry was working its way through Plum Gut. Enders looked down to a wide and shallow bay of bottom sand with patches of eelgrass in the shallows. On the opposite side of the bay was another rocky point, and a long white building and a railroad track beside it. "What's that? Looks like some kind of factory."

Spencer laughed and said, "Used to be the Niantic Menhaden Oil and Guano Company. Probably the most hated business anywhere in the state. They used to use leftover fish parts to make fertilizer. Made a stink beyond description. The locals tried to burn it down. Twice. We were accused of encouraging some of the arsonists. Can you believe it?"

"They still in business?"

"No, thank God. Just shut down this year. Should help our sales on this side of the rock, and at Black Point in Niantic."

****

Spencer drove back toward Sound View along the bumpy Shore Road. Enders picked up the Point O' Woods folder and glanced through several pages of building permits and sales notices. A postcard was attached to the back of the folder by a paperclip. He pulled it loose and read some of the commercial printing on the back: Two lots for $200. Your terms.

Spencer stole a quick look in Enders' direction. "Oh yeah, one of our private mailings. From 1917, if I remember. Guess you were still overseas. Now it's more likely to be ten percent down and four years to pay.

Prices have gone up."

Enders read, "A safe, sandy bathing beach, yacht harbor, running water, tennis court, deer park, et cetera." Turning to Spencer, he asked, "Yachts and deer?"

"Could be. Eventually. At least the tennis court is in. Water's coming along, but you know, it's hard to make it flow uphill."

"What does 'restricted as to cottages and nationality of purchasers' mean? Americans only?"

"Well, you don't want to share the sand with a bunch of Krauts, do you? Haven't you had enough of them?" Spencer chuckled. He slowed the car and pointed out the window. "Catholic church for Sound View. Which is right there," he said, still pointing toward the Sound. "Interesting mix of public beach and private homes."

"Yeah, I heard it's a popular place with weekenders coming down from Hartford."

"Now, this next beachfront coming up is some of our competition. Hawk's Nest Beach. A private beach association right from the get-go. Started by a man named Garvin about twenty-five years ago. Nice place. Couple of windmill water towers. A general store. Baseball field for the kids." He glanced at Enders. "Ride through there sometime. Take a look at the shoreline of cottages from the edge of the marsh back toward Sound View. All the same design—porch, second-floor dormers, left-side chimney, and staircase—but every one painted or roofed a different color. They call it Rainbow Row. Think we'll try to do the same thing over to the Woods."

They drove past a marsh thick with salt hay and cattails. A brackish creek snaked through the tall grasses searching for the Sound. Beyond the marshland, Spencer turned the truck onto another narrow road of sand flanked by wild blueberry bushes and Concord grape vines.

The property director waved his hand across the windshield, taking in the area ahead. "Used to be a campground for the National Guard. Then it was a potato farm. Now, as of last August, it's becoming a private beach for middle-class buyers and renters. A little bit of summertime paradise, just a short trip from Hartford or Springfield or New Britain."

Spencer stopped the truck in front of a pack of other open-bed trucks parked randomly before another flat field of survey stakes and strings. White-painted merestones were set at what appeared to be future street intersections. Lumber and roofing tiles were piled in the backs of two of the trucks. Spencer jumped out and pointed to one of the parked trucks. "Ah, good. The surveyor's here. Let's see how many more lots he's managed to squeeze outta these old potato fields."

They passed a truck with a stenciled door declaring, Cody & Cody, Civil Eng. A man standing beside a theodolite mounted on a steel tripod made notes in a hardbacked notebook. He looked up at their approach.

"Cody and Cody." Spencer raised his hat in salute. "What do you have for us?"

Mr. Cody closed his notebook. "Hundred and eighty-seven lots. Final map. Think that will be enough for JJJ?"

"We're happy. Mostly hundred-by-forties?"

"Almost all but a few oddballs that had to be stretched or squeezed around some uncooperative bit of geology." Cody extracted a pile of papers and legal-length documents from his notebook and handed them to

Spencer. "For the clerk's office. Signed and dated."

"Great." He turned to Enders. "This is Dave Enders. New foreman for the White Sand project. His first day, so don't hand him any problems."

Enders stepped up to shake Cody's hand. "Nice to meet you, sir."

Cody waved his arm toward the largely treeless property and the geometric spacing of survey stakes. "You're gonna be busy, son. You already got three dozen people wanting cottages built and ready for the summer."

Spencer corrected him. "Thirty-eight. Thirty-eight one-hundred-by-forty-foot lots sold to date. And we're building fast. The more cottages finished this year, the more families go home at the end of the summer to tell their friends and neighbors what a wonderful time they had here. Then they'll come wanting to buy too."

Spencer waved the documents at Cody. Then he and Enders walked toward a nearby house emerging on its one-hundred-by-forty-foot plot. The walls and roof of the little house were up; two men were fitting framed screens into a front porch.

"Tight space," said Enders, looking at the property lines.

"Remember, it's about the sand and the surf, not mowing the lawn." He pointed to the half-built house. "It's seasonal. Cold water. Some electric. A place to escape to on those hot summer days in the city."

Enders nodded in reply as he watched half a dozen men walk toward them, seemingly summoned by some silent command. Spencer started working on one of his lean Cuban cigars as the men gathered around. His cigar glowed. He looked at the workmen.

"Boys. New foreman for you." He glanced at

Enders. "Dave Enders from Milford. He's new to the real estate game, so be nice to him for a few days."

Everyone chuckled. The men stepped forward to offer names and hands; Enders grabbed at dry, rough hands and tried to remember a tumble of mumbled names.

"So, any future complaints or problems, talk to Mr. Enders here. He'll get you what you need. Okay?" He turned away without waiting for any replies or comments from the building crew. Enders gave them a quick wave and hurried after Spencer. They wandered down to the beach.

Spencer sucked on his cigar and expelled a warm cumulus cloud of aromatic smoke. They stood at the edge of a wide shore of brilliant white sand. To the west, Enders could see the outer lighthouse at Old Saybrook.

"Another great view."

"That's why we bought it. The view. Flat, dry land to build on. Sandy waterfront. Perfect. The other side of that outcrop there"—Spencer pointed his cigar to the east—"there's a boy's summer camp. Camp Rainsford. Poor New York kids. So, if you hear a lot of noise and see gangs of kids running around this summer, that's the reason. Too bad we can't put 'em to work."

He looked at Enders. "Here. Survey papers and deeds for the town clerk. Make sure he gets them before the end of the week. Need to get this stuff registered with the town. Any buyers come through, just show them around, explain the lots and the location, show them the beach, and send them up the road to the office or back to the Saybrook office. Wherever I am."

Enders glanced at one of the deeds. "One dollar for a lot. Twelve hundred dollars for a cottage?"

"If we build it. Yeah, that's standard. So, what do you pilots say, 'flying solo'? You're on your own now, kid. I need to get back to the office."

"I flew with a squadron."

Spencer guffawed and strode away. "Don't crash. I can't be looking for another foreman this week."

Chapter 3

Enders survived the fifty-hour work week.

After Spencer left him, he unfolded the surveyor's lot map and searched around the property to identify the already-purchased lots. Then he inspected the few completed houses, noting their overall simplicity of construction and similarity of design.

*Yeah, good enough for summer living. God knows I've flopped in much worse.*

At noon, the builders sat together eating their lunches. Enders realized he had not thought about lunch. Or dinner, for that matter. Rather than look foolish or hungry or both, he asked the crew about the lumber and supplies still piled on the trucks.

One of the men, a local named Sammy Gross, said, "Yeah, gotta come off and be stacked here today."

"All right." Enders took off his jacket and started moving braces and wallboard and rolls of roofing paper from the pickup trucks to the yard.

*I better remember lunch tomorrow. And hunt up some dinner tonight. And transportation. Hope they enjoy the show.*

One of the other men leaned toward Sammy, "He might be okay if he's willing to tote and haul when it's needed." Sammy nodded as he chewed his cheese sandwich.

At the end of the first workday, Enders went back

up Shore Road to Sound View Beach. Walking down Hartford Avenue, he stopped at the Sound View Inn for dinner. Afterward, a few doors back up the street, he found a two-story building, the first floor of which was an Italian grocery. He bought a stock of bread, crackers, cheese, apples, and bottled soda. He realized he needed a thermos, and he should take greater advantage of the Manor House breakfast.

****

Wednesday evening, he strolled the length of Sound View's sandy main street to the casino on the edge of the beach. It was a barn-sized building with a barn-like entrance. It also served as a dance hall and movie theater and frequently provided surreptitious gambling. The Hartford police raided it at least once a summer; the local constables tended to look the other way for a small fee.

Inside the large building, a solid door near the back seemed to have an unusual traffic pattern: people went in, hurriedly, but did not come back out. After watching the door traffic for a while, Enders strolled over to one of the casino employees and casually lamented the absence of a cold beer on a warm night. The man told him it was against the law, but after a series of questions to Enders about who he was, why he was there, and who he worked for, the interrogator said, "Of course, if we had any beer these days, it'd cost you fifteen cents a glass."

Staring at the floor, Enders said, "Prices are up, I see. Still, I could drink two cold beers after a busy day." He turned to the man. "Got change for a dollar?"

"I do." The man took his dollar and handed back seventy cents. "Follow me."

Behind the mystery door, he found a surprisingly

large, well-lighted room of men and women enjoying cocktails and beer. A phonograph played *Three O'Clock in the Morning*. At a corner counter, he asked for a beer. As the bartender set it down, Enders ordered a second one. When the bartender returned, Enders had finished the first beer and now was ready to nurse the second one. He leaned on the counter, watched the room, sipped his beer. *This is what Bobby needs: more space and some music.*

****

Late Friday afternoon, Sammy drove Enders into Old Lyme so he could drop off the White Sand property deeds and survey maps with the town clerk. Sammy pulled in front of the town hall. "It's off on the right side. You want I should wait for you?"

"No. We're done for the day. I'll catch the next train back to Sound View." Enders climbed out of the cab and shut the door.

"Okay, boss. See you Monday." Sammy pulled the JJJ truck away in a low cloud of gray smoke and fine dust.

In the town hall, he found the clerk perched on a high stool in front of a long, tilted desk of scarred wood and iron braces. The slender man wore a collarless white shirt with purple sleeve garters. A creased visor held back a shock of gray hair. Gold-rimmed bifocals perched above two small nostrils that flared periodically. The man glanced between a property deed and the huge ledger he was writing in with the steady beat of a metronome.

Enders knocked on the top railing of a gated partition that separated most of the office from the common entryway.

The clerk looked up and Enders thought, Bob Cratchit in summer. Enders waved his file folder. "Afternoon. Final survey maps and new property deeds for White Sand development. James Joyce Johnson Realty."

The man straightened up on his stool and motioned for him to come in. Enders handed him the folder, and the man glanced through the deeds. He looked at Enders and asked, "Know what you need to do this job, son?"

Enders looked at the huge ledger and the man's neat, almost machine-like cursive. "Really good penmanship?"

"Patience." He adjusted his glasses to better see Enders. "Used to be I'd get a sale or transfer deed or a new survey once or twice a year. Now I seem to be getting them by the hour. You developers are building faster than the town records can keep up. What's the hurry?"

Enders shrugged. "I guess people like the shore." He looked back at the clerk's neat recording of the deed on his desk. "Aren't all our sales deeds pretty much the same? Word for word? Can't you reference the language from an earlier deed? Save some ink and time?"

"The law won't allow. Every word matters. Or so every lawyer insists. Course, if you invent a better way to copy out property deeds and surveys, I'd be happy to give it a try." The clerk turned back to his ledger. He picked up his pen with thin ink-tipped fingers.

"Speaking of standard deeds." Enders took the file folder he had given the clerk and flipped it open. "Is this common language for properties around here?" He read, "...properties herein conveyed shall not be sold, leased, or rented in any form or manner directly or indirectly to any person or persons: (1) who are not of the Caucasian Race; (2) who are not acceptable either to the Grantor or to the Directors of the Beach Club Association..."

"Common enough language for JJJ. It's all private properties you boys are building. People generally do with their own homes and businesses as they see fit."

"Yeah..." Enders scratched his chin. "Still, it seems like wording that might lead to all kinds of trouble down the road."

\*\*\*\*

The next morning, Enders jumped and landed on the last step of the last carriage as the local train pulled away from Sound View station. He stood outside the car, watching the scenery and hoping the two-and-a-half-mile trip to Old Lyme station would end before the conductor found him.

At Old Lyme, he jumped down and strolled up McCurdy Road until it turned into Lyme Street, otherwise known locally as The Street. Beyond the imposing congregational church, he found a pharmacy. On the opposite side of the street from it, and a few yards farther up the street, was a general merchandise store called Rowland's. The two businesses seemed to constitute a good portion of the town's commercial enterprises.

*I need to telephone Mom. And buy a bicycle. And a thermos.* He looked at the library. *I need something to read at night. At night... Yeah, I need a place to sleep this weekend. Should have taken the whole week at the Manor House. I better start planning things out. Can't keep doing this random crap from day to day. This isn't France. I'm not him. Not anymore.*

He walked to the pharmacy, noticing the dusty

trolley tracks running the length of the street. On the plank sidewalk, he found a pay phone attached to the front of the building. He dropped in a dime and got the operator to connect him to Enders' Lumberyard in Milford. After a largely monosyllabic conversation with his father, his mother came on the line to tell him about his sister. Nothing had changed since he'd seen her last at Yale-New Haven. He told his mother about his job, asked about Brian Lonergan, and his brother, and said he would try to be home the following weekend.

Inside the James Pharmacy, he was surprised to find a Negro man in a white coat compounding pills behind the counter.

*Guess I can't sell him a cottage.*

He bought toothpaste, a bottle of aspirin, a better hairbrush, and, thinking it was only a matter of time before he cut himself at work, a box of adhesive bandages. He asked the pharmacist where he might buy a bike.

Morris James put down a graduated cylinder and said, "The only place in town would be across from Rowland's." He pointed up the road. "Man named Morley has a bicycle shop there. And caskets too."

Enders raised an eyebrow, but he did not get a chance to say anything before James said, "He's heard all the jokes already. So, if I was you, I'd just buy a bike and not comment on the other business."

Enders chuckled. "Okay. But the caskets don't give me much confidence in his bikes."

"He's heard that."

****

Across the street in Rowland's, he bought a thermos and added all his purchases to his rucksack. Next, he went to the library to look for some books Lonergan had mentioned at Bobby's garage/bar. He found F. Scott Fitzgerald's *This Side of Paradise* and his short story collection, *Flappers and Philosophers*. At the checkout desk, the young librarian asked him for his library card.

"I don't have one yet. Or a town address. I'm just getting settled in here. But I guess you could use my work address. James Joyce Johnson Realty on the Shore Road."

The young woman looked at Enders for a moment. "Yes, that will do." She smiled and stamped his books and said, "My, such…modern reading tastes, Mr. Enders."

He leaned toward her and whispered, "You should read *Chéri* by Colette in the original French. Shocking." He smiled back at her.

"Oh, that doesn't sound like something the town would buy us."

An older woman materialized beside Enders. She cleared her throat and asked, "Johnson Realty? You're the ones buying up all the farmland for summer homes. Old Lyme has been old Yankee and honest farming for centuries."

"Ah, yes, ma'am. We have bought some farmland. People want to go to the beach in the summer. Things change, I suppose." *God, how they've changed.*

"Well, young man, just remember what the Bible says: 'And every one that heareth these sayings of mine, and doeth them not, shall be likened unto a foolish man, which built his house upon the sand.' That's from Matthew."

Enders gave her a tight smile and said, "Maybe Matthew was referring to desert sand. We're building on beach sand." He picked up his books, waved them at the young librarian, and hurried out the front door. Saturday morning was too early for sermons.

At Morley's shop, he did his best to ignore the caskets lining the back wall and the ones still being assembled on sawhorses. Morley had a stock of new and used bikes, and Enders haggled with him over the price of a three-year-old Reading Roadster. He paid twenty dollars and watched Morley inflate the tires with a hand pump.

*That's almost half the week's pay. And setting aside something for taxes—Dad said Wilson started the income tax again. It's hard to be poor in this country. Still, probably better than back in Europe. Germany occupied. Ruined French and Belgian towns everywhere. Unexploded ordnance waiting for someone's plow or shovel. German food riots. The dead still being found. The war's not really over.*

Outside, he pedaled along the empty street. The day was warm, and riding under the elms lining Lyme Street he thought if he had a baguette and a bottle of wine in his pack, the day could not be better.

He stopped on the Bow Bridge and watched the tidal water of the Lieutenant River swirl among the cattails. In the distance, he saw several men in neat boaters and shirtsleeves standing in front of tall wooden easels. Enders crossed the bridge, pedaling along the road to the drawbridge that crossed the Connecticut River to Old Saybrook. Automobile traffic was light. The trolley tracks were empty. He took his time crossing the bridge, stopping here and there to watch the river traffic, to stare at the down-river lighthouses, and to study the riverfront power plant that raised two sections of the bridge for ships and sailboats.

He rode into Saybrook, forming a plan to sleep in the JJJ office and return to the Manor House on Sunday evening. He had the office keys but felt like he might be taking advantage of both the keys and his brief time with the company.

At the upstairs office, he was surprised to find Ann, Spencer's secretary/assistant.

"Hey, hon. You're not working today, are you?" she asked.

"No. I'm surprised you are. And that's fortuitous. Seems I did a poor job of planning my weekend. I've no place to sleep, so I was wondering if I might flop here tonight?"

She giggled and said, "You're already behaving like Mr. Spencer. You're not hiding some New York girl for the weekend, are you?"

Enders felt himself blush. "Regrettably, no. It's just me."

"Well, Mr. Spencer's cleaned up his act too. His family's here now, with a house at Saybrook Manor. So he's got no more excuses for *sleeping* at the office." More thoughtfully, she said, "Maybe he'll try to in Niantic sometime."

He pointed at the back door. "So I won't be ruining your own plans, will I?"

Ann pretended to be shocked. Laughing now, she said, "Well, I should slap your very rude face." She stood and sauntered to the back door. "Want the tour?"

Enders followed her into a small room with a water closet and a kitchenette. A wide Murphy bed was set in the back wall and a round dinette table and two chairs occupied the rest of the space.

"When the company started in this part of the state, it was a bit like the Wild West; work, sleep, eat; it all just sort of blurred together. Mr. Spencer never seemed to stop."

"This'll do. Sure it's okay?"

"It's jake."

"Thanks very much. It'll save me a few dollars this week."

"There should be coffee in the cabinet, along with some sheets and hand towels. Snoop around a bit and you might find an illicit bottle or two."

Having found a free bed for the night, Enders explored the town on his bike, pedaling to Saybrook Manor to see another of the company's beachfront developments and wander by Spencer's new house. He read his books in the little park marking the original site of Yale College. Later, he had an early dinner at a clam shack beside the steamboat dock.

Hours before dawn, alone in the unfamiliar backroom of the office, he jerked awake in the dark. He could not remember where he was and threw his left arm off the bed to touch the floor. It was close. And solid. And still. His breathing eased and after a while, he slept again.

****

In the morning, Enders pedaled back to Saybrook Point where a roundhouse once stood and the trains had been turned and sent back up to Saybrook Junction. Across the river, he could see the marshlands of Old Lyme. He rode across the former railroad causeway, now paved for cars, and stopped to look at the summer mansions at Fenwick, a narrow peninsula jutting into the mouth of the Connecticut River. A small sign described the neighborhood as a private association. Enders took the hint and pedaled away, amused at the idea of building private beaches even as he was being shut out of other private beaches.

He followed the hardpacked road along the high, rocky coast. In the distance, he saw what looked like a castle of light-colored fieldstone and red-tiled roofing. At the roundabout entrance to the seaside castle, he found a sign for *Hartlands at Cornfield Point*. Behind the huge building, the land had been cleared and several new houses and a water tower were set beside newly marked roads of hard-packed dirt. He pedaled behind the building and was surprised to find a JJJ flatbed truck.

Two men carried wooden cases from the truck to a narrow basement door at the far end of the castle. He lowered his bike to the ground and leaned on the truck bed waiting for the men to return.

As they emerged from the cellar, they were surprised to see Enders. They hesitated, looked at each other, then approached the truck.

Enders waved. "Morning. Didn't know anyone was working on a Sunday."

One of the men, wearing a torn denim shirt and a newsboy cap, said, "The company keeps us going."

"Me too. I'm Dave Enders. Foreman for the White Sand development area over in Old Lyme." He pulled away from the truck and put out his hand.

The men hesitated to move or say anything. Enders dropped his hand and looked back at the truck. "What's going on, fellas?"

The talkative man slapped his hands against his legs. He had made a decision, and asked, "Mr. Enders, you wet or dry?"

Now he had an inkling of the situation and said, "I'm wet," meaning he was against Prohibition.

The two men relaxed and told Enders the enormous stone house was closed and awaiting a buyer. The JJJ Company was hoping a new owner would turn the costly castle into a hotel, which then might serve as the centerpiece of the cottage colony now emerging on the neighboring cornfields. During the war, the former owner had leased the castle to the Army for a dollar a year. Now it attracted a different kind of tenant: fast boats from the other side of Long Island Sound dropping cases of Canadian whiskey, English gin, French champagne, and Caribbean rum.

The man with the cap said, "Lot of that goes on around here. I heard of some running up the river to the Essex dock. Others, clear up to Hartford."

The man in bib overalls suddenly came alive and said, "You're over to Lyme. You musta seen the Hatchetts Point mansions."

"Yeah. East of Sound View. Five or six of them."

"They got a big ol' dock the boats can run up to when no one's around. Those rum runners hide stuff there too. It's like a game of hide-and-seek." The man laughed.

The man with the cap jumped into the bed of the truck and pried the top off one of the remaining cases. He looked around, then handed a bottle of Canadian Club to Enders.

Enders looked at the bottle and thought about where to get some ice. "Listen. No one cares if you have a drink or where you get that drink. But you can't be using company trucks or property. Don't involve JJJ. So get this unloaded, get it out of here…and thanks for the bottle."

He stuffed the bottle into his rucksack, grabbed his bike, and walked toward one of the new houses. The men watched him go. The man in the truck said, "Seems like a reasonable cat for a foreman."

****

Enders stopped between two identical two-story cottages. The water tower loomed across the new road. He could see the shoreline and a stretch of new concrete seawall. A jetty of small boulders poked out from the shore. Several young boys dashed in and out of the chilly April water. It did not seem like the kind of place to attract smugglers and speedboats. But to Enders, everything still seemed oddly new and therefore surprising. He thought he had made the right call with the JJJ men turned smugglers—telling them to do what they wanted, but not to involve the company, which then might come to involve him.

He opened his pack and pulled out a company map and brochure. The new 1922 survey map showed a vast area of 550 lots for future summer homes. All but three acres around the castle were designated as forty-by-one-hundred-foot lots that would constitute the "restricted" Cornfield Point Beach Club.

"Ambitious building," said Enders. "Five hundred and fifty? All these clubs and colonies might just keep me employed for decades. Yeah, that's good. Nothing worse than searching for a decent job."

He looked around. He was alone; no one would wonder about him talking to himself. He opened the sales brochure, which showed blue-tinted photographs of the castle, the inner lighthouse on the river, and the curve of the coastal road above the gravelly shore. There was the usual JJJ guarantee of "ten percent down and four years to pay." The brochure promised a purchased plot "will rapidly increase in value and you should not neglect this opportunity of securing one. Every cottage constructed and improvement made will add to the value of your purchase. This estate will soon be a veritable City by the Sea."

On the reverse side, Enders read, "Every purchaser becomes a member of the Beach Club, but the privilege cannot be transferred without the approval of the Board of Governors. Thus will be secured for all time a desirable class of cottagers." On another page, he found the succinct addendum he had been looking for: "Plots will be sold only to genuine Americans."

Enders folded the map and brochure and remembered the many Belgians and Frenchmen he had fought beside in their mutual air war. He thought of the reserved Swiss he had met on the border and the boisterous Portuguese and Greek fishermen he had drunk with, and fought with, in Marseille. No summer cottages for them. And the German-speaking woman who had calmed his nerves and his nights: no beach for her, either.

*The Palmer raids scooped up every radical with an accent, and the Emergency Quota Act is keeping everyone else out of the country. No summer homes for anyone but us genuine red-blooded Americans. Land of the free, home of the restricted.*

He gathered his things and rode back into town.

\*\*\*\*

Enders' planning got better. He was organized now, at work and in his free time. He kept his Manor House room through the weekends, and Mrs. Kloss started packing him a lunch. He pedaled his bicycle to work at

White Sand or sometimes to the Point O' Woods development, which was downhill there and uphill back. He caught the train to meetings at the Saybrook office and once to another association site at Black Point just outside of Niantic. If it rained, he borrowed a company truck to take permits and deeds to the town clerk, whose name he was ignoring in favor of referring to him—surreptitiously—as Bob Cratchit. He drove lumber from the yard near Saybrook Junction back to White Sand and ice from the Sound View icehouse back to Spencer's diminutive office-house, or to the Kloss Manor House as a favor to his landlady.

He showed potential buyers around the developments, and hearing the rare, affected French phrase tossed off by moneyed, finishing-school wives, Enders would respond and engage them in French. The language barrier left husbands in suspense until they found themselves agreeing to double lots close to the beach, and the JJJ construction unit doing the building of Madame's design. Hearing about this novel sales approach, and signing off on those deeds, Spencer gave Enders a military salute, a bottle of English gin, and orders to keep chatting with the wives.

Dave Enders went home one weekend to pick up more clothes and have a drink with Lonergan. On the train to Milford, he stopped in New Haven to check on his sister and was surprised to find his parents there too. His mother fussed with Carole's sheets and blankets and then sat holding her hand as she whispered endearments to her silent daughter. Fred Enders surveyed the small ward of patients, young and old, male and female. Enders heard him mumble, "Looks like hell's slumber party," before he went to stare out a nearby window.

Carole seemed little changed from when she was first delivered into the care of the hospital's *lethargica* clinic. Her doctor was still as animated as he had been during their first visit, but his clutch of patients remained much the same: inert, silent, almost frightening in their somnolent incommunicativeness. Enders' brief conversation with the doctor did nothing to diminish his angst. He and his parents left depressed.

A visit to Bobby's speakeasy did not lift his spirits, though he did admit to the beer being better than on his first visit. Even Lonergan's breezy banter was but a brief anesthetic from the reality on display in the Yale clinic.

He left Milford in a restless, unhappy mood. His sister's near-vegetative state gnawed at him. His father's presence continued to stir old resentments. The town, with its familiar streets and houses and people, depressed him. He wasn't sure why. It was, after all, home. Familiar. Safe. Predictable. Maybe it was the sameness of the town and its people. He had changed; they had not. And why not? There had been a worldwide war. *La Grande Guerre.* And a pandemic. One or both of these monumentally destructive events should have shaken established life to its mundane core.

But his mood began to lift as he rode farther east, back toward Old Lyme. Here was something different. It wasn't a bustling city—there were less than a thousand people in the area and most of them were content to farm, fish, or sit quietly on old money. Maybe it was just the "newness." A new job. New people with whom to work. New money in his pocket. The magic of watching a scruffy bit of land transformed into a new house. Or maybe it was the morning air, laced with the brine of the sea, which seeped into his room each morning, providing some mysterious stimulus to a tired spirit.

The warm breeze of a May morning woke him. Enders rolled out of bed and put aside the empty whiskey glass and book that had been his dual nightcaps. He shaved, dressed rough, and was about to bound down the stairs to breakfast when he looked out the back window. In the distance, he saw Spencer standing with an old man resting on a cane. Behind them stood a polished silver Duesenberg. Its uniformed driver rested between the car's gleaming front headlamps. Spencer waved his arms left and right as if to banish the browsing cows and conjure a row of already bought-and-paid-for cottages.

*Spence is up early. Fancy car. Must be the old man. J. J. Johnson himself.*

On the far side of the field, behind a break of budding trees and a swampy creek slowly dripping into the Sound, Enders glimpsed a smattering of summer cottages that had spilled off the Sound View streets and now were coalescing into an independent association called Old Colony. He wasn't sure why they didn't call it New Colony—the owners had declared their independence from Sound View Beach. That was new. Maybe Spencer was worried the spreading colony might cross the creek and establish a footing on the Kloss farmland he was expecting JJJ to purchase. Maybe it was why the old man was up and out here so early. Spencer was showing him the looming threat of other potential buyers.

*I'll hear about it soon enough.* He checked the time.

He went downstairs to breakfast. After Mrs. Kloss' pancake breakfast, he took his bike and coasted down the hill to the little field office on the side of the road. The Duesenberg was gone, but two company trucks were parked there, along with a familiar bicycle. Inside, Enders found Spencer, Jesse Martin from Point O' Woods, and the two foremen from Black Point, and Cornfield Point in Saybrook.

It was a rare bit of formal management, which the director may have felt compelled to act out following his own earlier meeting with the company founder. The foremen from the various sites in the Lyme and Niantic area sat in chairs scattered around the desk. They were white men in working clothes, dirty boots, and battered fedoras who had never walked across a college campus. Most of them smoked cigarettes or sipped coffee, or both, as they waited for Spencer. Two of them, hunched forward in their chairs, held their burning cigarettes clasped between a thumb and their first two fingers. Enders marked them as veterans of France. He pulled up the collar of his shirt and found a seat.

Spencer stirred a tin spoon through his black coffee with enough force to serve as a signal to his audience. The talking, sipping and puffing stopped for a moment, and everyone looked toward his desk.

He laid the spoon on his desk. "Okay, gents. Met with Mr. J this morning. He's pleased with our progress to date and with some opportunities to expand our operations in the state. We're doing good. But reassure me; let's get a rundown on each site. Progress and problems."

Each of the foremen took a few minutes to describe their respective development sites. Several men pulled out lists of supplies they needed to maintain the building pace. Spencer, nodding periodically, announced their monthly sales figures and his general satisfaction with those dollar amounts. Jesse Martin, from Point

O' Woods, again mentioned needing to hire more men. A man from Black Point said, "The shad season will be winding down soon, so no more nighttime fishing; the locals will be looking for daytime work till the fall."

Spencer nodded again. "Hire 'em. Farmers know how to work. And school will be out soon. We can get some cheap high school labor for the summer." He turned to Enders. "Dave. You might walk over to Griswold Point. See who's camped out there and on Poverty Island. When the shad run's finished and just the clammin' is left, you might find some guys wanting a steadier paycheck. At least for the summer."

"Sure. I've been wanting to walk that stretch of shore."

The Black Point foreman said, "Be polite out there and you might get a free drink. I heard those Swamp Yankees have a still."

Spencer grunted. "Hard to believe there's enough solid ground to support a still. Isn't that why the shacks are on stilts?"

The meeting broke up as quickly as it had started. Men started filing out the door. Truck engines revved to life and rolled away. Enders stepped to the back wall of the office to look at a large, exaggerated map of the Black Point Beach development. Neatly drawn cottages lined the shorefront. The city of New London appeared off to the east, and Hartford was a smear of white buildings in the truncated north of the map. In the sky above the beach club, a biplane banked above the water. A caption read, "Live Days of Delight in a New Atmosphere." Enders stared at the plane until Spencer said, "I think I'll have it framed for the Saybrook office."

Enders tapped the middle of the print. "It's colorful.

I think you need more imaginative street names. I keep seeing Sea Spray, Saltaire, Billow, Brightwater, Sea View, and Sea Breeze on all these maps."

He waved a dismissive hand. "Ah, they're just placeholders. Anyone wants, we'll just rename the street from where they come from. New Britain Avenue, Hartford Street, Meriden Lane. Springfield Road. Whatever. Someone buys enough property, we'll name a street for them."

Spencer turned to a door in the back wall. "Hey, you want some more coffee? I think it's done. Maybe burned at this point." He stepped into a narrow backroom of filing cabinets, shelving, and a mammoth green safe. An electric percolator sat on top of the safe. He poured two mugs and handed one to Enders.

"Any money in that thing?" Dave Enders pointed his mug at the massive steel box.

"Not enough to warrant hiring a peterman." Spencer stopped smiling. "So, what's on your mind?"

"Nothing." He sipped the black coffee, which he didn't need.

Spencer sat behind his desk and thumped his arms on the cluttered desk. "I'm a salesman. I read people. You've got something you want to ask me. So, ask."

Enders hid his face behind his coffee mug and settled on one of the vacated chairs.

*What's he been reading on my face? I'm not telegraphing anything. Am I?*

An eternity of silence seemed to fill the little house. Finally, he said, "So, I've been reading the property deeds for White Sand and some of the other projects. You know. The clauses about 'genuine Americans,' Caucasians only. No Negros, Jews, Greeks, Poles,

Italians, et cetera. No lots sold to 'undesirable people.' "

Spencer started searching his desk for an early morning cigar. "Look, kid. We didn't start this exclusivity business. Hell, all these damn Yankee coastal towns started their own residency restrictions. Didn't want the colored cooks and nannies of wealthy weekenders at their town beaches." He put a match to the slender Cuban wrap and blew out a dense cloud of white smoke. Enders watched it drift toward the nearby window.

"You've seen Fenwick over to Saybrook?"

"Yeah. I rode my bike by there a while back."

"The Fenwick Beach Association. Dates back to the late 1880s. Bunch of rich families got the state legislature to allow them to raise their own taxes and set their own zoning restrictions around the beachfront. Hell, they got a railroad spur laid to take them to their front doors."

Enders swallowed the last of his coffee. "I saw the sign at the entrance gate."

Spencer puffed out another cloud of Cuban smoke and looked at Enders. "See the five mansions at Hatchetts? Now that's exclusiveness. Those families have their own golf course, tennis courts, bowling alley, docks, vegetable gardens, waterworks. Hell, they have their own communal dining hall. It's like the Paris Commune. You want in there? You need to marry someone's daughter."

*Where would Spence have learned of the Paris Commune? I only heard about it three years ago.*

Enders placed his empty mug on the desk and sat back. "Ever hear of a guy named Eugene Bullard?"

Spencer shook his head.

"Colored guy. Escaped from the South. He

eventually made his way to France. Fought for the French at Verdun and the Somme. Somewhere along the way, he learned to fly Nieuports and Spads. French fighter planes. Then he joined the Lafayette Flying Corps—where I knew him. He did about two dozen combat missions and received a lot of war medals and ribbons. An impressive guy. I liked him."

"What happened to him?"

Enders shrugged. "I'd like to think he had the sense to stay in France."

Spencer leaned across his desk and said, "I'm not the bad guy here. You've been to Sound View." He used his cigar to point out the door. "I have a name for you too: Harry Hilliard."

"I haven't heard of him."

Spencer jumped out of his chair and went into the back room. Enders saw him open a filing cabinet. From the back, he shouted, "He's the biggest socialist in Connecticut. Practically a commie. He's been buying coastal farmland here since the '90s. Sells 50-by-100 parcels to anyone. Poles. Hebrews. Italians. That's why you can get a decent meal just off the beach." He returned to his desk, chuckling at his own joke.

He sat and looked at the pages in his hand. "But even he has limits. This is one of his deed restrictions: 'It is distinctly understood and agreed that neither the said lot as a whole nor any portion thereof shall be sold to a negro, nor shall it be rented or sublet to a negro, and neither shall any cottage or building thereon erected be rented or sublet to a negro.' Even with Hilliard, your Eugene friend is out of luck."

"I guess it's hard to avoid racism…"

"That's the point. People want to come down here

to escape the city, escape work, forget the KKK and refugees and immigrants. They don't want to get here on Friday evening and find the League of Nations."

Spencer was enjoying his speech. He leaned into Enders again, saying, "We're building for the middle class. The guys doing hard work every day. We're offering them a sense of having made it. A second home. A vacation home at the beach. It's their reward, their right to have a little privilege, a little exclusivity. They want to see their names in the *Here for the Season* columns. There aren't a lot of middle-class guys at the Newport Yacht Club or the Yale Club. But we can offer them a sense of financial prosperity and social status."

Enders couldn't think of anything to add. *Maybe I shouldn't. This could turn into an argument, which I'll lose. Maybe lose my job too.*

He started to stand, but Spencer said, "In a way, we're just in step with the government. You probably haven't heard of the Better Homes in America campaign yet. Just started; I think Hoover's running it. It's intended to promote national home ownership. Even the campaign is saying new home buyers should consider the types of people living in the neighborhood before they buy in."

Spencer seemed satisfied with his lecture and sat back in his chair. He snuffed out the half-smoked cigar and glanced at the wall clock behind Enders. "Listen, I like you. You work hard. You got your crew working without being a bastard about it. You're making sales and talking up the West Hartford college dames. You could be running the whole company construction unit in a couple of years. So, what do you want to do, change the world or build houses?"

Enders had seen Spencer glance at the clock. The

lecture was over. He stood and said, "I was in France trying to change the world."

"Yeah, how'd that go?"

He placed the palm of his hand against the scar on his neck. "Not too well."

"It never does."

"I'd better get to White Sand." He turned to go.

"Hey, I'd been meaning to ask." Spencer looked like he was waiting for the punchline of a joke. "You said you got shot down three times. Once seems plenty. How come you kept going back up?"

Enders shrugged again. "Persistence?"

\*\*\*\*

It was an early Saturday morning. Enders was in the just-opened town library. Wandering through the stacks, he seemed to be alone and wondered if it was too early for church ladies to be around quoting Matthew to the library patrons. He picked up *Main Street* by Sinclair Lewis.

*Well, F. Scott showed how the beautiful people live. Let's see how the other half do.*

He took the book to the front desk, where the same young librarian checked his new library card, stamped his book, and gave him an inviting smile. Enders hesitated for a second, imagining her with bobbed hair, dressed in a dark, sleeveless flapper's dress of fringe and sequin, with a lasso of pearls revolving around her neck as she did the foxtrot.

Outside, he laughed to himself. *I need help. Or something.*

He looked up and down the street. *North or south? East or west?* He climbed on his bike and pedaled north, up the street, past the town hall. Beyond the center's buildings, he came to a long, shingled edifice with skylights and wide double doors. A sign in front read, Old Lyme Art Association Gallery. Several women were setting out tables and chairs for a little outdoor party. Farther up the road stood a tall, columned Georgian mansion. Beside the house, several men and women sat or stood before wooden easels to paint on small canvases. He stopped and looked around. Across the street from the mansion was the new Lyme Auto Service garage, a setting that seemed unlikely to attract the interest of serious artists. An aged barn sat farther back from the garage.

He turned the bike around gracelessly. He pedaled back to a narrow path between the gallery and the mansion and glided across a rail-less footbridge, which led to a wide field of grass and flowers and solitary trees. Near the far end of the field, close to the edge of the Lieutenant River, a woman stood by a large easel, hands on her hips. Enders jumped off his bike and walked to her.

"Good morning," he called to her back.

The woman turned at the sound of his voice, a look of frustration still on her face. She relaxed her features and gave him a casual wave.

Enders stopped and stared at her for a second too long. She was beautiful—not movie star beautiful or conventionally beautiful—but she had an undefinable look that interested him immediately and kept pulling his attention back to her engaging face. She wore a checkered tunic dress that failed to hide her curvaceous shape, a floppy straw hat that sometimes concealed one eye, a pale cotton kimono with tiny splatters of paint on it, and black-and-white Oxfords dusty with pollen.

"Hope I'm not disturbing you. I was just coming over to see the river." He glanced back toward the brush-fronted riverbank and glimpsed a small dock protruding into the sluggish river. Three flat-bottomed rowboats were tied to the wooden dock.

She sighed almost to herself. "It's all right. Things just are not working." She stared at the half-finished painting on the easel. "I have a heavy hand today."

Enders stared at the canvas. He recognized the painted tree in the foreground, the fence posts behind it, the bend in the river, and the bridge in the upper right corner of the canvas. It looked fine to him. Bright smears of color gracefully brought together to form recognizable features of the landscape.

"Maybe it needs people or some animals? Something lively?"

"Everyone's a critic." She laughed. "But I've never stooped to bovinity."

"Bovinity?" He repeated the word like he was tasting it. "Bovinity?"

"Cows."

"Yes. I just never heard that version of bovine before."

"There used to be an artist here—William Howe—who would rent cows from local farms whenever he wanted a more bucolic scene."

"I can't see a cow being a very cooperative model."

"What time is it? Do you know?" she asked.

He looked at his wristwatch. "Eleven-ten. I'm sorry. Am I keeping you from something?"

She shook her head and looked back at her canvas. "I'm not going to fix this today." She glanced at the sky. Enders looked at the almost stationary cumuli too. She started packing her paints and brushes and took off her kimono. She piled her things into a light wheelbarrow and placed her canvas on top of her equipment.

"Want to trade? You roll my bike; I'll push your wheelbarrow."

"That's very nice of you." She stepped forward and offered a paint-smeared hand. "Karen Bates. Unhappy artist."

Enders took her warm, dry hand. He didn't want to let go of it. "Dave Enders. Happy to meet the unhappy artist."

She took hold of his bike, turned it around, and headed back across the field toward the mansion. Enders lifted the wheelbarrow handles and followed her. On the other side of the field, they stopped beside a shingled shed behind the mansion.

"This used to be Childe Hassam's studio. And the thing in the middle of the orchard"—she pointed to what looked like a man-high pushcart with colorful wagon wheels and glass windows—"that's Ben Eggleston's portable studio. I don't know why he built it. What's the point of painting *en plein air* if you're going to sit in a tiny house?" She turned to him. "It means…"

"'Outside,' yes. I recognize the French."

"Do you know about impressionist painting?"

"Not a thing. But I saw a few such works in France."

"Oh, were you in Paris? That's so exciting. I'd love to go."

"Occasionally. Mostly I was in the east or down on the Med."

She cocked her head and stared at his face. She reached up and laid a finger over the scar on his neck, which was visible from his open shirt collar. Enders almost flinched at the unexpected intimacy of her touch.

She withdrew her short-nailed finger and said, "Well, you were somewhere. Tell me about that. You were a soldier."

He could not believe the boldness of this woman; this woman with her sagging hat and paint-splattered clothes and pollinated oxfords.

Behind him, he heard an automobile horn and the crunch of tires on gravel. He jerked a thumb in the direction of the Lyme Inn's driveway and said, "I was a pilot. Come to lunch with me and I'll tell you about France. Or whatever you want to hear."

"Oh, I can't. I'm supposed to attend the gallery party. But tomorrow…"

"Tomorrow's good. Where can I meet you?" *I can't believe I have to wait another day for this woman. Christ, what if she wants to paint instead?*

"I'm staying with Miss Florence." She pointed to the mansion. "Come over and we'll walk to the Inn. I haven't eaten there, so it'll be fun. Yes?"

"Yes." *I can be bold too*. He reached out a hand as if to shake her hand, but instead kissed it, saying in French, "Karen, I look forward to the pleasure of your company."

She withdrew her hand, staring into his smiling eyes. "Well, *monsieur*, I look forward to lunch. And stories. Lots of stories. Otherwise, I might bore you with talk of canvas undercoats and complementary colors. And bovinity."

Chapter 4

Sunday eventually arrived. Enders sped down the noontime road in a cloud of dry spring dust. He pulled the company truck in a tight U-turn and parked in front of the mansion. She stood on the front steps, leaning against one of the round white columns. She eased away from the column and sauntered toward the truck in a sleeveless floral-print Davis dress and T-strap heels. Her dark brown hair fell loosely around her narrow face. He met her on the edge of the lawn and wondered at the color of her eyes: somewhere between a light blue and a pale green. He was sure she would have a proper name for their color.

She glanced at the stenciled company name on the truck door. "Ready for lunch, Mr. Enders?"

"I was ready yesterday." He waved his left hand in the direction of the Inn and they stepped back into the street. Enders looked left.

"There's no traffic. You could take a nap in the middle of the road and be perfectly safe," said Karen.

"It is a quiet little town. Maybe I'm being overly generous with the word 'town.' More like a village? Or a hamlet?"

"You're not going to change that special smallness, are you?"

He told her where he worked, what he was doing, and where he was living. "I promise not to move any cows or knock down any barns until you've painted them."

"I do like that big white Manor House. I thought I might try to paint it this fall with the changing leaves and an autumn sky."

The Inn's desk clerk guided them to a sunny dining room along the south side of the building. They ordered steamed mussels, chowder, and *tautog*, the local blackfish. Enders bemoaned the absence of a properly chilled white wine.

"All the more reason to go back to France. Now tell me about you in France. You were a pilot. You were hurt? Shot while flying? And…"

Enders loosened his tie and pulled at his collar. He straightened his suit coat and leaned back in his chair.

****

"Well, the Germans, with their hobnail boots and pointy steel helmets normally make a lot of noise moving around. But they do know how to tiptoe through the clouds. And that's how one of them snuck up and shot me from behind."

Enders held out his left hand, palm down. His right hand descended toward his left wrist.

"Planes have machine guns, but it's funny, I only remember hearing one shot. That shot burned my neck—made a mess of my scarf, by the way—punched through my instrument panel, and ruptured the fuel tank. Now, suddenly, gasoline is pouring into the cockpit. My pants and boots are getting soaked with gas. One spark, one bit of static, and I'm a bonfire in the sky."

Enders started playing with his fork. He shook his head. *This isn't something I want to remember. Why am I telling her this stuff?*

"Oh, my. That must have been terrifying. What did you do?"

"What did I do?" He asked himself as if he wasn't sure. "Banked left and down." Enders tilted slightly to the left in his chair. "One of my squad mates engaged the German. I shut off my engine, worried that sparks or heat would ignite the gas."

He looked at her blue-green eyes, which stared unblinking at him. "I was scared to death. We were at twelve thousand feet. I was gliding now. No engine. But the wind, for once, was with me. I got archied—shot at with anti-aircraft fire—as I crossed the line again. Then I started looking for a place to put down. I couldn't be too choosy—my machine was dropping fast."

He stared up at the blue-painted ceiling. "It was so quiet without the engine. I smelled the gas. My neck hurt. The ground was coming up fast. There was a fenced field to the south, and I angled that way a bit. I didn't think I'd reach it. The plane was so low my wheels smashed into the top railing of the fence. I hit the ground and rolled silently toward...a herd of cows."

Karen sniggered. "More bovinity."

Enders looked at her. His heart had stopped racing from the memory. "It wasn't funny," he said, smiling. "They didn't hear me coming. They were just standing there waiting to be hit and wreck my plane. I started yelling, *Bougez! Bougez!* and waving my arms. Finally, they scattered, and I came to a stop at the other end of the pasture. I jumped out and ran to this farmhouse. They had a pump out back, and I started pumping water over my pants and boots. I didn't want some cigarette-smoking farmer to wander by and light me up. Fortunately, when the farmer did come around, he wasn't smoking. He just pointed to my bloody scarf and said, 'Hey, Lieutenant Pilot, you're bleeding.'" He pointed to his neck. "So that's how I knew I'd really been hit. Just a scratch, considering what happened to so many others."

Karen was serious again. "I'm sure it was unnerving...terrifying, up there. People trying to kill you. Crashing to the ground."

*That's twice now I've told someone about that shoot-down.* Enders went back to his fish. After another bite, he asked, "So, how did you come to be a painter here in Lyme?"

"Old Lyme. There's a difference. Well, it's not nearly as exciting as your life." She touched the corner of her lipsticked mouth with her starched napkin. "My parents packed me off to Miss Porter's. In Farmington?"

*Porter's. I might have guessed.* He nodded. "I grew up in Milford."

"It didn't do my parents any good. I fell in with a catty group of girls; we spent all our time ranking our classmates. You know, most likely to marry rich. Most likely to marry a Hartford insurance exec. Most likely to leave in the middle of the school year. We were terrible."

Enders smiled. "Positively evil."

"Still, something good came out of it. In town, I came across a few impressionist paintings by a man named Dawson-Watson. I thought they were just...wonderful. So bright and colorful. I loved his *In the Shallows;* it felt like me. I persuaded my parents, begged really, to send me to the Women's Art School at Cooper Union. That's where I learned to paint."

Enders put his elbows on the table and folded his hands under his shaved chin. "And then you came out here to paint?"

"I went to the colony in Cos Cob first. Close to home. So many painters. And writers. But a little too New York. So, I came out here. More pristine. More 'Old New England.' More cows."

"Well, I'm glad you did. I don't suppose I could get you to come to the Sound View Casino or O'Conner's Dance Hall some night?"

"That would be fine. However, I first need to find a place to live. The season is starting, and Miss Florence has a house full of regulars. I need to look for another room. I can't be running to and from my parents' place in Port Chester.

"I'll build you a cottage."

She leaned toward him and whispered, "Take me to Paris."

He could not believe the boldness of this woman.

\*\*\*\*

After a lunch Enders had prolonged as long as he could, they strolled back toward Miss Griswold's estate. Karen was right, there was little chance of being hit by a car as they strolled up the middle of the lazy, dusty street.

They stopped in front of the walkway. A couple of artists remained before their easels in the shade of the mansion.

"Well, I had a lovely time. Thank you for lunch," said Karen.

Enders smiled and asked, "Aren't you going to invite me up to see your etchings?"

She laughed. "That line didn't do Stanford White any good. Are you sure you want to risk it?"

"Well, it did wonders for Evelyn Nesbitt's career. She's still around, yes?"

"Oh, yes. Very busy these days." She glanced back

at the mansion and the working artists. "How about if I find a place first? Do you have a telephone you can use?"

He gave her the numbers for the two JJJ offices and his home number in Milford.

"I'll call as soon as I can."

"I drive in to see the town clerk regularly. I'll look for you." He walked back to the truck, waved, and drove away. She stood on the walkway until he was out of sight.

****

Enders did not drive to the field office or the Manor House. Instead, he impulsively pulled into the Lyme train station and stopped.

He looked at his watch. *Another westbound in three minutes.* He jumped out of the truck and ran onto the platform. *I've got time. It's a quick trip. I've been away for years; I can spare the rest of the day.*

The train pulled to a stop and Enders climbed aboard, paying the conductor for a two-way ticket to New Haven. He sat in the car, drumming his fingers on his legs and staring at the empty seat in front of him as the train chugged along the coast.

In New Haven, he strode several blocks to the Yale-New Haven Hospital and began searching for the neurology ward. A nurse led him to the six-bed ward overlooking a weedy, bricked-in courtyard. He signed the visitors' log, spying his mother's fluid signature from last Friday. The little ward was filled with three girls, a child of uncertain gender, a teenage boy, a middle-aged man, and Carole. He hesitated, then stepped to her bed.

She was propped up with an extra pillow. Dressed in hospital whites, she lay on her back, seemingly asleep, awaiting but a gentle noise or her whispered name to awaken her. Enders tried her name. She didn't move. He called her again. Louder, but with no response. He glanced around the room, then shook her shoulder, almost shouting, "Carole."

Her eyes opened. Carole blinked several times and turned to look at her brother. "David."

Her eyes fluttered shut.

He shook her again, shouting her name. Her eyes opened again. She looked at him and asked, "David, where have you been?"

"Carole… I was in the war. In Europe. But I'm home…"

Carole moved her head and her eyes slammed shut as if she had finished with all visitors for the day.

*She's awake!* He grabbed her by the shoulders and shook her again, shouting her name until another voice stopped him. He turned to find her doctor, the one he had met when they first brought her to Yale.

"She's probably had enough for the moment. They wake up, but they can't stay awake. But the stimulus may help." He stepped closer to Enders. "I remember you from the intake appointment."

Reluctantly, he released his grip on his sister. "Yes, Dave Enders. Did you see her? She opened her eyes and said my name."

"William Hoffman." The doctor put out his hand. "It happens. We try to get them awake, and up and around, as much as possible."

Enders shook his hand. "Is she improving? Carole. Is she…"

"No. Not that I can tell." Hoffman surveyed the room, taking a quick inventory of the ward's occupants. "Do you have a moment? We can talk in my office."

He stared back at his sister. "Yeah, sure."

He followed the doctor down the tiled corridor and around the corner to a small office with a large desk and several floor-to-ceiling bookshelves crammed with textbooks and dark green file folders.

Enders dropped into an upholstered chair. The doctor began to fiddle with a hot plate and a glass flask. "Tea?"

"Sure."

"Back in medical school, I found tea was cheaper than coffee. Especially if I took the time to extract as much flavor as I could from every teabag and infuser." He handed Enders a chipped porcelain mug. "Sorry, no sugar or milk. Just the warmth and flavor of a good black tea."

Enders sipped from the mug. He felt drained now and hoped the tea might give him a jolt. "So, my sister?"

"Is part of a medical mystery. I think I mentioned at your first visit these cases have been appearing since 1915. Worldwide, there now may be several million cases of this *encephalitis lethargica*. In fact, you might say it has reached the level of a pandemic."

"Jesus, we just got over one pandemic. So now the influenza is causing this second pandemic?"

Hoffman propped himself against the bookshelves and cradled his tea mug. "As I might have said previously, influenza is coincident with cases of *encephalitis lethargica*, but may not be the cause of EL. Initially, some doctors suspected the culprit was the Pfeiffer's bacillus, which they also thought for a time was the agent of influenza. But they were wrong. And many of the first reported cases were diagnosed as botulism because of the floppy, drowsy presentation of the patients. But that's clearly wrong too."

"So, it's a process of elimination? Like Sherlock Holmes dismissing one explanation after another until…"

"Well, yes, I did say it was a mystery." Hoffman straightened up and went back to his desk. He opened a stiff green folder. "One intriguing possibility is scarlet fever. The diplococcus that causes it… but your mother says Carole never had scarlet fever. Correct?"

"Yes, I think so. I was away until recently. I never had it either, but I remember the red-and-black quarantine notices on a couple of houses in town when I was a kid."

Hoffman sat in his desk chair and folded his hands on its polished surface. "Sadly, we are likely to have many new cases to study in the coming years. There is no sign this thing is going to just disappear. There was an uptick in cases in November 1919, again in November 1920, and in January 1921. Including many fatal cases."

"What about this year?"

"We're still waiting for all the case numbers."

"So, it's more common in winter?"

"That's not a surprise. It's colder outside. People are crowded indoors staying warm. Passing around flu, pneumonia, scarlet fever, common colds, et cetera."

Enders set aside his tea mug and stood. "So, you've no idea what's going to happen with my sister?"

"Honestly, Mr. Enders, I couldn't guess."

Enders noticed a small painting on the opposite wall and stepped over to it. He pointed at the framed picture. "This looks like one of your patients. My sister, maybe."

The painting showed a young woman dressed in white, her head wrapped in a white scarf, lying on a narrow bed with writing materials resting on her lap.

Hoffman got up and walked to the painting. "It's called the 'Seeress of Prevorst.' Painted by a German artist named Gabriel von Max. I think he's dead now. Anyway, this woman in the painting was a real person. I forget her name, but a fascinating neurological case. Or maybe a fascinating psychiatric case."

Hoffman turned to Enders, an eager look on his face. "She had frequent convulsions and would fall into these coma-like or dream-like states in which she would speak in a bizarre, unknown language. Each time she awoke, she would claim to have been in communion with the spirit world and to have had prophetic dreams. The local village people believed she was a mystic. A seeress, if you will."

Enders looked at Hoffman's lively face. "What happened to her?"

"She died. Very young."

****

The Kloss Manor House did not have a telephone. Neither did Florence Griswold's boardinghouse for artists. He had to wait. Restlessly. Wondering about Karen.

*'Take me to Paris.' Who says that? And what would she do if I had the means and the inclination? Start packing?*

He thought of her as "the artist" and sometimes as "the painter." He wasn't sure if there was a difference in title. He remembered the painting in Hoffman's office. *The Seeress of Prevorst*. Karen might be interested in hearing about the painting and its history. But she'd want to know how he knew about it, and he'd have to tell her about Carole.

*I need to find less ghoulish things than war and disease to talk about on future dates.*

On Monday, he went back to work at the White Sand site. Once the crew had settled into the day's tasks, Enders walked to the beach and out to the end of Griswold Point. It was a pleasant walk on a warm May morning with the Sound on his left and the broad mouth of the Connecticut River directly ahead.

He followed a compacted path along the top of the dunes. As he neared the end of the Point, he saw three high-peaked army tents set behind the low dunes and nestled among clumps of beachgrass. Beyond them, across a shallow inlet separating the Point from low-lying Poverty Island, three shacks stood on rotting stilts above the brackish water. The tide was out, and he saw two men digging clams, clawing the muddy bottom with short steel rakes, and dragging along slat-and-wire baskets floating in black inner tubes to hold their catch.

*Now, this is a hard-scrabble life. Despite the fantastic view. Don't I know it.*

He turned to gaze at the ocean. Small waves lapped at the sandy peninsula. Just offshore, Enders could see the waves cresting along the length of a sandbar. He wondered if the men living here knew about all the building going on near them. Did they resent the intrusion? Would they come to resent the summertime influx of people with money and automobiles and the freedom to sit idly on a stretch of sand they once might have considered a part of their natural domain?

He was here to offer them work, a decent wage for decent work—work he was doing too. From the looks of things—the tents and stilted shacks—he imagined they might be happy for the wages. But maybe not. He had met fishermen along the Marseille coast who had been content to live a low-cost life of subsistence fishing and sporadic labor for the chance to do whatever they wanted on their own idiosyncratic schedules. Maybe these men did too. As a way of living, it had an appeal Enders could understand.

He passed the tents. A pair of dirty feet stuck out from the first tent. Enders walked on, finally stopping near the two men clamming.

"Morning," he called to them.

The two men stopped their work and straightened up in the shallow water. One of them waved a casual hand. The other nodded.

"I'm Dave Enders. Building foreman for White Sand." He inclined his head in the direction of the beach.

"The old troop beach," said one of the men.

"Yeah. Building cold-water cottages now. We're looking for some summer construction help if you're interested. Twenty-five a week. At least through the summer. Maybe longer."

"What's the particulars?"

"Digging foundation pilings. Pouring cement. Tacking tarpaper and wires. Pounding nails, sawing lumber."

The two men stepped out of the water and approached him, their waders squeaking with stray water. One man squeaked forward to extend a hand. "Tom Davidson." He was a thin man with short black hair, flared ears, and a shave so close to the skin it was hard to tell any hair had grown on his angular jawline.

Enders shook his hand, then turned to the second man.

"Hi there. Rick McMurphy. Nice to meet ya." He

shook Enders' hand with impressive force. McMurphy was a heavier man with close-cropped red hair. He wore a not-so-old army shirt with corporal's strips. Enders noticed a wedding ring on his left hand and wondered at a wife who would tolerate living in a tidal shack that lacked every convenience and essential known to American modernity.

Davidson said, "Be a nice addition to the clam and eel market at Saybrook Point. You want us, and maybe a third fella?"

Enders looked back at the tent with the protruding feet. "That him?"

"Nah. That's Tommy. Been here forever and a day. Just clams and drinks. It's a mystery how he lives in the winter."

"Well, three upright guys would be welcome. Come over to the site tomorrow. I'll sign you up and get you started. Eight o'clock."

"This a cash job?"

"Yes. Pay's every Friday afternoon."

Enders saw a rowboat round the tip of the island and start through the channel. Two kids were in the boat, one rowing, the other dipping a wire cylinder in and out of the water.

He pointed to the boat. "How are the kids at clamming?"

Both men glanced at the rowboat. One of them said, "That there's eel pots they're pulling. Good market for 'em 'cross the river."

"Okay. I'll see you in the morning. Just follow the noise. And bring a lunch for yourselves." Enders shook hands with the men and started back along the beach to the work site.

Eels, he thought. *Couldn't eat the glass eels in France. I'm sure not gonna eat the black eels here.* Swimming in the Sound around Milford, he and his friends would sometimes scare up eels hiding in the slender green eelgrass that grew in the sandy shallows. Their long black forms would slither away between the underwater stems, like snakes through an uncut lawn. *No sir. No snakes. No eels. My personal menu has limits.*

\*\*\*\*

Davidson and McMurphy showed up the following morning with a third man Enders didn't recognize. He was short and dark—either from the sun or his ancestors—wearing leather work gloves, a wide-brimmed hat, and a dark beard. Enders thought he would make an excellent pirate. He checked the names and spellings of the first two men; they were local farmhands who rented the island shacks during the summer and went back to farming, haying, and lumbering in the fall.

The pirate gave his name as Vasco Silva. He had an accent Enders could not place. He asked, "Spanish?"

"Portuguese."

Enders nodded and said, "*Bom Dia*," remembering the phrase from the Mediterranean's cosmopolitan coast.

He introduced them to some of the regular crew, then led them to a sold lot gridded with string and stakes and marked with wooden squares to show the placement of piling holes. Enders picked up one of the two-by-two-foot wooden frames.

"Okay. Pilings for the house. Dig down two feet. Make sure the hole is wide enough for a two-by-two foot of cement or block. Twelve pilings here. Twelve more at the next lot."

He pointed to another lot of strings and markers

across an imaginary street. "Once the digging is done, we'll pour some concrete, let it set, and then get to work framing that one back there." He pointed back to the regular crew at work on flooring the joists of a nearby cottage.

"Questions?"

There were none. The men picked up shovels and started digging.

*Farmers and clammers. They know shovels.* Enders went back to the house where more of the crew were at work. He and Sammy Gross talked for a few minutes about septic piping, electrical wire, and the need to buy more joist lumber before the end of the week.

Enders made some notes in a cardstock notebook. "Got it." He looked at Sammy. "I've got to see Mr. Spencer sometime today. Any ideas, complaints, high praise you want me to pass along?"

"Nothin' comes to mind. Less'en he wants to give us all a raise?"

"Yeah, I'll check on that." He waved the notebook at him and sauntered to an almost-completed cottage with an across-the-street view of the Sound.

He stepped inside and looked around at what would be the living room. A brick fireplace stood in the middle of the back wall, separating two bedrooms behind the wall. Two closets stood on either side of the fireplace. A short hallway to the right led into a kitchen and an open back porch. A narrow water closet stood just before the kitchen. Enders looked up between the roof rafters to the underside of the roof. Windows were in place, but most of the walls still needed to be paneled over to hide the framing and the exterior walls.

Enders flipped open his notebook to a list of final

details he would run through. He called it his "walk-around" after the pre-flight inspections he did before climbing into his warplane. The septic pipe was in place. The sink's cold-water pipe and drain were done. An electrical outlet was set in every room, though he knew the town did not have regular 24-hour power. The fuse box was nailed in place and awaited a couple of screw-in fuses. He stepped out the back door to see a shower head and pipe tacked to the back wall of the cottage. He grinned at the shower pipe, imagining kids trying to wash sand off themselves without getting too wet from the cold-water spray.

Back inside, he checked the chimney flue—the fireplace would be the only source of heat in the spring and fall. On the front porch, the tall wire screens were in place, offering a mosquito-free but not a rain-proof view of the neighborhood. Enders imagined chairs and rockers on the porch, the owners sitting out in the evening, listening to the ocean and waving at neighbors passing by. The thought stopped him. He stood there for several seconds. Enders stepped back into the living room and looked around. "Imagine," he said out loud and wandered back into the kitchen to look at the empty space.

****

Spencer was laughing into the phone when Enders knocked on the doorframe and stepped inside the Sound View field office. Still looking amused, Spencer hung up the phone and asked, "Dave Enders, you ever been to our Rogers Lake site? Beautiful spot. If you prefer lakes over salt water. I was just reminiscing." He glanced back at the telephone. "Back then I went door-to-door in Hartford, selling lots at the lake for ten cents apiece."

Enders sat in front of the desk. "Sounds like a bargain."

"Nah. Worthless swamp. A muskrat won't live there. But people came to look at their new property. See the lake. Naturally, they weren't happy with what their dimes had bought, so I would say to them, 'How about trading up?'" A nice piece of lakefront for fifteen hundred, or a hillside view on the west side for a bit more? You'd be surprised how many decided to 'trade up.' So, they wind up spending fifteen hundred and ten cents.' He laughed again. "Rogers Lake, it's a boomtown up there now. Pretty soon lakefronts will be going for four thousand. It was a great idea. If I do say so."

Enders took his hat off and rolled it around in his hands. "Clever sales pitch. Sounds honest enough, though there's just something about it that feels…a bit shifty? Maybe?"

Spencer leaned back in his chair. "'Though I am not naturally honest, I am sometimes so by chance.' Shakespeare. *The Winter's Tale*. Ever read the Bard?"

Surprised by Spencer's obscure quote, Enders felt he had to defend his own erudition. "*Julius Caesar. Romeo and Juliet. King Lear. Hamlet*. Some of the sonnets."

"It was honest enough, let me tell you. A dime for a muddy bit of land. And a chance to buy something better. So, what brings you in today?"

Enders told him about the three men he had hired and gave Spencer their names so they could be paid on time. "And I have an idea."

"Okay. Entertain me." Spencer rested his chin in the cup of his right palm, his elbow planted on the desk.

"Well, we're selling people empty lots. Some of

them are ugly-looking, with all that sand and rock and scrub. And all the buyers have for getting a sense of what they're buying are the company sketches and blueprints of the standard cottages. It's hard to imagine living in a sketch. But what if we built a complete cottage? Painted it. Stocked it with furniture, a stove, and an icebox. Pictures on the walls, knickknacks on the shelves. Potential buyers could walk through it, look around, really imagine themselves in it. They would be able to see exactly what a summer house could be."

Spencer jumped up. He started walking diagonally across the office room, reversing and marching back. "Yeah. Yeah, like walking through someone's already lived-in house. See the layout. Okay. We'd say this is the typical summer cottage…"

"They could ask for changes. On the spot. Maybe expensive changes," said Enders.

He was still pacing, digesting the idea. Enders had been turning to follow his course, but gave up knowing he would eventually come back into view.

"Architects, they make small models of the stuff they're going to build. We could make a life-size model. A model home—the beach model—you could walk through. Furniture. Curtains. Everything." He turned on his heels and sat behind his desk. "I don't think anyone's done that before. Not so I've heard. And it's not like we can ask people already living there to let us troop strangers through their bedrooms regularly." Almost to himself now, he said, "Yeah…model home."

"So, it's a good idea?"

Spencer looked across his desk. "Hell, yes." He scribbled a note. "I'm gonna send over three guys from Black Point. Put 'em to work building the single-story, then the two-story standard. Pick some nice lots, not prime, but nice. We'll stage a couple of model cottages and see what happens."

"We'll need to buy things…to decorate the insides. Maybe from a consignment or secondhand store."

Spencer stared at the low ceiling. "Maybe my wife. She likes to decorate. Or spend money, I'm not sure which." He looked back at Enders for a long moment. Then he grinned. "Speaking of money, Lieutenant Enders. How about a five-dollar-a-week raise?" He pointed a wagging index finger at him. "I knew you'd be good. You're not looking to take my job, are you?" Spencer raised an inquisitive eyebrow at Enders.

"No. Thanks. I appreciate the confidence. And the raise."

"It's a very good idea. I like it." He made a note to the Saybrook office to have Enders' weekly pay increased. He lifted an eyebrow at Enders still sitting before the desk. "Anything else?"

"Yes. My brother mentioned real estate commissions when I telephoned him the other night. Shouldn't I get some kind of commission for selling those two cottages to the French-speaking women? The socialites?"

"Yeah, maybe. If this was 1919. Things have changed. The speculators and curbstoners are gone. Now you need to be a state-licensed real estate broker. Like me."

"Oh."

Spencer looked at Enders' disappointed face and drummed the fingers of his right hand on the desktop. He came to a sudden decision and yanked open the center drawer of the desk. Spencer pulled out a large blue check ledger, flipped it open, and started writing.

He glanced at Enders again, mumbling, "I am not naturally honest…" He tore a large check from the ledger and handed it to him. "Still, good work should be rewarded. Here's two hundred. It's not a proper commission, but you're not a proper realtor."

Enders skimmed the check off the desk, folded it in half, and stuck it in his shirt pocket. "Thanks. I appreciate the consideration." He put his hand on the triangle of polished wood on the desktop that advertised his boss: John A. Spencer, Property Director. Smiling, Enders tipped it forward and said, "That Shakespeare quote. Maybe you could use this side to let potential buyers know you're sometimes honest. You know, forewarned is forearmed." He smiled to let his boss know he was joking.

Spencer seemed to give the idea serious consideration. He glanced at the triangular wooden name plate and said, "Yeah, it might fit." After a second or two, he grunted, got up, and went into the back storeroom. He came back with a cup of coffee in one hand and a file folder in the other. He handed the file to Enders.

"Drop these deeds with the town clerk sometime this week. Woods and Black Point sales." He sat again and sipped the burned black coffee. "Okay, go build some model cottages before my honesty dissipates." Enders headed for the door.

****

Carole Enders died on May 19. Spencer's secretary/assistant in Saybrook took the telephone call from Enders' mother. Then she got on the train and made her way to the White Sand development to find Enders.

Dave Enders sat on the back of a truck for a long

time thinking about the coma-like patient he had left at Yale-New Haven Hospital. In that state, and after his six-year absence, Carole had seemed more like a stranger, or maybe an artifact, than like his younger sister. His clearest memories of her were as a fourteen-year-old girl before he left for France in 1916. He decided to hang onto those earlier memories and forget the bedridden patient who could barely acknowledge his return.

Enders slid off the truck bed and gathered the nearest members of his crew. He told them he'd be away for a few days to deal with a death in the family. "You guys know what to do. Get the sold lots built. Get the model cottages going. I'll be back as soon as I can."

There were muttered condolences, and Sammy said he would drive him wherever he needed to go. Silva, in his leather work gloves and hat, bowed his head and made the sign of the cross. Sammy drove Ann and Enders to the Manor House. Enders threw some clothes into an overnight bag, left a note for Mrs. Kloss, and then they were on their way back to the Sound View station.

Ann got off the train in Saybrook. Enders thanked her for taking the trouble to come find him with the news. He had meant to ask her about being away from the job. Would he be paid for the missed days? Did he even have vacation days? He had never asked, thinking only to be away from Milford again and busy at some work other than his father's store and mill. He would have to check on such details when he got back.

Alone on the train ride to Milford, he thought of his mother's grief and what other emotions might surface at home in the coming days. *I hope Bobby's still got his speakeasy going. I'm gonna need a couple of shots.*

His thoughts turned to Karen Bates. She had

telephoned the other day to say she had found a room on Library Lane with an elderly woman. He hoped it wasn't the Bible-quoting woman from the library, which led him to wonder how many elderly women were sitting comfortably in mansions in Old Lyme. Karen had gone home to Port Chester to collect some more clothes, so the only time he could find to be with her had been a hurried Wednesday breakfast in Old Lyme.

*Who has a breakfast date*? But Enders had been glad to see her even for an early morning moment over toast and eggs. Now he would miss her again while he was in Milford.

His jumbled thoughts ended with the conductor's announcement of their arrival back in town. *Home again, home again. Again.* He pulled himself upright, collected his bag, and headed to his family's house.

Chapter 5

Enders had eight days of paid vacation time, as long as he didn't take it during the prime building season, plus the usual holidays. He stood in one of the still fictitious streets of White Sand Beach Association, thinking how he might have to divide his few remaining vacation days between family and Karen Bates. Around him, his building crew dug piling holes, bricked chimneys, and nailed up wallboard. The company had placed new cottage advertisements in newspapers in Hartford, Springfield, and Meriden, so more potential buyers could be expected during the course of the summer.

Enders' two model cottages—he was thinking of them as his, his idea, his models—were going up as fast as ten men could dig holes, lay brick, and cut wood. *I need to hire more men, high schoolers if nothing else.*

One morning, he stopped one of the Poverty Island workers. "Mr. Davidson, how are things?"

"No complaints. Work's easy enough and I like the extra money."

"I heard rumor there was a still over your way."

Davidson looked around the yard. "Might be." He lifted his cap and rubbed his forehead with the back of his callused hand.

"What do you suppose is being brewed out there? I might be interested in a bottle of something that won't blind me."

"Like potato vodka? Taters and skins are cheap. A monkey could make vodka. Nice clean copper distillation rig. Makes pretty smooth stuff. So I hear."

"Well, if you hear anymore, I'd consider buying a bottle sometime." Enders smiled at the man and walked toward one of the company trucks.

He drove into town to leave some newly signed deeds with Bob Cratchit. Taking advantage of his proximity to Florence Griswold's estate, he drove to her house. From the street, he saw a few artists in the field beyond her yard. He parked, hopped over the roadside creek, and stepped into the field. Close to the riverbank, he started searching for Karen.

She was standing before her easel in the same spot where he had first met her. Enders stopped and stared at her for a minute. He watched her move as she painted. He wanted to touch her. He had a sudden image of the two of them lying in the field, in each other's arms.

Reluctantly, he ended the fantasy and stepped closer. "Hello. Is it finished yet?"

She turned at the sound of his voice. "You're back. How are you? How is your family?" She put her palette aside and wiped her hands with a small rag. She reached out a hand to touch his sleeve. "Was it awful?"

"No. Not awful. Painful enough. I guess it was a cruel reminder the Spanish Flu isn't done with us yet. Or maybe something new is stalking us." He told her about the funeral and the Yale doctor who had surprised them by attending the service.

"Was it his penance?"

Enders shrugged.

"Did he say anything more about your sister? I don't understand how someone in a coma can just die."

"He said they die from brainstem inflammation. And maybe increasing cranial pressure." Enders held out his hands, his fingers spread apart as if he was squeezing a basketball. "Anyway. My mom… She'll never get over it, I'm afraid. She and Carole were close. At least they were before I left." Enders looked to the river, trying to hide whatever his face might be showing.

She tugged on his sleeve. He turned back to her. "Perhaps we could do something less grim this Friday or Saturday?"

"Yeah, I'd like to. That's why I drove by. I wanted to ask you. We could go to O'Connor's Friday. I could meet you at the Sound View station. The 7:10 train. It'll give me time to clean up and practice my foxtrot."

Karen gave him a quiet laugh. "What of your tango?"

"Without a couple of drinks in me, it looks like a waltz. That reminds me, you never told me how old you are. Or what year you graduated from Porter's."

"No, I didn't, did I." Smiling, she returned to her painting.

"Okay. Friday. I'm looking forward to it."

She glanced back at him. "So am I, David." It was the first time she'd spoken his given name. She sounded nervous using it. "You can tell me more about your life in the air."

"No." He smiled at her.

"About France?"

"I'll see you Friday. Karen." The sound of her name lingered in his ear. Enders hiked back to his truck. He felt her eyes on him and turned to see her watching him as he walked back across the field. He waved.

Enders reached the truck, jumped on the runner, and

waved madly at her. He wasn't sure if she saw him this time. He climbed in, started the motor, and turned to drive across the street to the Lyme Auto Service. Enders asked the attendant to fill the tank and stepped aside to let the man work. Hands in his pockets, he bent toward the front windows to look in the office. On the back wall, he spotted two photographs of familiar airplanes. He went around to the side door and into the little office. The first photograph showed a De Havilland biplane in flight. The other showed a pilot standing beside the plane.

"It's a De Havilland," said a voice off to Enders' right. He straightened up and turned to see a tall man with a rough shirt and a smooth tie standing with a clipboard in the garage bay doorframe. The man limped into the office.

"Yes, a DH-4."

"You know planes?" The man set his clipboard on the desk and leaned on the edge.

"I flew Nieuport 17s for the French. Were you in the war?"

"Naw. Flew for the mail service until two years ago. Then I crashed." The man stuck out his hand. "Fred Winsted, former pilot."

Enders reached over and shook his hand. "Dave Enders, former pilot."

Winsted spread his arms and said, "You look fine. Nary a scratch on you. You must have been an ace."

He shook his head. "Just real, real lucky, Mr. Winsted."

"Fred. You fly anything bigger than the one-man Nieuport?"

"The British RE-8, late in the war—courtesy of the *Aviation Militaire Belge*. And a Jenny JN-4 in 1919 doing recon for the occupation for a few months. Both good machines. Once you got used to them."

"Plenty of Jennys and DH-4s in Mitchell's air derby back in '19. You try to get in?"

"I was still in France. But I read every word I could find about it. Heck of a race."

The two men talked for a while. Winsted did not offer any details about his crash, and Enders knew not to ask. Enders told him he was working for the JJJ Company. Winsted pointed at the stenciling on the side of the truck. "I see as much."

Finally, Winsted said, "If you're interested in getting up there again, there's a guy over to Niantic, just up from the Guard base. He's been buying Army surplus and selling them off to flying circuses and barnstormers. I think he's still got some Jennys. Nice thing about flying around here is no one's shooting at you."

"I'll keep that in mind." Enders looked at his wristwatch. "Better get back to work before I'm looking for another job." He shook Winsted's hand again. "Nice to meet you."

Driving back to White Sand, Enders glanced at the truck's simpleton instrument panel, comparing it to aviation panels he knew. He wondered if he ever would "get back up there." He pulled into the nearest White Sand construction lot and stopped. *No. Why would I?*

****

Work ended for the week. The sun was still high in the sky as Enders watched his crew scatter by truck or foot for the coming weekend. He slipped his cotton shirt back on and found his hat, then followed the trail of the Griswold Point men as far as the beach. The beach was empty, but likely to attract a few cottage-owning families by evening. Near the water's edge—it was high tide—he took off most of his clothes. The Griswold men now were far enough away not to see or comment on his European boxer shorts. Enders stepped into the chilly saltwater, shuffled along the sandy bottom, dodging the occasional rock, and finally dived under the clear green water. He surfaced sputtering and swam out from the beach for a minute. The early evening Sound was calm, and he floated on his back, thinking about O'Connor's Dance Hall and Karen. He rolled over, slipped under the water again, and swam for shore. He paused, face-down in the water, to watch a large sand crab side-stepping its way between two kelp-covered rocks.

Back on the beach, he stood in the sunlight, wishing it would warm him faster. The orange sun seemed to balance itself atop the outer lighthouse in Saybrook. The wet breakwater glimmered in the angular afternoon light.

*Yeah, maybe Spencer is right. This is the life. I can see why someone would want a beach house here.*

When he was dry enough, he slipped on his clothes, picked up his boots, and started walking. *Quick shower. Pour some gin in the flask. Quick bite in Sound View. Up to meet the train, and… And see what the night brings. I do like that girl. If anyone asked, I couldn't say why with any honesty. Looks, absolutely. And something else. I think she's hiding things from me. Am I supposed to ask or just find out over time? Ha. I wonder if all romances start as detective stories with too few clues?*

****

Enders waited at the Sound View station, freshly shaved and neatly dressed in white linen pants and a blue jacket. He reached down to brush coal dust from his white leather shoes. The train pulled in on time, and when it stopped, he offered a hand to help Karen onto the cement platform.

"Well, you look very nice," he said. "Spectacular, actually." She wore a sleeveless, ivory tea dress that showed plenty of leg. In her hand, she held a beaded, cream-colored purse. With her stacked heels, she was almost as tall as he.

"Thank you. You do too."

He led her across the tracks, and they strolled down Hartford Avenue, which now was filling with weekender automobiles.

"Did you eat yet?"

"A finger sandwich with my landlady. Did you?"

"Not enough to get through the night." He pointed to an Italian grocery that also served as a casual restaurant. "A triangle and a Coke?"

"Marvelous. You know, I've never been here. I knew the beach was here, I just never came down."

"All that painting…" He led her inside, waved to the women behind the counter, and took a small round table covered with a checkered cloth and supporting a candle in a chianti bottle that would never again see any legal chianti.

A young girl with dark Italian eyes approached the table. Enders said, "Gianna, two New Haven triangles and two Cokes."

After she left, Karen said, "I think she likes you."

"She should. I'm in here a lot of mornings for an espresso and a sugar-coated sinker."

"You're tanned."

"Like you, I work *en plain air*."

Their order arrived—the Coke bottles wet from the melting sink ice, the pizza thin and lightly charred from the coal fire. They ate in silence for a moment.

"This is good. Will they be open later?" she asked.

"Probably. Catch the late-night crowd and just-arrived weekend folks." He lowered his voice. "If we can find some tonic at O'Connor's or the Casino and a bit of lime or a splash of Sunkist, I have some very good British gin. You are twenty-one?"

"Yes. But does it matter, with Prohibition?"

"One crime at a time." *Ah-ha, a clue.*

Finished with their pre-dance snack, they walked across the street to the dance hall. Orchestra music blared out from the open doors, along with the heat of electric lights and energized dancers.

An orchestra of sweaty black and white men pumped out a steady stream of popular songs—*Lovesick Blues, I'm Forever Blowing Bubbles, Someday Sweetheart.* Karen led Enders onto the floor, where he showed a competent foxtrot. Later, he held her close for a tango and a waltz. Karen shouted near his ear, "You're a regular Oliver Twist."

"I have a great partner."

Later, he leaned toward her and asked, "Drink?" She nodded, and they squeezed through the dancers to reach a sidebar selling soft drinks. Enders got two tall tonic sodas with slices of lime and slipped behind a wooden pillar to perform a bit of illegal alchemy with the contents of his flask.

"To the Eighteenth Amendment." They clinked glasses and sipped their gin-and-tonics, Enders resisting the urge to pour it all down in one long thirst-quenching gulp. When they finished, they went back to the dance floor, moving with the music from a band whose members seemed never to inhale. He got two more tonics, performed his sleight-of-hand with the gin, and they stepped outside for cooler air. Other couples strolled toward the beach. They followed the slow-moving throng.

They passed a man in a rumpled brown suit. He had a pockmarked face that reminded Enders of smallpox survivors, and a solid-looking paunch that might have suggested gluttony but for the man's otherwise rail-thin frame. A deputy's star was pinned to his suit coat. "Evenin', folks," he said. Enders nodded in reply, gave the deputy a closed-mouth smile, and continued toward the beach. Glancing at a shop's window and its reflections, Enders watched the deputy staring after them.

Near the water's edge, Karen stopped, dropped her purse, and asked him to hold her drink. She placed a hand on his shoulder and undid the straps of her shoes.

Keep going, he thought.

"That's better," she said and stepped into the ocean.

"Wait." Enders placed their glasses in the sand and pulled off his shoes and socks. He rolled up his pants and joined her in the ankle-deep water; tiny wavelets lapped at their legs.

"I heard they sometimes have midnight swims and sailing here. Maybe I should have brought my bathing suit."

"It's dark. Why do you need a bathing suit?"

She laughed and looked around. "It's a crowded beach."

Enders spread his arms to point east and west. "It gets real private in either direction."

She tittered, stepped closer to him, and kissed him. He put his hands on her shoulders and kissed her back.

For a long time.

She pulled away, and he asked, "Those catty girls at Porter's. What were *you* voted most likely to do? You never said."

"Rebel."

"Against?"

"Everything. My mother, for example." She lifted her dress to show off more of her legs. "I shaved. She'd be shocked to death." She dropped the hem of her dress and raised her arms over her head. "Shocked."

*A huge clue for the detective.* "Yes, I noticed your legs. Lovely gams. And arms. French women everywhere would be surprised too." He muttered something in French.

"They don't shave?"

He shook his head, thinking about her smooth legs. He had not seen legs, hairy or otherwise, for a long time.

She led him out of the water, and they sat in the sand, finishing their drinks. Enders sat close beside her, hip to hip, feeling her move and breathe. A light flashed far out across the Sound. He pointed to it and said, "Out that way, a couple of miles beyond Orient Point, is the infamous Rum Row. Fast boats waiting to drop booze along the coast here."

"Was the light the rum runners or the police, do you think?"

Enders shrugged. "Seems like a lot of work just to keep people from having an after-work beer or a champagne toast at a wedding."

She leaned against Enders. "I hope we can do this again."

"Every night, if you want. Every day if I didn't have to work."

****

They returned their glasses to the dance hall and walked barefoot back to the Italian store. Enders went inside to order the same things they'd had before. Outside again, he showed Karen a hand pump on the side of the building where she could wash the sand from her feet. By the time they had their shoes back on, Gianna came outside with their hot pizza and cold pop. He paid and tipped her, and he and Karen worked their way up the avenue, balancing food and drinks as they went.

At the station, she took hold of his wrist and looked at the radium dial of his watch. "Close. We might have missed it."

Enders wanted to say, 'Then you'd have to stay with me,' but he held his tongue. Rebel or not, he did not want to put her off by being too forward.

She turned to him. "Wait. How are you going to get home? This is the last local. You should stay. I can walk from the Lyme station."

"I don't want to leave you yet." He kissed her lips, oiled and peppery from the pizza. "I'll walk back. It's not far."

The train's headlamp swept across them as it eased into the station. They climbed aboard and sat by an open window, feeling the shore breeze cool their damp skins. Too quickly for Enders, they were at the next stop, and they stepped off onto the deserted street. They ambled past the country club, the Duck River Cemetery, and the congregational church, which—according to Karen— had been painted at least once by every artist in America. At the corner of Lyme Street and Library Lane, they stopped in the quiet dark. "The house is there on the left."

She started to say something else, but Enders

stopped her, asking, "Are you painting tomorrow?"

"I don't have to…"

"No, please. Do your work. I was going to ride over to Niantic to see someone about some things." *Am I?* "We could do something tomorrow night or Sunday?"

She considered the idea and said, "Maybe Sunday? We could get some food, go down Ferry Road. Sit and watch the river traffic and have a picnic?"

"Perfect. I'll work out the details." He pointed up the street. "I'll find you there at the shingled house with the cut-stone out front?

"Mrs. Foley's place, yes."

They stood awkwardly for a moment. Then Karen the Rebel pushed herself against Enders, kissed him hurriedly, and sauntered up the road.

"Good night," he said. She waved. He watched her until she slipped through the front doorway. He knew the walk home would be easy.

****

Enders rolled his bicycle off the train onto the Niantic platform. Clearing the station, he pedaled along Shore Road, turned onto Smith Avenue, and rode past the boatyards and marinas. It was a warm and sunny day, and when he reached the perimeter fence of the National Guard camp, he followed the road around to a flat, squared-off peninsula dotted with grassy fields and little farmhouses.

He saw them. Colorful biplanes parked in a row in front of a large barn that looked like it might serve as a hangar and repair shop. A small office with a fluttering windsock on its roof stood out from the barn. On the opposite end was a gasoline pump and an above-ground tank.

If someone had asked him why he was here, he could not have said. It was not nostalgia; he did not need to reminisce about terror and death and near-fatal misses in the skies above France. It was not curiosity; he knew all he needed to know about planes and flying. And crashing. All morning, and on the train, he had not given a single deliberate thought or reason as to why he was coming here. But here he was, standing on an airfield, familiar warplanes before him.

Enders cruised to the office. He propped his bike on the side wall of the building and looked up. *Warm sky. A few cumuli. Light wind steady from the east.*

Inside, a man in shirtsleeves sat at a desk, staring at a new fuel pump. Enders knocked and stepped inside.

"Morning. I see you've got a couple of Jennys down the line."

"You fly?"

"I did. For *Lafayette Escadrille* during the war. I flew a Jenny for the occupation."

The man stood to shake Enders' hand. "Robert Beaumont. Barely a former pilot, myself. Now I'm a buyer and seller of fine aircraft. You here to buy?"

"Could be." Who is saying that? Enders asked himself. He felt as if there were two David Enders in the office, one wanting to climb into a plane, the other wanting to kick the first one. "I was hoping I could take one up for a quick turnaround." *Take one up? Jesus Christ.*

Beaumont leaned on his desk and adjusted his suspenders. "When'd you fly last?"

"Early 1919. Over the Alsace-Lorraine area. And the Rhineland."

"Pay for the gas?"

"Of course."

Beaumont considered Enders for a moment. "Okay, Ace, I'll show you the Jennys and do the walk-around with you."

They stepped outside. Walking the line, Enders pulled ahead to stop beside a yellow biplane with its rudder painted red, white, and blue.

"A JN-4. Hispano-Suiza engine?"

Beaumont nodded. "Beats out the old OX-5. Though the barnstormers like the slower OX. Guess they don't want to get blown off the wing."

"You expecting action? You've still got the Lewis gun's Scarff ring in place. And the camera mount."

"Yeah, I have to pull those off sometime. Nothing but added weight."

Enders reached into the rear cockpit. The baseball bat-shaped control stick moved easily. The rudder bar looked new, as did the cylindrical batteries. He moved forward to the wing, touching the wires, and mumbling their names as if they were long-forgotten colleagues: Drift, Anti-drift, Flying, Landing, Incidence. He opened the engine cowling and looked at the wiring and the fuel line. No sign of oil spray. Enders ran his hands over the copper-sheathed propeller, walked around the left wing, and ran his hand along the length of the painted fuselage, counting the spruce ribs. Behind the plane, he moved the flaps up and down and swung the rudder back and forth. He squatted to get a better view of the skid. He wrapped his arms around the tail section and lifted the plane, feeling its forward balance.

He looked at Beaumont. "She looks good. Ready to fly."

"You know your planes."

Enders stared at the machine, remembering the view from ten thousand feet. The abandoned German lines, ancient villages reduced to rubble, Groves of trees sheared down to stumps by massive artillery barrages. Vast bomb craters turned into deep green ponds. The iron wreckage of industrial warfare abandoned where it had died.

"So, you going up?" he heard Beaumont ask him. Maybe for the second time.

"Uh, yes. Sorry. Just thinking."

"Good. Think down here. Act up there. I've got some helmets and goggles."

"No need." He shucked his rucksack and pulled out a worn leather helmet, a pair of goggles, and a green canvas field jacket.

Smiling, Beaumont asked, "You're not going to fly off with my plane now, are you?"

Enders shook his head. "I've got a girl in Old Lyme and a boss near Sound View. I work for the James Jay Johnson Realty Company. Probably seen the signs along Shore Road?"

"Sure. JJJ. Drive by them all the time." He watched Enders pull on his jacket and toss the empty pack behind the second pilot's seat. "I'll get my mechanic to spin you up." Beaumont headed toward the barn.

Enders climbed in and strapped himself to the seat. He looked at the fuel gauge, tapped its glass front, and did the same to the center compass. The plane's clock had stopped; he checked the time on his wristwatch. He put his feet on the rudder bar and pushed it to port and then to starboard. He pulled the throttle all the way back and wiped a bit of dirt off the Triplex windscreen.

"All set?" a voice asked.

He looked up to see the mechanic standing in front of the prop. He gave the man a thumbs-up signal. Enders flipped the magneto switch and shouted, "Contact."

The mechanic shouted, "Contact," and grabbed the end of a propellor blade. He jerked it around and the engine caught. The prop spun in a blur of noise. The man hurriedly stepped to the side. Enders nudged the throttle and checked the fuel valve. He gave another thumbs-up and the mechanic bent down to pull the rope holding the wheel chocks. The plane lurched forward.

He turned to the right. Ahead lay a wide, empty field ending in a line of trees. The Niantic River waited just behind the trees. His hand was sweating on the control stick. He heard himself say, "Go." Eventually, he did.

He pushed the throttle to its limit. The plane sped across the field, its fuselage shaking from the engine vibrations and jumping from the lumpy field. The trees were close. Behind him, Beaumont slapped both hands to the top of his head as he watched the plane drive toward the trees.

"Up. Pull up, dammit," said Enders. At the last second, he did. The wheels kissed the tallest branches. Then the plane was out over the river. He was in the air.

He knew he had hesitated. Hesitated far too long. He rolled the plane around and headed back to the airfield. Enders rocked the machine back and forth, a reassuring wave to Beaumont on the ground. Beaumont waved back, and Enders flew over the town and out to the bay. Above the water, he laughed and turned west, following the coastline.

He lifted his goggles and settled back in his seat. His whole body relaxed, and he forgot the noise of the engine and the mechanical burping of hot gas fumes. He forgot about himself and his doubts and just flew without thinking. Pulling back on the stick with a loose grip, he climbed through the clear air, applied pressure to one side of the rudder bar with a casual foot, and banked the plane, moving through the morning sky as easily as the gulls, skimming above Long Island Sound, feeling wildly alive but less a man in a machine and more like an amalgam of the two, fused into one aerial creature, moving at will and ease against the tyranny of gravity and bodily fragility.

He climbed through a natural palette of colors: green water, blue sky, white clouds, brown sand, pink stone, and gray-barked trees with red and green leaves. A disorganized flock of gulls glided below him. Two lobster boats rocked on the offshore currents as boys pulled the day's pots.

"No archie. No shells. No cordite clouds. No burning planes on their way to the ground."

Enders turned back toward the shoreline and flew over the Black Point Beach Association. Cottages dotted the broad flat land. He dropped low, skimming the water between the rock islands of Giant's Neck. He crossed the bay and headed straight at the high rocky outcrop of Point O' Woods. Enders pulled up, leapfrogging the high point of the peninsula, and dropping again to follow the emerging line of beachfront homes his company was building. Soon he was over the marshlands that formed a barrier to the half-dozen mansions of Hatchetts Point.

In the distance, the Manor House stood alone in a field above the empty shore. As he roared past Sound View, children on the beach stopped to wave at him. He drifted back out over the water to get a better view of the Rainbow Row cottages as he passed Hawk's Nest.

"Yeah, does look nice," he said to no one.

He moved inshore again, passing the Mile Creek marsh and some old farmland. He slowed the plane to a crawl as he circled above White Sand, looking at the staked-out street lines, the empty lots, and the half-built inland houses. The beach sand was bright in the morning light. A few people outside their new waterfront cottages looked up and waved. He dropped as low as he dared and flew along the length of the white shoreline.

Enders was above Griswold Point and its oddball collection of canvas tents and shotgun shacks with low-tide legs. He turned north, followed the Connecticut River, hopped over the railroad bridge, up to the new automobile drawbridge—new to him—and rolled east to cut across the Lieutenant River into Old Lyme. He circled the Congregational Church's lofty steeple in a tight orbit, hoping Karen was out painting and might see the plane.

From there, he glided down to Shore Road and followed it east, back to Niantic. He flew over the town again, past the Guard base, and spotted Beaumont's field. Enders spotted the limp windsock, starved for wind, and dropped the machine onto the grass. He shut off the engine and rolled to a quiet stop in front of the office, feeling like a bird now forced to walk.

Beaumont rushed out of the building as Enders climbed from the plane.

"You had me worried."

Enders lied. "Yeah. Thought I felt a catch in the engine. At the last second everything seemed okay, so I pulled up hard. Good machine."

"Well, you're both on the ground again in one piece."

Enders stepped closer and said, "Don't sell the plane." *Why not?* "My company might want to rent it from time to time." *Wait till Spencer hears this.*

Beaumont paused, considering that option. "These are going cheap. Less than fifty, 'cause it's used. You'd probably be better off buying outright than paying fuel and the mechanic."

"Fifty dollars?"

"The Army's got thousands of JN-4s it doesn't need or want. There's a rumor they might stack them in a heap and burn them."

Enders was silent for several seconds, thinking. *I can't afford an automobile yet, but I can afford a plane? How is that?*

He unbuttoned his field jacket. It was hot back on the ground. "Well, let me talk to my boss. In the meantime, don't sell it without calling me first. I'll give you some phone numbers where you can reach me."

\*\*\*\*

"That was you?" she asked. "I thought you were done with flying after being shot down."

"Actually, I was forced down three times. I was curious to see if I still could fly." *Still had the nerve.* He took her hand. A bold move rewarded with her easy acquiescence. "Guess what? I can. It was fun again." His face took on a serious appearance. "It hadn't been fun for a long, long time."

She gave him a skeptical look. "And I was going to ask if you'd teach me to drive. My father won't. But now… You've crashed three airplanes?"

He laughed. "Well, technically, the Germans crashed the planes. I just happened to be in them at the time. As for driving, I can teach you. But right now…do you know how to use a camera?"

"I have a Kodak Autographic. Do you need a camera?" They were standing beside his company truck parked on Lyme Street.

"I have something more complicated. A German Leica. I can show you how it works. I want you to take some pictures of the cottages we're building. And the beachfront."

"Why can't you do it?"

"Because I have to fly the plane."

\*\*\*\*

They drove back to the Manor House. Along the way, he explained he wanted some aerial photos of the properties as possible advertisements for the company. JJJ might like the idea, and then he might have regular access to a plane, paid for by JJJ.

Mrs. Kloss met them in the foyer. A train-traveling salesman was coming down the staircase; Enders had met him on earlier visits. A newly married couple staying at the House sat in the parlor drinking iced tea. He introduced Karen to his landlady and then excused himself to find his camera. She stood in the entryway talking to Mrs. Kloss about Miss Florence's summer house guests until Enders called down the stairs to her.

She turned to Mrs. Kloss, who smiled, nodded her head, and walked off toward the kitchen. Karen went up the stairs and around the railing toward his voice and his open door. She found him standing before an open trunk on his bed.

She stepped in and surveyed his room. "I could paint this. Bright window light. Books on a nightstand; I like that. The open wardrobe. Neatly hanging clothes. The dresser with scattered coins, a pocketknife, and a hairbrush. The fedora dangling from a bedpost."

*This scene would be better with you in the bed.* Enders hefted the camera in one hand. "I bought some 35mm film when I arrived back in New York. Seems hard to find in the U.S."

Karen glanced in the trunk. "And what's all this?"

"Things from the war. From France. Odds and ends." He looked back at her and said, "It's funny. All my wanderings around France after the armistice, I always managed to hang onto this thing."

"It must have been important to you."

"Was it? I think I just realized it's mostly full of things from dead men." He weighed the camera in one hand. "German officer." He lifted a pair of binoculars from the trunk. "German pilot." Enders picked up a surveyor's compass. "French squad mate." He pulled out a Webley pistol, drew back the locking latch, and broke open the frame to expose an empty cylinder. "British pilot." He snapped the gun shut. "Saved my life toward the end of the war. And this…" He moved his hand to show the wristwatch. "…same British pilot." He picked up a silk scarf. "My bloody scarf." He tossed it aside. "We didn't loot the dead or the prisoners for valuables, but for things that might keep us flying. Keep us alive. Like a reliable watch or a pistol."

"A grim treasure chest," she said staring into its dark interior.

"Not entirely." Enders picked up a Greek fisherman's cap and placed it on Karen's head. He leaned back and looked at her. "Yes, very fashionable. Very much the *artiste* look."

"I hope the owner's not dead." She touched the cap.

"Not that I know of." Enders remembered the man

in Marseille. He also remembered waking in the morning, still drunk, with bruised knuckles, a black eye, and the Greek cap on his head. How he came by the hat and the wounds were mysteries he didn't care to explore.

Enders shut the trunk. "Enough of this. It's over." He glanced at the open door and stepped closer to her. He kissed her. He pulled her closer. Then they were locked in a smoldering embrace that left both of them breathless.

Enders blinked several times, searching the room as if he had never seen it before. He stared back at Karen with unfocused eyes. "We need someplace private."

Still wearing the fisherman's cap, she leaned toward his ear and whispered, "Yes," which set off another round of open-mouthed kisses and searching hands, the likes of which would have paralyzed Mrs. Kloss on the spot.

****

"So, you brought along a gunner this time," said Beaumont as he grinned admiringly at Karen. "And here Mac's already pulled the gun mount."

"My photographer. A little aerial recon today. Can we borrow a helmet and goggles set?"

"Sure." Beaumont turned away but stopped again to ask, "Think you'll clear those trees again?"

Enders gave him a thumbs-up. He looked at Karen, who was dressed in palazzo pants—which fluttered in the light air—flat sandals, and a light jacket. "Nervous?"

She studied the plane. "Yes. What trees?"

"It's a joke. Once we get up, you'll be fine. The take-off is always noisy and bumpy. You'll think the machine is coming apart. Don't worry. It's not."

"How fast can we go?"

"Top speed is about ninety. But we'll cruise at fifty or so today."

"That's so fast. Faster than any express train." Her eyes widened. She seemed alarmed at the idea of the plane's speed. "How long can we fly?"

"Almost two-and-half hours. There's an auxiliary fuel tank."

Beaumont reappeared with a polished leather helmet and attached goggles. "Mac's not around. I shouldn't be either, but here I am."

Enders got the sense Beaumont did not want to spin the prop. "It's fine. I'll get it going and hop in. Done it plenty of times before."

He helped Karen into the rear cockpit with the aid of a stepping stool. She had the Leica dangling from a strap around her neck. He said, "Don't touch anything. I'll control everything from the front seat. We'll fly down the coast to the river. You can relax and enjoy the view. On the way back, we'll see if we can get some pictures. Okay?" He bent and kissed her. Tight-lipped, she nodded behind the goggles.

Enders jumped down. Leaning into the front cockpit, he opened the fuel valve and flipped the magneto switch. He hurried around to the front of the plane, waved to Karen, and yanked the propellor around. The engine fired, and he stepped away to pull the wheel chocks. He jumped onto the wing and slid into the cockpit as the plane rolled forward. Laying the rudder over, he opened the throttle and raced down the field.

They were in the air in seconds, clearing the trees, and leveling off above the river. Enders yelled back to Karen. Behind him, she threw out her arms and yelled, "We're flying." She gripped either side of the cockpit and turned her head left and right to take in the hidden view of the world from a low-flying airplane. She tightened her grip.

They flew along the same invisible path Enders had followed the previous day. He called out landmarks to her, dropping low sometimes, and climbing over small islands or rocky peninsulas laid bare by the last glacier. They flew to the mouth of the Connecticut River. He banked the machine above the railroad bridge and headed back out along the coast.

"White Sand is coming up," He called to her. She nodded, twisted a bit in the seat, rechecked the leather seat harness, and raised the camera. Enders slowly rolled the plane to the left and throttled back. Karen braced the camera on the edge of the cockpit, looked through the viewfinder, and depressed the shutter. He circled around and she took two more photos of the front cottages and the construction in progress farther back from the beach.

They repeated these maneuvers around the Point O' Woods project and the Black Point development. She used all the film. After, she sat back to enjoy the spectacle of soaring along the coastline toward New London.

Karen shouted, "We're flying east?"

"Yes."

"Stop when we get to Paris."

Enders laughed out loud. "We might need gas in Bermuda and the Azores." He chuckled at the idea of flying a tiny plane across the immensity of the Atlantic.

****

The workweek was hot and sunny. David Enders stood in the shade of a cottage wall looking through his list of building supplies and things to buy in the

Saybrook or Niantic lumberyards. The shoreline trains were crowded now with weekend beachgoers. The roads too. People were staying for weeks at a time in their newly bought cottages and in rented rooms. Now, any of Enders' after-work swims would require a bathing suit. He wondered what Karen would look like in a bathing suit. He knew she was painting in the mornings and gossiping with other artists and the gallery staff at lunchtime. Enders had not seen her since their Sunday photo flight along the shore. But Friday would come, and they would find a movie in Saybrook or another jazz band in Sound View.

An automobile, kicking up sand and dust, ended thoughts of Karen in a bathing suit. A Case sedan with the top down jerked to a stop near Enders; some of his crew looked at the arrival. A man jumped out, followed by his wife and two children. He had curly hair, a neat mustache, and a broad smile. He stuck out his hand as he approached Enders.

"Hi, there. You the agent? I'm Alonzo Guarino. Al. Just down from Hartford. We've been seeing the JJJ ads in the *Courant.* The missus and I thought it time we spent some of our hard-earned cash on a little fun. So, what's available here?"

*God...dammit. A fine time for Spencer to be in Niantic. Now I have to insult this guy in front of his family. Goddammit!*

"Dave Enders, construction foreman," he said, shaking the man's hand. "Our sales agent, John Spencer, is in Niantic today, so I guess you're out of luck."

"Well, we can look around," said Mr. Guarino. His wife tried to shoo the kids off a stack of cut lumber.

Furious at the position he found himself in, Enders

put his notebook in a death grip. He looked off to the nearest cottage under construction and listened to the rhythm of a light hammer tapping home a line of finishing nails. *There's no delay here. Say something.*

"Well, sir, most of what's under construction is already sold. The rest…the empty lots, well, I think the company is holding them, waiting for prices to increase."

Guarino looked around. "You mean all this space is taken or being held? I've got cash. Ready and willing. Right now."

Enders felt sweat coursing down the middle of his back. He hated himself all the more for having to sweat through this disgraceful performance. He glanced at Guarino's face again, trying to make eye contact, however briefly. He pulled a pencil from his shirt pocket and wrote on a blank sheet of paper in his notebook.

"JJJ may not have anything right now, but up the road, at Sound View, ask for Harry Hilliard. He's got property for sale. Or try Patrick Breen. He'd be at the Old Colony Beach right next door." He scribbled faster. "And maybe Charles Garvin over here at Hawk's Nest. He's got land too. And the Rainbow rentals right on the sand." Enders tore the page from the book and handed it to Guarino.

The man stared at Enders for long, hot seconds. He snatched the paper from him and folded it twice over with the long fingers of one hand, looking at Enders the whole time. Guarino leaned toward him. In a whispery snarl, he said, "I know what this is. Know it all my life. If you were a decent man, you'd be ashamed."

"I am. A decent man. And ashamed. If I owned this land, we'd be signing the deeds right now. But I'm just the guy stuck in the middle."

Guarino stalked off, waving to his family to join him in the car. His wife looked at Enders' face as she pushed the kids toward the car. He watched them back up and pull away in a tire-spinning spray of sand.

*I am a decent guy*. He felt limp. He heard a noise behind him and turned to find Vasco standing nearby drinking water from his big glass jug. Vasco was sweaty in his gloves and hat and long-sleeved denim shirt. "Es hard to being different. Yes, boss?"

Enders had no sensible answer for him. He threw up his hands and strode away.

****

It happened twice more before the week was out. A Greek family from New Britain and a Jewish couple from Springfield appeared hours apart and drove off with the names of more liberal landowners around Sound View. Each encounter exhausted Enders' sensibilities, and each time he imagined himself yelling and screaming at Spencer for putting him in the position of company bigot.

The town's summertime constable appeared.

He remembered seeing the man on Hartford Avenue as he and Karen walked to the beach after dancing. The deputy looked even less hospitable in the unforgiving light of a summer afternoon. He climbed out of a Dodge two-seater, which needed new paint and several new wheel spokes. He leaned back on the driver's door, lit a cigarette, and waited for Enders to come to him.

Enders finally did but took his time doing it. He had had experiences with serious, professional police in France and Switzerland; this poxy, pot-bellied little man was nothing more than what he appeared to be: a part-time, small-time constable hired by the town for the summer crowds. Enders doubted he was worth the $300 Bob Cratchit said he was being paid.

"Afternoon," said Enders as he strolled over, hat set low, notebook in hand.

"You the crew foreman?" The deputy puffed out a faint haze of blue smoke. "Seen you about the town."

He stood close enough that the deputy had to look up into his tanned face. "What can I do for you, Deputy…?"

"Pierce. Down from Middletown for the summer. It's a regular town gig keeping an eye on things. Traffic. Bootleggers. Gambling. Gypsies. Lollygaggers looking for an easy buck."

"It's a pretty quiet town." Enders glanced back at the construction. "No one's nicked so much as a nail from us."

"I can help keep it that way. Drive by on the off hours to check around. Here and your Point O' Woods site. Talk to your boss; won't cost much for added protection."

Enders felt the bite. He nodded as if considering it. "I'll mention it to Spencer—our realty agent and site developer—next time I see him. till then, we're jake."

"Yeah, Spencer. Fast talker. Always on the move. Like he's runnin' from something."

"Could be his wife." The deputy didn't seem to get the joke. "Well, I'll mention…"

"Seen you with one of the Griswold artists. She got a manacle on you yet?" The deputy smiled, but the smile looked more like a leer.

Enders held up both hands to show the absence of a ring as he imagined throttling the scrawny little man and stuffing him back into his car through the driver's window.

*Someone call me with a problem. Any excuse to leave this guy. Please.* And then one of the Griswold Point clammers stepped out of a framed cottage and called him.

"Gotta go. See you around." He hurried to the cottage.

Chapter 6

On Friday, as the heat of the afternoon dissipated, Enders cut the work crew loose early. He headed down the dirt path to the waterfront, planning to walk along the shore to Sound View and have a quick beer at the Dance Hall before meeting Karen. At the edge of the water, he saw a man standing beside a sailboat resting on the sand. The man waved. Enders walked over.

"Afternoon, Mr. Bridges. New boat?" He knew the man as one of the first property buyers at White Sand. He was a mid-level banker from Springfield who had poured some of his family's money into a large house perched right on the beach.

"Mr. Enders. How is the building business? You're not making too many new neighbors for me, are you?" Bridges continued to admire his boat. "Yeah, just bought it. Used. It's in good shape, though. I hope the kids will have fun with it." He looked out at the Sound. "Winslow Homer's *Breezing Up* comes to mind," he said, tossing off some of his pricey Holy Cross education.

Enders leaned inboard to better examine the lines and deck tackle. "Nice catboat. Yeah, that would have been me and my friends; running out of Milford. And a couple of times across the Sound to Port Jeff."

Bridges tipped his straw boater back and looked at Enders again. "Sailor, builder, pilot. You do it all."

Enders shrugged and pointed at the boat's stern.

"You've got an engine mount."

The outboard's mount partly obscured the boat's name, *Close Hauled*. On the opposite side of the tiller were the painted words, Old Lyme, CT.

"Yes, indeed. Got a little Johnson to the back of the house. Don't trust the wind and the tide to get me home for dinner. Or it could be my sailing I don't trust." Bridges studied the space between the water's edge and his front porch. "Think it'll be all right here? There's no dock. Yet." Bridges gave Enders a smile and a questioning eyebrow.

"Pull the anchor line taut and bury the anchor in the sand. Barring a big storm, it should be okay. I walk by here often enough; I can keep an eye on it."

"Would you? That's wonderful." Bridges paused. "Listen, we may not be here much in August. Work. End-of-year bookkeeping. Taxes. The stuff I bought this place to get away from. Anyway, if we're not around and you want to take the boat…"

"I appreciate the offer. Thank you. In the meantime, I'll see it doesn't float away."

The two men talked for a few more minutes before Enders excused himself and walked off along the beach.

*Well, I've been shot down, but never sunk. I wonder if Karen likes sailing?*

\*\*\*\*

He met her at the Lyme station. They rode the train into Saybrook, where Enders collected his printed aerial photographs from a photographer's studio on the corner of Elm and the Boston Post Road. He might have spent half the evening there talking with the photographer about cameras, enlargements, costs, and airplanes, but for Karen's determination not to be late to the town hall's public meeting room.

"You don't want to miss the movie, do you?"

Smiling at her, he said, "No. I haven't seen many in the last few years. I've fallen behind the times."

"This is a comedy. *Rent Free*. About a penniless artist."

"Your life story?"

"Ha. I'm not penniless. Well, maybe. Most of my pennies still come from my father. But that's a different story."

Taped to the wall outside the public room was a black-and-white poster advertising Wallace Reid as the movie's leading man. Enders paid the doorman fifty cents. Inside, a bedsheet screen was stretched across the front of the room. A bulky projector with a lethal-looking electrical cable dominated the aisle, separating several rows of folding chairs. They found two seats away from the machinery.

"This is about an artist, and Wallace Reid, in real life, is a fairly good painter," Karen whispered.

Enders nodded a reply. The lights went down, as did the window shades. The projector reels began to spin. He placed a hand on Karen's thigh and leaned toward her. "If there was a balcony, we could sit up there and..."

"And what?" She stared at the flickering screen and tried to hide a grin.

"And not watch the movie."

****

After the movie, they strolled back up Main Street to dinner at the Coulter House. Over steaks and roasted potatoes, Enders asked her about sailing.

"I know rowboats. Sails are mysterious."

"Well, I might have access to a nice little catboat

129

come August. One of the people at White Sand. We could do a bit of sailing on the Sound and up the river."

"That sounds nice. You know how to work the boat and all those ropes and sails?"

"I do. Easy as driving or flying."

"What would I wear?"

"A bathing suit. We might get wet."

"I think I'd like to paint a sailboat. I'm not very happy with my pasture themes right now."

"I can grab a company truck tomorrow and we can drive over to White Sand and have a look at Mr. Bridges' catboat. I'm sure he won't mind if you want to paint it. Who knows, he might buy your painting."

\*\*\*\*

Spencer plunked an enamel pot of steamy coffee onto a warped card table occupying the center of his office-house. Around the table and the rest of the small room were the building foremen from six job sites in Lyme and Saybrook. Enders sat among them, cradling his folder of photographs and his notebook.

Spencer poured himself a cup of coffee and settled back in his rolling office chair. "Everyone seen the cottage models at White Sand?"

Nods all around. "Good. We're gonna do the same thing at POW and Black Point and the Castle. Stage some houses so they look like they've been lived in. Potential buyers won't have to imagine what their cottage might look like—they can see one, walk around in it, sign a deed right on the kitchen table."

He looked at his foremen. "My wife was at the White Sand models yesterday. She's buying second-hand furniture for them. Delivery should be sometime this week. Curtains, books, knickknacks. All kinds of stuff. They're gonna look like real lived-in places."

Turning to Enders, he said, "There was some woman by the Bridges' place, painting pictures. Know anything about that?"

"Yes." He raised his folder of photographs. "She's been helping me with an idea to promote the beach properties."

"Another idea? This gonna cost me money again? Supporting local artists now?"

Enders started passing around the photos. "We took these shots last week. I flew a plane out of Niantic and Karen—ah…the artist, took these photos."

Spencer lost control of his morning meeting as the other site foremen peppered Enders with questions about being a pilot and flying a plane. Finally, he said, "Okay. He's a flyboy. Now, what's the plan for JJJ?"

"I've got access to a plane. There's a professional photographer in Saybrook." Enders took back some of the photos and said, "These are only an experiment. Now a pro with a wide-view camera can get photos good enough to reprint as advertising in the newspapers. Summer's here, and we can get pictures of people at the beach. Umbrellas and chairs. Kids playing in the water." He looked at Spencer. "A picture's worth a hundred sales pitches."

Spencer nodded and rocked back in his chair. "Yeah, maybe. What's this gonna cost us?"

"Not much. Gas for the plane. The photographer's time shooting, and his printing materials. We could get some dramatic shots around the Castle at Cornfield Point and the outcrop at Woods."

One of the foremen said with a smile, "Sounds more like barnstorming than working."

"How low can you fly?" asked another.

"Might be a good idea," said Jesse Martin, the foreman from Point O' Woods. "If nothing else, it could be a good way for the company to record building progress. Or a nice company history in photos."

Spencer drummed his fingers on his desk. Everyone sat and watched him. After almost too much time had passed, he said, "All right. I'll send this to Mr. J. See what he thinks. It's his money. His company." He looked at the waterfront shot of Rainbow Row at Hawk's Nest. He studied Enders. "No barnstorming, no dogfights?"

Enders moved a steady palm above the table. "Nothing but pleasant cruising along the beaches."

Wednesday morning, Enders went to the field office and took one of the company trucks. He drove only a block before being stopped by two Gypsies leading four colorfully saddled horses across the road into Sound View. Enders glanced up Cross Lane. There was an encampment of bright tents and painted wagons spaced between Swan Brook and the railroad tracks.

*This must be what that constable was claiming to keep an eye on. Kiddie horse rides, day laborers, and tarot card fortune-telling. Can't imagine this is a source of much crime when we've already got speakeasy booze and gambling.*

He drove on, passing White Sand, and headed into the center of Old Lyme. He rolled into Library Lane to park in front of Karen's rental. She was waiting in the driveway. He jumped out and hurried to her.

"Is she looking?" Karen asked.

Enders surreptitiously searched the curtained windows for the wrinkled, possibly frowning face of Mrs. Foley.

"No."

"Kiss me."

He did. "That's the way I'd like to start every morning. Ready?"

He loaded her paints and easel into the back of the truck. She hopped into the passenger seat wearing loose pants, open-toe sandals, and her paint-marked kimono. Enders' Greek fisherman's cap clung to her piled brown hair.

They drove to White Sand and down to the Bridges' waterfront cottage.

"They left Sunday afternoon to drive back to Springfield," said Karen. "I think he might buy the boat painting. If I can finish it this week."

"Wonderful. The starving artist makes some dough." Enders carried her things to the beach where the catboat rested on the wet, low-tide sand. He placed her equipment above the tidal line and turned to her. "Okay, I'm up the road if you need anything."

"Come back for lunch?"

"I'll try. Depends on Spencer. And his wife may show up with furniture for the staged cottages. Or buyers looking around." He kissed her and said, "Finish the painting, collect two hundred dollars."

"I wish."

Enders returned at noon. He brought her a thermos of cold lemonade and an apple from the produce stand on Shore Road.

Karen stood before her easel, barefoot, mixing paints on one of her palettes. Her hat was off. The back of her long neck had a sheen of perspiration. Her cotton shirt looked damp from the day's heat. She turned at his approach. "What do you think? I'm almost done. But maybe I should wait for the early evening sun. Might be softer, more pleasant light." She pointed the tip of the brush west, toward the outer lighthouse in Saybrook.

Karen had pulled the mushroom anchor and pushed the catboat into shallow water, where its hull rested inches above the sandy bottom. She had painted a seagull sitting on the boat's gunwale. Wavelets of water were indicated in short, thick strokes of white or green. The boat's white hull was smooth, and the anchor line—a thin red line of paint—had a smear of green that might have been the soft green kelp that came ashore with the tide. The folded sail lashed between the boom and the gaff looked like folded layers of white paint and short dashes of yellow-brown to represent the wooden boom and gaff.

Enders stepped back, still looking at the painted gull. "Up close, it looks like you used a tiny putty knife to smear thick white, black, and orange paints here and there. But if you step back, it's clearly a seagull. And the waves—up close they're thick, stubby smears of paint. Step back and they're green and white wave tops." He turned to her. "I like it. Did a gull actually land here and model for you? Or is this some artistic license?"

"It landed. I told it, 'Don't move'"—she waved her brush at the long-departed gull for emphasis—"and went to work painting it."

"Well, it's a different way to paint, that's for sure."

"That's impressionism. One, painting outdoors. Two, no canvas undercoats, so the colors seem brighter. Though I'm painting this on a wooden panel. Three, follow the spectrum: violet, indigo, blue, green, yellow, orange, and red. And lots of white. Four, place complementary colors adjacent so they intensify one another."

She looked at her painting again. "I hope Mr. Bridges buys it."

"If he doesn't, I will." Enders stepped closer and put an arm around her shoulders, carefully avoiding the brush and palette she still held in her hands.

"No pity purchases. Besides, there's the end-of-summer exhibition and the art sale at the library in town. I'm hoping to sell some of my other paintings there. Including the one I was working on when we met."

"I remember it." He looked at his watch. "Well, you've got plenty of time. But I do not. Gotta get back." He kissed her. Lingered. Kissed her again. She smelled of warm sand and salt.

She slipped his arm with a graceful turn. "Go."

"Reluctantly."

He meandered past the single-story model cottage they had finished. A few blocks beyond the model, he stopped to watch a local crew of Niantic carpenters build a large frame-and-brick house on a double lot. The owners had bought two adjacent lots from JJJ and hired a local contractor to build an imposing two-story house in the middle of the property. The town driller already had sunk a well for the plumber's piping. Good crew, Enders thought as he watched them at work.

A Saybrook moving truck appeared before a cloud of fine brown dust. Behind the truck's dust was Spencer's car. Both vehicles stopped in front of the single-floor model; Enders turned and followed them. Expecting Spencer, he instead found Mrs. Spencer standing near the car, watching the movers unload furniture for the model.

"Good afternoon." He doffed his hat. "I'm David

Enders, the site foreman."

Mrs. Spencer, a slight woman with pale lipstick and a wide sun hat, stuck out her hand and said, "Oh, yes. The pilot. I've heard so many interesting things about you from my husband. Normally, employees are just employees, but you seem to have struck a chord with him. You keep surprising him. In good ways, apparently."

"Well, I guess that's nice to hear. Doesn't sound like I'm up for firing anytime soon." He waved a hand at the cottage. "Can I help with the move-in?"

"Oh, no. They can do it. After, I'll go in and have them arrange things...properly." She looked at Enders again and said, "This is very exciting. This building is a model people can walk through. I'll bet it catches on with the whole real estate business."

"Well, that'll keep you busy decorating."

"Oh, that would be fun. You know, staging these models for people."

Enders watched the movers bang a painted dresser up the porch steps. "I should get back to work. Please call me if you need any help."

"It was very nice meeting you, David."

At the end of the day, Enders went back to Bridges' cottage. Karen was packing up her paints and brushes.

"How's the work of art?"

"All done. What do you think?"

"What's the saying? Everyone's a critic." He stepped up to the easel to re-examine the seagull and examine the white smears of vertical paint that represented the Breakwater Lighthouse. "Very nice. Very *impressionistic*. I still like the gull."

She laughed.

"If you're done…" He grabbed the bow cleat and pulled the boat higher on the sand. He reburied the anchor.

Karen sat in the sand, leaning against the boat bow, with her back to the sun. "It was a hot day." She wiped her forehead with the back of her hand.

"The hazards of *plein air* art." He sat beside her and laid his arm on her shoulders.

"You know, Monet insisted he didn't have a studio. He said he did everything outside." She looked at him. "So, are you doing more aerial photos?"

He told her he was waiting to hear from the company owner. Then he told her about meeting Mrs. Spencer and arranging the model cottage with furniture and fixings. When she didn't comment on anything, he looked to find she had fallen asleep, her head resting in the crook of his shoulder and chest.

Enders sat still, letting her sleep. After a while, he remembered the tide was coming in, the quiet waves lapping their way farther up the sand with each passing minute.

*Time and tide… Wake her or get wet?* He watched the water creep across the warm sand. His pants got wet.

****

Debrie, the photographer, had never been in an airplane before. It showed, but once he concentrated on his equipment and the scenery rolling by beneath his feet, he forgot he was strapped into a fragile tube of stiff canvas and creaking wood and purring wires.

Enders rolled the machine to the shoreside; Debrie squinted through the viewfinder of his Goerz-Anschütz Ango large-format camera. He captured a centered image of the meandering Cornfield Point castle in

Saybrook. Enders came around again, higher, so Debrie could photograph the castle and the cornfield morphing into a private beach club of staked lots and water towers.

Enders yelled back to him, "We'll head home now. Got enough shots?"

"Yes, yes. I believe so. Marvelous way to see the town. Can we do it again?"

"Probably." Enders smiled and wondered where Debrie had bought his camera—a beautiful piece of German optics and engineering. Enders could have used it over the Rhineland in 1919.

Beaumont watched them land. With the engine shut down and the propeller no longer spinning, he approached the silent plane and helped Debrie unload his plates and camera. Enders hopped down.

"I do like this rental arrangement, I have to say," said Beaumont.

Enders pulled his helmet off and ruffled his hair back into three dimensions. "Glad to hear it. We'll want to keep using the plane. At least through the summer."

The photographer struggled out of his borrowed leather helmet to reveal a once well-oiled, carefully parted head of hair now reduced to a damp, squashed pelt.

Enders turned away to chuckle. He said to Beaumont, "If we use some of today's photos for a mailing brochure, we can mention not only the photographer but Beaumont Airfield too. If you don't mind a little publicity."

"That would be excellent. Maybe I should hang onto one or two planes for the occasional air survey. This aerial photography could be a regular sideline." He glanced around at the remains of his flying stock.

Enders looked back at his plane. "Now that you know I'm not gonna fly off with the Jenny, would you consider an overnight rental? Say, to Long Island."

"Don't see a problem. Why? You guys have a development site over there?"

"Just thinking out loud. Could be personal use."

\*\*\*\*

Enders stood on the shady front lawn of the Lyme Street gallery balancing a warm cup of tea and a cookie he worried he might never have a chance to sample. Karen kept introducing him to a parade of artists decked out in straw boaters and seersucker suits, and a few women artists in long summer dresses, bobbed hair, and sun hats. When they learned he was a builder, he was repeatedly admonished about despoiling the town with cookie-cutter cottages for bourgeois invaders.

In his defense, he said, "Well, we're building as slowly as possible. And away from the town's bucolic fields and streams. And cows."

She led him to an escape under an oak tree by the north corner of the gallery.

"Couldn't you have just told them I was a barnstormer or one of the idle rich enjoying the summer season? Apparently, I'm not good company around here."

"I like you." She was about to lean into Enders, but a voice on the other side of the tree said, "Good afternoon. Karen, how are you today?"

"Miss Florence. So nice to see you again. We keep missing each other since I moved across the street."

A woman of seventy years or so appeared from around the tree trunk. She had curly gray hair and a closed-mouth smile that still touched her eyes. Karen introduced Enders as a former pilot for the French Army.

"Oh, how marvelous. To fly like a bird. It seems almost magical to me."

"Well, it's more interesting flying around here with a photographer than in France with a gunner." He told her he had taken a local photographer up to photograph the Old Lyme shoreline and some of the larger houses perched above the Sound.

"Oh, I should like to see such pictures."

"I think that's possible. He may try to exhibit some of them in the library later this month," said Enders.

Miss Florence changed the subject, asking Enders if he had seen the permanent artwork in her house.

"Ah, no. I have not."

"Well, Karen must show you. Some of it is so amusing." With that, she excused herself and ambled toward the tea table.

"Come on." She took his hand and led him across the lawn to the Griswold mansion.

"We can just walk in?"

"Yes. People are in and out, up and down, all summer long." She guided him to a side porch—Enders placed his teacup and uneaten cookie on the railing—and through a screened doorway that led into a dining room.

"Look around."

He did. There were paintings everywhere. On the door panels. On the wall panels. Surrounding the kitchen pass-through. Along the fireplace mantel. Impressionist nudes. Caricatures of former resident artists. Paintings of cows and local scenery in summer and winter.

"You'd need a saw or a chisel to move any of this art," said Enders.

"It all comes with the house." She led him up the

hall, past Miss. Florence's apartment, into a front sitting room. "See? More permanent art."

He moved to one of the closets to admire several paintings made on the door's wooden panels. *More cows; must be the same artist.*

He turned to find her staring at him with a look so focused and so serious he froze for a second. "Karen?" Puzzled, then instantly worried he had said or done something, he reached out to touch her arm.

"You're not one of those men who decide to run off someday, are you?"

*What the hell? Where is this coming from?* He wanted to laugh at her question, to lighten a mood that had mysteriously darkened. But somehow, he knew that would be the absolute wrong thing to do. She seemed to have decided something. Something serious. Her question was like a fulcrum, and whatever he said now would tip their relationship. But tip it where? And why?

He went to her and took hold of her arms. "If I run off, it'll be to chase after you. If I go anywhere, we'll go together."

She put her arms around him and kissed the scar on his neck. "Good." Her face relaxed, and she led him across the room to an old double-head sofa.

Enders muttered, "The detective is baffled," and slumped on the sofa.

"What detective?"

"It's nothing." He waved a dismissive hand, but realized he had to explain himself. So, he told her about his silly little idea of new relationships being like a detective slowly gathering clues about the other person.

"Oh, I like that." She reached over and kissed him again. "What have you discovered?" Her blue-green eyes sparkled with amusement.

"Not enough."

She checked her dress and smoothed its lines with her palms. "I'm sorry. I'm not trying to be difficult. Or mysterious. I'm going to New York City for a few days. Your detective's case will be solved when I get back."

"Never mind my imaginary detective. *I'm* baffled."

"Don't be." She took his hand in hers. "I'll be gone about a week." More to herself, she said, "I should stop in Port Chester on the way in and back to see my parents. Would you like to meet my parents?"

Enders said, "No," like he was declining the offer of a second cup of coffee.

She leaned into him, laughing. "They're nice people. It's just they sometimes think it's still 1898." She pulled him off the sofa. "Oh, come on. They won't bite. Perhaps a little growling… Now, let's go have some fun."

\*\*\*\*

"Hey, flyboy."

Enders stopped sawing and turned to find Spencer standing in the yard, smoking one of his reedy Cuban cigars.

"More photos?"

"Nah. Not today, anyway. Could you fly to Port Jefferson? Long Island?"

He glanced at the sky to consider the distance and the fact the route would be over open water. "Sure, I can do it. When?"

"Right now. Mr. J went over there yesterday for an investors' meeting today at Stony Brook. Know where that is? So he forgot a bunch of drawings, surveys, and cost estimates. I was gonna have Ann try to run them over by train and then the Bridgeport ferry, but the time's not gonna work. So, I thought…fly. We've got a pilot. We've got a plane."

Enders brushed sawdust from his pants and jumped off the new flooring. "Okay. So I finally get to meet the man?"

"Unlikely. He'll probably have a driver meet you." Spencer puffed on his cigar like an idling engine. "Don't worry, he knows who you are. He's impressed. The model homes. The aerial ad photos. You're doing good, kid. I told you." He tossed away his cigar. "Let's go."

****

They stopped at the field office to retrieve the needed papers. Enders unrolled one of the company's large topographical maps of Long Island and the Connecticut coastline. He checked the distance to Port Jeff and took a bearing from the map's compass rose.

At the Manor House, he grabbed his jacket and flight gear.

On the road to Niantic, Enders asked, "There an airfield around there? I can't land anywhere. Actually, I can. I just shouldn't."

"Across from the ferry docks, there's a dynamo, and behind that some oil storage tanks. Now, the other side of those—the dynamo and the tanks—there's an open field. Pretty flat. Separates a neighborhood from the docks and stuff. You could fly right in from the shoreline there. A car can meet you at the top of the field." Spencer glanced at the truck's gas gauge and asked, "What about fuel? Will you need to buy more gas to fly back here?"

"No. I've got a range of a hundred seventy-five miles. It'll be a bit more than a hundred miles there and back."

"Hmm. I guess you could get to Florida with a bunch of stops along the way. Better than driving a car."

"If you want to send me sometime…"

"Yeah, yeah. Let's not get ahead of ourselves here. Let's get *this* little jaunt done first."

They stopped by the airfield office. Enders went to the Jenny; Spencer went looking for Beaumont.

By the time he finished his walk-around, Spencer had appeared with the briefcase of papers and the mailing tube full of rolled blueprints and maps. Enders tucked everything behind his seat. He climbed into the front cockpit. Spencer leaned over the empty back seat, staring at the wires and the instruments.

"You really know how to fly this thing?"

Enders looked back. "Hop in. I'll show you."

"Maybe later." The normally effusive real estate director stepped back. He searched his pockets for another cigar. "You know, a couple of years back there was a guy at Sound View with a seaplane. He'd land—well, land in the water—and give people rides over to Saybrook and back. Could be a nice side gig for you."

"Joy rides. That's a few steps down from barnstorming and aerial circuses." He looked at Spencer. "*Je suis un pilote sérieux.* I'm a serious pilot."

Spencer puffed out a fog of cigar smoke. "Maybe you're too serious."

Mac appeared. Enders signaled him to spin the prop and pull the chocks. He gave Spencer a thumbs-up too. In a minute, Enders was in the air again. Below, he could see Spencer watching the plane bank and head south.

Flying low over the Sound, he checked his watch and the compass. The clouds were high and thin. There was little wind and little chop on the water below. The machine hummed along under its maximum speed. Enders lifted his goggles and put his head back. It was a good day to be in the air. He smiled. *If I have to be a delivery boy, this is the way to make deliveries.*

He flew past a black channel marker a mile off the Old Lyme coast. Farther out he spotted a large yacht of polished teak and fresh paint drifting on the morning currents. It had a large center cabin and an open stern deck. Enders tipped the plane toward the yacht. Closer now, he saw a man in a suit, his tie flapping loose in the breeze, standing on the empty deck. He wondered who would wear a suit on a boat on a day like this. The man spun around at the sound of the approaching plane.

He pulled a pistol from under his jacket and fired.

Chapter 7

Enders saw the muzzle flashes. Two bullets punched neat little holes in the lower left wing. A third grazed the fuselage behind him. He stared at the man with the gun, not quite believing what he was seeing.

"Shit!" *This lunatic is shooting at me*! Enders came alive and rolled the plane away from the boat. He opened the throttle, gaining speed with every second. He climbed and jinked the plane around to throw off any more shots. Enders twisted around to see if he was still drawing fire. He rolled left to curl around the boat. He dug out his binoculars and tried to focus on the boat.

A second man had appeared on deck. He shoved the gunman and seemed to scream at him, waving his arms. Enders glimpsed the transom; the boat's name had been painted over. He flew through a thin cloud and lost the details of the boat.

"Goddammit. They shot at me. What the hell?" He punched the edge of the cockpit. He realized he was gasping, like in the war. He stopped, held his breath, and exhaled. Enders looked into the cockpit, watching his feet on the rudder bar. He glanced at the instruments. The engine hummed steadily. Everything was okay. The plane was okay. He was okay.

*That boat. Gotta be bootleggers. From the other side of Long Island. What the hell! They're supposed to be quiet. Sneaky. Not shooting at people. Not drawing attention to themselves. Must be the dumbest fuckers in the booze business.*

Enders was still shaken, and enraged, forgetting for long minutes to check his heading and get back on course. *I just got archied crossing Long Island Sound!*

He flew on, oblivious to the scenery or the time. Only after he noticed a ferry leaving the Long Island coast did he manage to focus on his location and destination. He flew by the ferry, crowded with summer tourists and truckers, and followed its wide wake into the harbor of Port Jefferson.

The dynamo and oil tanks were where Spencer had said they would be. He banked to the right and dropped to a hundred feet. He skimmed over a narrow gravel beach and checked the field where he was supposed to land. It looked flat enough; he saw no debris that might break a wheel or snag a wing. Enders came around again, cleared the beach, and dropped onto the field. He bumped to a stop near the top of the weed-and-bramble meadow, shut off the engine, and slumped back, feeling drained. His jaw was clenched. He felt his hands tremble. Disgusted with himself or furious at the rum runner, or both, Enders shoved his fists under his armpits and sat waiting for the car.

Minutes later, he watched the silver Duesenberg pull into a street parallel to the top of the field. A uniformed driver got out. Enders climbed out of the cockpit and retrieved the briefcase of papers and the cardboard mailing tube. The driver met him halfway to the plane.

"Dave Enders from Old Lyme."

"For Mr. Johnson," said the driver with a slight bow of his head. He held out his hands for the documents and maps.

Enders surrendered them, and the driver asked, "Do you require anything at this time, Mr. Enders?"

"No. Thanks. I'm set for the trip back."

"Very good." The man touched his cap, turned on his booted heels, and marched back to the shiny sedan.

The car pulled away, and Enders walked to a corner of the field shaded by a cluster of elm trees. He relieved himself. Looking around, he spotted a handful of old bottles. He picked up a heavy green wine bottle. Tossing it in the air with one hand, he thought this weedy corner of the empty meadow might have been someone's last stand against the advance of Prohibition. He dropped the bottle and went back to his plane.

"Stupid son-of-a-bitch," he mumbled to himself as he examined the bullet holes in the wing and the shallow scratch just behind the front cockpit. "Could've killed me. Crashed the damn plane." He leaned against the fuselage, thinking he could use a drink right now. Instead, he rooted through his rucksack to retrieve his pipe and tobacco pouch. He packed the bowl and flicked his IMCO lighter. The tobacco caught, and he drew in the cherry-flavored smoke.

*Maybe Spencer was right. This is a lot of work firing a bowl.* He looked at the lighter's casing, which was made from an old brass cartridge. *Now, wouldn't that bastard bootlegger have been surprised to see me come around and open up with both Vickers? I wonder if Beaumont bought any planes with the guns still in place?*

Enders pushed off the fuselage and went back to the shaded corner of the field. He picked up the wine bottle and rooted through the weeds until he found a lighter whiskey bottle. He hefted the bottles in his hands. "Yeah. These'll do."

He went back to his machine and snuffed out his pipe. He opened the engine cowling and then flipped open a small butterfly valve and bled fuel from the tank into the two discarded bottles. He set them on the ground, careful to keep them upright. There was a rag behind his seat, used to wipe the gauges and windscreen. He tore off two long strips of cloth and stuffed them into the necks of the bottles, leaving a few inches free to serve as wicks.

He brushed his hands on the rough grass and looked at his two firebombs. *They're criminals. If they were willing to shoot at me, they've probably shot at other people as well. Probably at closer range. With better effect.*

Enders glanced at the holes in the wing and shook his head. He lifted the full bottles and wedged them between his seat and the fuselage. He stowed his rucksack and pipe and slapped his shirt pocket, checking for the lighter. Walking around the tail, he spotted half a dozen kids emerging from the line of trees separating the meadow from a neighborhood of small houses. They ran toward the plane, waving and shouting. He found himself surrounded by excited voices, shouting questions about the plane.

'Can I have a ride?' was the most frequent question. Enders kept replying, "Not today. I'm working." He lifted a few of the kids to look in the second cockpit. A little girl in baggy pants and scuffed brown shoes asked, "Do girls fly?" She was shouted down by most of the boys, but Enders told her, "Sure. There are women pilots. Marie Marving and Bessie Coleman, for example." *Women in France, anyway.*

"Okay, who wants to help me turn the plane?" Everyone yelled again, and Enders led them back to the tail. He wrapped his arms around the fuselage and said, "All right, now. Let's lift and push the airplane."

When the plane faced the shoreline, he said, "I'm going to start the propeller. Everyone has to stay back here. A spinning prop is very, *very* dangerous. So, stay." He pointed an index finger at the kid gang for emphasis. Enders checked the cockpit valves and switches and then stepped around to the prop. He gave it a hard spin. It caught, and he scrambled to climb aboard. He looked back at the kids, waved, and settled into his seat. In a moment, he was racing through the field with six children in riotous pursuit.

Airborne again, he set his course for the Connecticut River area and climbed to ten thousand feet. He looked at the two petrol cocktails wedged in beside his seat. The relaxed muscles of his face tightened. *I almost hope they're gone. And if they're not…? Am I gonna be a target every time I go up? Or maybe they'll try to find the plane in Niantic. And me. What if Karen had been aboard? What if she was hit? I couldn't help her. Couldn't even reach her. She'd bleed to death with me just two feet away.* He checked the bottles again. "Fuck 'em. They shot at me. Time to shoot back." He nudged the throttle.

High up in a fair sky, he spotted the boat. It had moved. Now it was off the Saybrook Breakwater, a mile out in shallow water. Enders dropped the plane until he was skimming just above the water. He raced toward the painted stern, fumbling for his lighter. It sparked. He lit the wine bottle fuse and gripped the bottle in his gloved hand. No one appeared on deck. He was close now. He rolled to the right, released his bomb, and roared over the boat's bow. He kept low, presenting as small a target profile as possible.

Enders climbed and banked hard to come around and see what was happening. He still had his second bomb. No one was on the stern deck or bow. There did not seem to be any fire onboard.

"I couldn't have missed," Enders insisted.

As he got closer, black smoke emerged from the cabin hatch. The cabin windows blew out. Now he could see flames and thickening smoke. He noticed the anchor line, taut in the afternoon swell.

He came around again. *No one aboard? Did they go ashore? Someone pick them up?*

He could not loiter near the target; someone on shore would see the smoke. And he did not have the fuel. He turned north, heading for the river. He dropped his second bottle, unlit, into the water below. Enders flew up the river, almost to Essex, before dropping low again and flying over the fields and forests of Lyme and Rogers Lake.

*No sense letting anyone see me make a beeline for Niantic.* He worked his way south, finally spotting the Guard camp, and set down in Beaumont's field. He rolled past most of the planes, stopping at the far end of the line.

He found Beaumont in the office, talking on the phone, scribbling notes on a pad of expensive paper. Beaumont looked up, held up an index finger, and nodded at the telephone mouthpiece. True to his finger, he was finished in about a minute. "What's up? Good flight?"

"Yes, thanks. Great day for crossing the Sound."

Beaumont leaned back, relaxing his once firm body, tossing his long legs on the desk. "So, what do you need?

Besides a bill for the flight."

"Paint. I was thinking to paint the tail with a JJJ insignia since we're using it so often."

"Sure. As long as it's nothing garish or surreal or anti-American. Can't have the Guard coming in here to smash my planes. And I really don't get that surreal art stuff."

"I think we're safe. Just a couple of big blue or green J's."

"Mac's in the barn. He'll show you the paint locker. Think we have some tin stencils somewhere, too."

"Thanks." Enders turned in the doorway. "Send the bill to Spence."

Mac showed him the paint supplies and Enders got to work collecting the things he would need to repair the bullet holes and disguise the plane. He quickly brushed yellow paint over the tail, hiding the red, white, and blue pattern. He painted the short, lower wing tips blue. He crawled under the wings, stencil in hand, to paint a large blue "J" on both of the lower wings. He took some glue and rags from Mac's shop, coated a couple of small rag pieces with the glue, and forced them into the bullet holes. He sealed the holes, top and bottom, with short strips of cloth tape. Enders dappled the tape with the same yellow paint. The tail was almost dry, so he used a smaller stencil to paint three offset J's in blue on both sides of the tail.

Enders stepped back to examine the now-camouflaged machine. "Not bad. Not a perfect disguise, but probably good enough for bootleggers." He checked the scratch near the cockpit. *Just a bit of varnish here.*

He stared at the line of airplanes and the quiet field. But for the various colors of the planes, it looked like an army aerodrome. He held out his right hand, palm down. His hand was steady.

*Flying is fun again. I can't let those guys drag me back to when it was a death-defying duty. I can't go back to "nervous pilot" status.*

\*\*\*\*

Enders came downstairs to find Mrs. Kloss talking with a Bell Telephone man.

"Ah, David. Good news. We have a telephone," she said, pointing to the black candlestick phone perched on the foyer table.

He glanced at the phone. "Very nice."

"Mr. Kloss decided we could afford the three-dollar monthly charge."

The Bell man closed a leather pouch of wiring tools and said, "This should make booking guests easier, ma'am." He looked to the front door. "'Bye now."

Mrs. Kloss waved him off and Enders asked, "What's the number? I could give it to my boss. And my mother."

"And perhaps an attractive young woman from Port Chester?"

Enders beamed. "I thought I might. What's the exchange number?"

"Seventy-six, three. Old Lyme."

"I'll be sure to tell everyone." He started for the door but stopped and turned back to Mrs. Kloss, who was admiring her new telephone. "I noticed survey stakes on the edge of the dunes. Are you planning to build something?"

"Well, Mr. Kloss has been watching all these summer cottages popping up here and there. He thought selling a few beachfront lots would add to the value of the remaining property."

"So you're still thinking of selling…in the near future?"

"Like as not. There's milk competition upstate. And lower transportation costs to the bottling plants up there. And we're not getting younger. Though I should like to keep this house. I like the guests. Most of them." She flashed a quick smile at Enders.

"And I'm enjoying the fried chicken and club breakfasts." He gave his stomach an acknowledging smack and dropped his hat on his head. "I'm sure JJJ Realty will still be interested in the farm whenever you decide to sell." With that, he stepped out the front door and around the back of the house to retrieve his bicycle. On the Shore Road, he glided to the little blue house.

****

He found Spencer at his desk, staring into a half-empty coffee cup. "You're back. Mr. J called last night. Said he got everything he needed for his meet. He was very pleased. I like this having a plane on hand. Coffee? You'll have to make it."

Enders sat across from the desk. "No. I've had enough for the morn." He told Spencer about the staked lots on the Kloss Farm.

Spencer sat back and rocked his chair back and forth. "Interesting. How many staked lots?"

"Four. Maybe five. Right behind the grass and dunes. Get some vacationers in there next year and they'll have their own model homes to show off."

"Yeah." He stared at the low ceiling. "I'll have to mention this to Mr. J and the New York office. We want that property." He looked across his messy desk to Enders. "Good to know. You get this from aerial reconnaissance?"

"Kind of. I looked out my back window."

Spencer chuckled. He came to rest in his chair. "We had a little meeting here yesterday with the foremen. Seems our print ads have been working too well. Guys, and me, have been spending too much time turning away…undesirable buyers."

Enders lost the humor on his face. "I had to turn away three last week." He looked past Spencer to the back hallway. "I didn't like doing it."

"I heard. Sent them off to Old Colony and Sound View."

"How'd you hear that?"

"When I'm not talking, I listen. I hear things. That's okay, send them somewhere else."

"We're just helping other people sell their own lots. Is that good business?"

"No. That's why I think we'll go back to private mailings. Like 1917. More selective clientele. And use some of your aerial photos in them."

Spencer freed a cigar from the closed box on his desk and proceeded to fire it. "Look. We keep building. We get enough people on the property to call themselves an association or private beach club. Let them make the rules. A few years down the road, we help get them a special act from the state legislature. Codify zoning, taxes, roads, water, et cetera. Then it's fixed. Blessed by the state, the association can be the bad guys. Keep out whoever they want. It's not our problem. We're just developers. Builders."

Enders stood. "I still don't like it. But whatever, I don't want to have to tell some guy and his kids they're not welcome."

Spencer puffed on his cigar like he was trying to hide behind a fog of white smoke. "Build faster, you won't have to. The White Sand cottage models are done. Check 'em out. Show 'em if any buyers—suitable buyers—come by when I'm not around."

He slid two brass skeleton keys across his desk. Enders scooped them off the desk and left.

****

Her voice came through the telephone wire, sounding more distant than the actual space separating them. It felt as though she were whispering to him in the dark; the idea of her invisible presence aroused him. He looked around the Manor House foyer for casual eavesdroppers.

"Would you come in for Saturday dinner?" she asked. "Just a quiet family dinner."

He remembered his family's evening dinners—his father at the head of the table—as anything but tranquil. After a moment of soft static in the line, he said, "Yes. I can make it."

"I have the train schedule," she said, though her tone seemed to suggest he could not use the excuse of a missed train for skipping dinner with Mr. and Mrs. Bates of Port Chester.

Enders smiled into the phone's black mouthpiece. He glanced around the foyer again. "I've missed you this week." *Thank God you weren't on the plane.* "Karen, I'll catch the local from Milford. I might as well stop in Friday evening to see my mom. Maybe call my brother. Then come out to see your parents. I'll get through two families with one visit. Like two birds with one stone."

"Well, there shouldn't be any reason to throw stones or kill anything."

"You haven't met my father." Enders checked his wristwatch. Three minutes were passing fast. "All right. I'll call again Friday evening or Saturday morning from Milford. Looking forward to seeing you again. Wait." He remembered her going into the city. "What happened in New York?"

"Me too," came a faceless whisper through the dark earpiece. The static faded. The line went dead.

****

Enders slipped the key into the new lock, twisted the doorknob, and pushed on the newly varnished door. He stepped into a small living room that smelled of new pine panels. Behind him was an open porch staged with wicker furniture. The living room contained a heavy Stickley table desk and matching chairs, shelves of books and trinkets, cheap nautical artwork on the walls, a mirror above the mantel, and a wood-burning fireplace awaiting a match. An old Craftsman sofa sat under the side window. The overhead electric light worked. He opened the closets on either side of the chimney. The three bedrooms were made up with iron-frame beds and painted dressers. In the back, the kitchen had an icebox, a side-by-side oven and burners, and a sink with running water. Fishing poles hung from a rack behind a long picnic table on the screened back porch. Enders stepped out back to check the water faucet and the showerhead pipe attached to the back of the house. Cold water gushed from both outlets as he turned the valves.

*Okay, this looks good. I could see spending a summer here. Walk to the beach. Fry up some dinner. Cold bootleg beer in the box. Good decorating job, Mrs. Spencer.*

He stood still in the empty backyard. *Should I buy*

*one? Why not? I can be a builder and a customer, can't I?* He tucked that fantasy away and crossed the imaginary street to look over the staged two-story model.

\*\*\*\*

Enders distributed the week's pay, and the men dispersed to their various weekend destinations. Davidson, the renter of one of the Poverty Island shacks off Griswold Point, lingered around the job site.

"Hey, boss."

Enders looked up from his notebook.

Davidson opened his battered canvas tool bag and pulled out a bottle wrapped in a green terrycloth towel that once had been clean and fluffy. He held it up. "A gift from the sea."

Enders took the bottle. Canadian whiskey. The label was wrinkled from moisture and was about to peel away. "Very nice. How much?"

"No charge. Like I said, a gift from the sea. Two cases washed ashore the other day. Wood looked a bit charred, but the whiskey is just fine."

"Charred?" Enders held his breath.

Davidson shrugged. "Warehouse fire? Or set too close to some rum runner engine? I ain't asking too many questions regarding two cases of northern whiskey."

"Well, I guess I won't either. Thanks. Ah, anything else wash in with the tide?"

"Flotsam and jetsam. Nothing as valuable as that," said Davidson, pointing at the bottle.

Davidson walked off and Enders stuffed the bottle in his haversack. *No bodies washing up either. Lucky for me.*

\*\*\*\*

"I think I want to go to Paris."

Enders shook his head, a wan smile on his tanned face. "Why? You don't speak the language. What would you do there?"

Brian Lonergan sipped his warm beer and said, "Same thing I do here. Report. Write. Become a famous foreign correspondent. Write books."

"For the *New Haven Register*? Their idea of 'foreign' is Cape Cod and New York. They're not sending you to Paris."

"I could freelance."

"You could starve."

"You're not being helpful."

"Fine. I'll teach you how to say, 'More wine,' 'More beer,' and for the ladies, 'How much for an hour?'"

Lonergan choked on his beer and began laughing loud enough to draw the attention of everyone in Bobby's speakeasy.

Friday night was busy. Bobby's backyard speakeasy had not been shut down yet, and if he was making any money from it, he wasn't putting the profits into a more sophisticated ambiance or a better selection of beverages. Still, he had regulars, and they did not seem to mind the *ad hoc* atmosphere.

"Why do you want to go to Paris?" Enders leaned back in a rickety chair and stared at his friend. "The war's over. You missed all the action."

"Yeah. Thank God for small mercies. But that's good; the war's over. The French economy is… Well, they could use a few tourists spending dollars there. Better than here, where you can't buy a legal bottle of wine or read what you want. You know *Ulysses* is banned? And *The Little Review* was declared obscene for publishing some of it. Damn the New York Society for the Suppression of Vice." Lonergan raised his beer glass. "A toast. To Comstock, may he rot in hell, and to Congressman Volstead, the living, breathing reason we're drinking in Bobby's garage."

Bobby appeared at their table, looking like he had just chopped two cords of wood. "Gents. How's tricks? Stayin' outta trouble, Davey?"

"I'm sitting in your so-called speakeasy. Whatta ya think? Speaking of which, how about two more?" Enders drained his glass and set it on the scarred tabletop.

"Long as you got cash," said Bobby as he turned and headed back to his makeshift bar. He returned with two more beers and a tin can tucked under his arm.

"What are we donating to this week?" asked Lonergan.

"Boy Scouts." Bobby held out the can with a hand-printed label: Boy Scouts of America-Donations.

Enders said, "Good cause," and dug some coins out of his pants pocket. "Worth every beer."

After Bobby left with their donations, Enders asked, "What were you complaining about before Bobby interrupted your diatribe?"

"Hey, you don't have to use big words with me. I'm a writer; I'm not impressed. Wilson. That's what I was talking about. He's gone, but it's like he still has a death grip on the country." Lonergan started counting on his fingers. "Espionage Act. Sedition Act. Immigration Act. Palmer raids scooping up anyone with an accent or an opinion. The Committee on Public Information. Banned books. The Red Summer."

"I've heard of the Red Scare. What's the Red Summer?"

"Coast-to-coast race riots in '19. Pretty ugly. Lotta

people got killed. Wilson made sure the federal government sat on its hands. Again, just last year, hundreds of black folks killed in Tulsa in a part of the city called Black Wall Street. 'Wall Street' because everyone there was so rich. Richer than a lotta white trash locals."

Enders nodded. "Yeah. Guess we're all still waiting for Harding's 'Return to Normalcy.'"

"I'm tired of waiting. I'd like to live a little. A bit of the Bohemian. The *Avant-Garde*. In *Paris*. Jazz, writers, journalists, painters, war correspondents, no censors. French wine, French cigarettes, French girls. I need to get out of here."

Enders sat there chuckling. "I'm trying to picture you in a beret, baguette in one hand, Berlitz guide in the other."

Lonergan waved him off with a dismissive hand. "Hey, how's that artist girlfriend of yours? When do I get to lay eyes on her?"

"Never."

"Come on. I'm harmless. Charming, even."

"She wants to go to Paris too. There must be something in the water around here. Everyone wants to leave. I just got back."

"You should have stayed."

"I needed a real job. I had a sick sister. My mother was worried about all three of us." Enders twisted around in his seat to signal Bobby.

Lonergan got serious for a moment. "Tell your mom I'm thinking of her. And Carole. She was a good kid."

Bobby arrived with two more beers just as the corner gramophone spring gave up the last of its wound-up energy and the music faded into the babel of voices in the room. Bobby jerked a thumb in the machine's direction and said, "Ah, that's how I'm feelin'. Run down. It's a hard business keepin' the town wet."

"You'll get no sympathy from me. Unless you want to clear my tab," said Lonergan.

"I need your money more than your sympathy," said Bobby. He pointed at the gramophone again and asked, "Any requests?" But he wandered off before either man could reply.

Enders picked up his beer. "My last. Got to be clean and sober tomorrow evening."

"Right. The big job interview…"

"Dinner."

"…for future son-in-law. Does the family have money?"

"Maybe. Her father's a lawyer. New York practice. But I have my own money now. A job. A raise. A two-hundred-dollar sales bounty. Ten percent for those aerial photos I told you the guy was trying to sell. And I may sell him my Leica camera, too. Probably get fifty for it."

"You're so flush you could retire the rest of this bill."

"Ha. Forget it. So, Scoop, what's the news on these rum runners and bootleggers operating in the Sound? They dangerous? Do they tend to shoot people?" *Like me?*

"Yeah, we've published some stories about muscle in the booze biz. You know, leaning on buyers to buy only from one syndicate or another. Lot of bribery when it comes to the local fuzz. But it's not like there's been many people killed outright. Why?"

"Just wondering. Seems like some of them are running ashore near where I work. I don't want to get involved. Ya know?"

"I think you're safe. Smuggling's generally a nighttime operation. They want to avoid running into regular citizens. Not to mention the coppers."

Enders stood, slapped the rafter above his head with one hand, and drained the rest of his beer. "Let's blouse."

The gramophone was playing *I'm Just Wild About Harry*. Lonergan stood and danced his way to the door, his tall, lanky form slipping between a few tipsy couples dancing in the spaces around the tables. Enders followed at a normal gait. Outside, they cut through the backyard to the sidewalk and then up the street. At the corner, Lonergan stopped and said, "I'm serious. Paris. I need to breathe free air."

"Yeah, yeah. I'll meet you there."

Lonergan poked Enders with an index finger. "You better." He turned away but stopped to say, "And I expect a detailed report on that future son-in-law dinner tomorrow."

"Get stuffed."

\*\*\*\*

The Saturday train left Enders on the Port Chester platform with time to spare. He looked around the emptying side lot and got his bearings behind the switch tower. He drifted up King Street to the corner at Summerfield Place, where he spotted his target: A gray shingled house with a wide front porch and a square tower bisecting a steeply pitched roof. The house sat on a hill with a wrap-around stone wall, which kept the yard from sliding into the road. Enders climbed a curving cement staircase to the front porch. He took a deep breath and raised his fist to the decorative front door. It flew open before he could knock. Karen held the door, smiling.

"I saw you climbing the steps."

He looked behind her into the interior. He pulled her onto the porch and kissed her. "I've missed you." He glanced back into the house. "Your father, is he for or against Prohibition?"

"Why? He's generally against these kinds of national morality laws."

Enders lifted a small paper bag. "A bottle of red wine and a bottle of Canadian whiskey. Dinner and dessert."

"I'm sure it will be fine." She pulled him into the foyer. Karen studied his nervous face, his hand needlessly pressing flat a brightly colored green-and-blue tie inside a seersucker suit jacket. "Relax," she whispered. "I said they won't bite."

"I'm not afraid of being bit." He glanced around the foyer expecting her parents to appear, surrounding him with probing eyes and nitpicking questions.

She led him into the front parlor where her father sat reading the afternoon newspaper.

"Daddy…"

Mr. Bates looked up and then ejected himself from a winged chair of red leather. "Ah, the pilot. Landed at last." He stuck out his hand and Enders stepped forward to shake it.

Bates was a tall man with slicked-back hair, gold-rimmed reading glasses, and an expensive three-piece suit of summer wool. He did not look old enough to have a daughter of Karen's age.

"Dave Enders. Very nice to meet you, sir." He reclaimed his hand and presented Mr. Bates with the wine and whiskey.

"Well, this is very welcome, indeed. And just in time." He glanced at the mantel clock. "Shall I pour us some drinks while we await dinner?"

"Sure."

Karen slipped away to find her mother. Her father went to a corner cabinet to find glasses and a corkscrew for the wine. Enders, suddenly unmoored, drifted about the room, taking in the formal furniture, the Persian rug, the polished wood, and the wall art. A watercolor portrait drew his attention. It was Karen, in profile, with a different hairdo.

"It's a self-portrait. From art school." Karen had reappeared with her mother in tow.

"You look…pensive. But I like it." He turned his attention to her mother and said, "Mrs. Bates. I'm David Enders from Milford."

"Very nice to meet you, David." Karen's mother was elegant, dressed in a dark blue dress with a pearl necklace but still wearing a spotless white apron from the kitchen. Her reddish-brown hair brushed her shoulders. A trace of lipstick highlighted her lips.

Mr. Bates came across the room holding a silver tray. "Whiskey for the men, wine for the women."

Everyone took an appropriate glass, and Mr. Bates raised his tumbler. "Cheers, all."

****

Enders complimented Mrs. Bates on her *art de la table.* He kept to his hard-won French dining etiquette as he worked his way through roast beef, roasted potatoes, a light gravy, and, surprisingly, fresh tomato slices drizzled with olive oil and dusted with freshly ground pepper. He sipped his wine, stole glances at Karen sitting—out of reach—across from him, and fielded her parents' questions about him, his work, and the war.

"You stayed in Europe after the war," declared Mrs. Bates.

"Yes. There was flying to do for the occupation in 1919. And later, I…enjoyed traveling about and not being shot at while I was doing it."

"You must have a completely different perspective of the war compared to all those men in the trenches. You were above it all. Literally. With a bird's-eye view of things," said Mr. Bates.

"That bird's-eye view wasn't always a welcome or reassuring vantage point. There was that long dangerous line of trenches to cross." He let out a sigh. "The trench line. It looked like a gash on the otherwise green face of the world."

"That's very poetic," Karen whispered.

Enders looked past her father to focus on nothing in the dining room as he recited his memories. "On artillery observation flights over the trenches… sometimes you could spot the moving black dot of a shell as it arced across the line." He looked back at Karen. "You'd see it begin to wobble and then tip toward the ground. You knew it was going to land on your guys…and there was nothing you could do about it but watch. Worse was getting hit by one of our own shells headed for Hun-land. The plane…would just vaporize in a yellow-white flash. They called it 'friendly fire.'"

Mrs. Bates chimed in to say, "The newspapers often compared pilots to mounted knights fighting in single combat; warrior against warrior, airplane against airplane." She glanced at Karen. "You pilots all looked so dashing in your scarves and leather jackets."

"Ah, the press and their colorful copy. Well, we flew

in squadrons, so we weren't alone. And in the case of a two-seater machine like the British R.E.8., you had a tail gunner with you. Just two feet away. As for the scarves, well those were more about keeping your neck from chafing against coat collars as you searched for enemy contacts." Enders turned his head from right to left and pulled at his shirt collar, trying to mimic the desperate searches for prowling enemies.

"Karen said you were shot down," said Mr. Bates.

"Did she?" He looked across the table at Karen, who was staring back at him, a hint of a smile on her face.

"It seems terribly irresponsible for the military brass not to have provided you flyers with parachutes. After all, if sailors have their ship sunk, they still have lifeboats and life jackets. You poor devils had nothing," said Mr. Bates.

Enders nodded. "Yes, the generals were pretty slow about the chutes. But late in the war, I did get my hands on one." He placed his knife and fork on the plate and lifted his wine glass.

"You didn't tell me about a parachute," said Karen.

"It fell into my hands. Literally. The Brits didn't start issuing parachutes until September 1918. The Germans had started in April. One day in October, a German pilot was shot down near our forward airbase. His plane was on fire. He had to jump. And when he did, a great big white shroud opened above him. He came floating down into our waiting arms. I guess he didn't like the reception committee. He drew his pistol and thought to shoot at us, but several of our guys raised their rifles and he reconsidered the matter. He dropped his pistol and started yelling in French, 'Don't shoot.'

"We grabbed him. Took papers, his pocket

compass, his binoculars and map, and rolled up his chute, and marched him off to our mess tent. I happened to be the ranking officer on site at the time, so I interrogated him. He was from the western Rhineland area and spoke pretty good French. I gave him a cup of coffee while I checked out his parachute and the harness system. After I got some idea of what I was looking at, I asked him to show me how it worked and how it was packed together.

"He said, 'Why should I help you?'

"'Come here,' I said and went to a roll-up window in the tent. He followed me and I pointed to a tool shed about fifty yards away. 'I'll lock you in there tonight. A child could push the door off the hinges. And maybe you could slip your compass back into your pocket when I'm not looking. Understand? Pilot to pilot. Or we can call in the *Service Général des Prisonniers de Guerre* now and they'll ship you off to a prison camp in Corsica or North Africa.'

"He stared at the wooden shed. 'Yes, I like this shed confinement. Very good. Much preferred to the African deserts and the colonial troops.'"

Mrs. Bates interrupted to ask, "But isn't that providing aid and comfort to the enemy?"

Karen, sounding exasperated, said, "Mother. He's not a traitor, for God's sake."

"It's all right. Really, it wasn't any different from not shooting at enemy soldiers trying to retrieve their dead and wounded, or troops getting out of the trenches to sing carols on Christmas Eve. And we sometimes flew over the German lines to drop message bags telling them which of their airmen had crashed and died or been taken prisoner. They did the same for us."

"So, this German pilot, he was the one aiding me. I

was just giving him a chance to be picked up by another allied patrol or shot by his own people as he tried to cross over No-Man's Land. I put him in the shed, and he disappeared during the night. I have no idea if he ever made it back to his side. But I got a working parachute out of the deal."

"And you had to use it?" asked Mr. Bates.

"A week later, yes. My squad went on a raid. I climbed into the German rig. My observer saw me and said, 'Lieutenant, you are planning to abandon me up there?' I said, 'Not at all, Cabal Renard; I'll wait until you're dead. Then jump.' Well, he didn't think that was my funniest joke. I told him, 'If the plane's coming apart, we'll jump together. I'll reach back, you grab the harness here and here'—and I touched either side of my chest— 'and we'll go together. Whatever happens.'"

Karen interrupted to ask, "Did he go with you?"

Enders shook his head. "No." He hesitated, but said, "Coming back over the line, we ran into a ferocious dogfight. Screaming planes everywhere. Machine gun fire like rainfall." He drank more of his wine and said, "We got hit broadside. Shot through from tail to engine. I don't know how it all missed me. I looked back because I didn't hear our Lewis gun. Renard was dead. The engine was smoking. I didn't have any rudder. The lower left wing was shot to pieces—it looked like it might tear away any second. I knew I couldn't land my machine."

Enders looked around the table at his immobile audience. He shrugged, trying to look and sound as casual as another dinner guest might in discussing afternoon golf. "There was nothing left to do. I unbuckled my seat harness and wiggled half out of the cockpit; the parachute took up a lot of room in there. I was half-standing when the left wing broke away. The plane rolled over and…I fell out."

Mrs. Bates let out a soft gasp.

"I was falling, head-first. I must have closed my eyes because when I looked again, I saw my boots. I was right-side up. Then I looked up…" Enders eyeballed the dining room ceiling, "and there was this big beautiful white canopy of silk lowering me gently to the ground. Which happened to be in the allied zone, lucky for me. The chute snagged in a tree branch and left me dangling a foot off the grass. A squad of French soldiers saw me come down and rushed over thinking I was a German. But they saw my uniform, and I was shouting at them in French anyway. They helped me down that last foot, back onto solid ground. And that was my only parachute jump. The war ended three weeks later."

"Not a moment too soon," said Mr. Bates. He shook his head and tossed his linen napkin on the table.

"I'm very sorry to hear about your sister." Mrs. Bates inclined toward Enders. "We lost many friends and family members in '18 and '19. It's so…distressing to find this pestilence still lurking about, ruining so many young lives."

"Thank you. It's been hard on my mother. She and Carole were close. I don't know what Mom's going to do now, without her."

Dinner finished and the wine bottle empty, they moved back into the front parlor where Mr. Bates became the center of attention. He opened a closet door and retrieved a small metal box and something that looked like a black musical horn of some kind. He set them on a table under the bay window.

"David, what do you know about radio?"

Enders looked over his shoulder at the equipment and wires. "I know it's impossible to fly, shoot, navigate, and send Morse code messages to the ground at the same time."

"You had radios in the planes?"

"Briefly. They were heavy and hard to use and took up most of the gunner's space. Much easier, and safer, to scribble a note, stick it in a message bag, and drop it with a bright streamer so someone could find it."

"David, I guess you weren't back yet for the Dempsey-Carpentier fight last summer. RCA drew in three hundred thousand listeners. For one fight. Amazing." Mr. Bates looked at the mantel clock again. "It's early still. Someone will be transmitting from Manhattan."

"Daddy, the radio people call it broadcasting, not transmitting."

"You're right, kiddo." He attached two wires from the black sound horn to the crystal set and made minute adjustments to a screw apparatus on top of the box. Music suddenly burst from the horn.

"Ta-da! Magic." Mr. Bates turned to the room. "It *is* magic when you consider this thing has no electric power. Those invisible radio waves are the source of power for this set."

Enders sat on the sofa next to Karen. "That is almost …spooky: an invisible wave turning on your radio so you can hear things at a distance. Imagine if it could listen, too."

Mrs. Bates said, "Well, at twenty-five dollars it is certainly a cheaper hobby than golf."

Mr. Bates looked at his wife. "We should think about some RCA stock. This radio business is nothing but a growth market."

Mrs. Bates turned back to Enders and asked, "David, you never mentioned why you were with the French and not the Expeditionary Force during the war. Was the U.S. too slow in getting into Europe's mess?"

Enders looked away from the radio speaker and said, "No. I was interested in flying back in high school, but the Wrights had a legal stranglehold on aircraft design and building, and neither the government nor the War Department had much interest in aviation. But France and Germany did. They took it seriously and put a lot of time and money into developing new planes and flight control methods. The Wright brothers may have shown it was possible to fly, but in France, men like Louis Blériot, Armand Deperdussin, and the Voisin brothers made it practical. France had the best planes and engines, and soon, the best pilots. The Brits came to France to learn to fly. And when the war began, the Brits were flying French planes. So, I had my classroom French and a few joy rides in planes here, and off I went looking for adventure."

Karen said, "I guess you found more than you were expecting."

Enders smiled at her. "Yeah. I did. I didn't give the war much thought until I found myself in it." He looked off in the distance, remembering a youthful, naïve boy who maybe had wandered too far and too fast. "The war was already on. I was learning to fly at the *Blériot* school. Paying, begging, borrowing, and helping British students who had less French and mechanical knowledge than I did. I got my *brevet*—my license—and immediately joined the *Escadrille Americaine.* The American Squad. Forty or so of us were in France at the time. All of us wound up flying frontline missions near Switzerland. By the time the AEF arrived in the summer of '17, there were maybe two hundred Americans flying for France. Most of those guys transferred to the American Army in 1918 where, unfortunately, there were no planes and no other experienced pilots. It just seemed more practical for me to stay where I was as an almost-Frenchman, from a French flying school, flying a French airplane with the French Army."

The music faded away and Mr. Bates searched for another magical source of entertainment. The talk turned to the Old Lyme art colony and the cottage-building industry that had taken root all along the shoreline. But now Mrs. Bates' questions kept returning, artfully, to probing Enders' interest in her daughter. Eventually, he remembered to look at his watch.

"I should think about getting to the station. Otherwise, it's a long walk home."

Karen jumped up and said, "I'll walk you there."

In less than a minute, Enders had managed to thank his hosts, congratulate Mr. Bates on his wireless hobby, and reach the front door. Karen, standing behind him in the foyer, slipped back into the living room and returned with something tucked under her arm. She placed a covert hand on his shoulder to urge him out the door. Descending the steps, he unbuttoned his suit coat and pulled his tie loose.

"See, now, that wasn't so bad. No bite marks." She laughed at his discomfort.

They were below the stone retaining wall, and Enders stopped her on the sidewalk and began kissing her. "This is my dessert."

She pulled away and said, "I have something for

you." She held up the framed self-portrait from the living room. "You said you liked it."

He took it in both hands. "I do. However, *pensive* you look."

"That's the same word in English and French. And you'd be *pensive* too if you had to paint yourself with a couple of instructors staring over your shoulder."

"I'll hang it by my door. That way I'll see you every morning."

They continued down King Street. Karen took his hand and said, "I was in the city."

"Yes. I've been meaning to ask. So, tell me. Why?"

"You know who Margaret Sanger is, don't you?"

He stopped and looked at her. "The birth-control lady."

"Do you know what a Dutch diaphragm is?"

He stopped breathing. The memory of the woman in Lyon flashed through his mind, and he, waiting for her, eagerly, as she slipped into the WC to do something mysterious before coming to bed. *Do I lie? Tell her I don't know what it is and look naïve? Or tell her I know, and she asks me how I know?*

He sucked in some of the evening air and looked at her as he tried not to smile. "Yes… They're…common in Europe."

"Well, Mrs. Sanger has a clinic in Brooklyn. And a staff of some nice Jewish women doctors—they couldn't get regular hospital jobs—to help other women with, you know, birth control. I went there." She stared at Enders' flushed face. "I bought one. I think they're smuggled in from Canada."

He leaned in to kiss her again and whispered, "I don't care where they're smuggled from."

Karen pushed away and said, "Now maybe we can find a place to use it?"

Enders nodded his head in an almost mindless acknowledgment. All he could think to say was, "Wow." *I cannot believe the boldness of this girl.* Then, "Yeah. A place."

She pulled him along the sidewalk. "We have to go. The train."

Walking silently to the station, he began imagining and discarding places where they might be alone. The Manor House. A no-questions hotel. The overnight room at the office in Saybrook. A nighttime beach. At the train platform, he stopped and laughed.

"I'm an idiot."

Karen looked at him. "I hope not."

Laughing at her response now, Enders said, "I know a place. I just built it. And," he reached into his pocket, "and I have the keys." He reminded her about the recently finished and furnished model cottages at White Sand. "They're perfect. Right down to running water, lights, and…beds."

He jiggled the keys in his hand until he noticed the oval disk on the key ring. Enders slid the disk off the ring and handed it to Karen. "A souvenir from the war."

She held it in her palm and read his name and birth year engraved on the metal.

"My Army dog tag. My mother has the duplicate."

"You don't want to keep this?"

"I want you to have it. I wore it long enough."

The train rolled in and squealed to a stop. Enders said, "I want to pull you on the train with me right now."

"I'll be back tomorrow." She kissed him a last time.

"That's not soon enough."

Chapter 8

Monday, at lunch, the crew scattered themselves around the job site, finding spots in the shade, easing back against piles of fresh-cut lumber, and perching on nail kegs or tarpaper rolls, to enjoy the noon quiet and the surprising midday breeze.

Enders sat on a saw-cut stump, bent over yesterday's copy of the *New York Times*. Immersed in the newspaper, he did not hear Sammy Gross and McMurphy, one of the Griswold Point clammers, approach. After a moment of silence, Sammy kicked at a stone in the sandy ground. Enders looked up.

"Fellas?"

"Gonna walk back to the two-story for the ladders," said Sammy.

"Sure."

"Must be some good readin' in the papers, Mr. Enders," said McMurphy.

"Not really." He flapped the paper in his hands. "Just reading about the influenza."

"Come and gone," said Sammy.

"Maybe not. According to these reports, it's still around. There's a chart here. Says for the New England area—that's us—there's been about a hundred 'excess deaths' from flu and pneumonia per hundred thousand people. So, I guess there's a normal level of deaths and last year there were more deaths than the normal number.

Sounds like the Spanish Flu is still here. Still killing people."

"That's what took your sister?" Sammy asked.

"Yeah. Well, afterward. A post-flu sleeping sickness. Whatever it is." Enders turned a page in the *Times* and read, "'There were few cases of *encephalitis lethragica*'"—that sleeping sickness—'reported before 1920,' and 'No statistics are as yet available which show the percentage of cases in which complete recovery takes place.'" He looked at the two men. "No one knows anything."

"Terrible," said McMurphy.

Enders folded the paper and let it fall to the ground. "Sorry, fellas. Gloomy news on such a fine day. Those ladders?"

"Yep." Sammy and the Poverty Island clammer walked off.

Enders drank the last of his lemonade and started to lean back before he remembered where he was sitting. He leaned forward, elbows on knees, and wondered if Karen was back in Old Lyme. Enders imagined she would be painting today—she'd been gone for a week and probably wanted to catch up on her work. He wanted to call her, but he didn't want to badger her, either.

*Probably won't get together until Friday, anyway. Not until this place is cleared out for the weekend. Patience. Patience.*

****

"This is marvelous," said the man from New Britain. "I'm ready to move in today. How 'bout it, hon?"

His wife stuck her head out of the front bedroom. "It's very nice. A bit cramped with the kids. And if your parents drop in on weekends."

"The kids'll be at the beach, and I'll only be showing on weekends. It'll be fine," said the man. "And the *Courant* can announce every spring, 'Mrs. Deerfield will be summering in Old Lyme this season.' It'll be grand."

Enders leaned to one side of the porch doorjamb and let the young couple talk themselves into buying a summer home.

"I can't say I care much for the artwork on the walls," said the woman.

"You'll find some excellent local paintings and photographs in town. This stuff…" Enders waved his hand around the living room, "…it's just to give you an idea of what a lived-in cottage might look like. I'm sure you folks will do a better job of decorating than we have." He smiled at the woman.

The couple looked at each other. An unseen message passed between them, and the woman said to Enders, "Yes. We'd like a cottage just like this. On the lot we looked at earlier?"

"Of course." Enders stepped forward to shake both of their hands. "Congratulations and welcome to the White Sand Beach Association." He scribbled the lot number on a piece of paper, along with a note about the single floor model and handed it to the man. "Just get back on Shore Road, head past Sound View, and you'll see our little blue office on the left. Mr. Spencer's there and he'll fill out the deeds and building permits. Then we'll start building your cottage." *And we'll see if Spencer writes me another sales check.*

Enders watched them drive off and stood for a moment, smiling at how happy they were to be building something for themselves and their children. Much the same thing had happened earlier in the day when he showed a family of five the staged two-story model. The kids—two boys and a girl—had run up and down the narrow staircase, arguing over who would get which side of the cottage. Their parents closed the door to the larger bedroom behind the kitchen and decided the distance between them and their kids was worth the added cost of a second story.

The rest of the week was uneventful: good weather, steady construction work, and regular drop-ins by potential buyers. Karen had left a message for him at the Manor House, and he made quick use of the Kloss' new phone to call her back. As he expected, she wanted to paint—had to paint—all week, making up for lost time in the city. But there was something in her voice, something at times almost breathless about the delay and the distance between them. And there were other moments, maybe imagined moments, when she sounded coy and hesitant.

Enders had no such uncertainty or hesitation. He knew falling into bed together would change them, or her, and there would be some unexpected consequence perhaps, but he was willing to follow that uncertain future, wherever it took them. They made plans to meet in Sound View on Friday.

He met her at the train stop above Hartford Avenue. She wore a green dress—almost a flapper's dress—and heels. She had a small purse on a light chain and a curious tea-green headband with dark green-and-blue feathers clustered to one side of it.

"You look…amazing. You've been gone so long." He kissed her for as long as she would let him.

She smiled and touched his jacket. "No tie? Very college casual. Or are you trying for drugstore cowboy?

Either way, I like it, David."

He led her to the company truck, and they drove down the length of Sound View to stop on the edge of the wide flat beach. The sun had not yet faded from the horizon, and Enders pointed to knots of people standing on the sand. Some of them had binoculars; others pointed out to sea.

Karen and Enders joined the crowd as they watched a fast-moving boat several miles offshore. A large cutter, blowing coal smoke from its stack, was in pursuit.

A regular Sound Viewer in the nearby crowd declared, "They're way past the hootch pier at Hatchetts."

Another man said, "Could go up the river or hide among the Thimble Islands till the heat's off. They better move."

Karen turned to Enders. "Bootleggers?"

"Yeah, probably with booze straight up from the Bahamas to Rum Row to here. All that commotion just for a drink. Which we should enjoy later tonight." He surveyed the beachfront hotels and other businesses. "Shall we try Doyle's tonight?"

She took his arm, and they strolled over to Swan Avenue. Enders wondered how long they would stay and what excuse he, or she, might make for leaving early. And then what? He needed a drink. Did she? She looked calm. Not a hint of pensiveness.

Doyle's Pavilion was a ramshackle building, part restaurant and bar, part bathhouse and store. Had Doyle also rented rooms, there would have been no reason for customers to leave the premises. A sign at the entrance to the defunct barroom announced the Satriano & Tassilo Orchestra. He could feel the music before they moved down the hall to the large barroom-turned-dance floor.

They danced among some forty other couples, all tanned from the beach, and perspiring from the self-contained heat of the room. Eventually, the orchestra slowed the music, and the dancers slowed too.

Karen leaned into Enders and asked, "Did you remember to bring the keys?"

"I did. Why? Are you interested in buying a cottage?"

They both laughed longer than Enders' joke warranted.

"How about we get a drink and then drive over?"

He bought two iced tonics and supplemented both glasses with some of the contents of his flask. They leaned against the bar, sipped their drinks, and watched the dancers waltz around the polished floor. Enders gulped at his drink, crunching bits of ice, and looking everywhere but at Karen. After a moment, he groped for her hand, held it tight, and turned to look at her. *Why aren't you nervous?*

They finished their drinks, Enders resisted the urge to down another, and they headed back out into the early night. The street was crowded with weekenders and seasonal locals. They strolled toward the truck, Enders waving at the occasional familiar face. At the end of the street, he spotted the summer deputy, Pierce. Enders nodded at him and opened the passenger door for Karen.

\*\*\*\*

She slid across the seat to lean against him. The one-and-a-half-mile drive passed largely in silence, both of them focused on their own thoughts. Pulling off the Shore Road, she whispered in his ear, "Don't crash." He almost did as he swung into the development entrance.

Enders stopped the truck near the two model cottages and hopped out. He helped her out of the cab, kissed her, and held up his door keys.

"Any preferences? Two-story? Basic model?"

"No stairs." She took his hand.

They headed toward the cottage, the silhouettes, and shadows of other half-built homes surrounding them. Lights from several occupied waterfront homes lit patches of the rough ground. They stepped onto the open front porch of the model, and Enders unlocked the door to the living room. He led her into the dark room.

"Are there lights?"

"The electric's not on yet. There's an oil lamp on the front table. Careful." Enders shuffled to the table, struck a flame from his lighter, and lit the new wick in the heavy glass lamp. He picked up the lamp, took Karen's hand, and led her down the short hallway to a bedroom. He set the lamp on a three-drawer dresser and looked around the small room, pretending not to see the wide iron-frame bed. "Well, this is it."

"Yes." She kissed him and then they were locked in the kind of passionate embrace neither had experienced since that day at the Manor House.

She broke away. In a breathy voice, she asked, "Oh…the WC?"

"Right across the hall. There's running water," Enders felt like he was panting.

"Don't go anywhere," she whispered and disappeared across the hallway and behind the bathroom door.

"Don't go anywhere," Enders muttered. "Are you kidding me?"

He stood there for a moment, wondering what to do.

*Stand here? Like an idiot. Get in bed?* He glanced about the small room. *The hell with this. I know what I'm doing.* He yanked off his clothes and left them in a pile on the floor. He slid into bed, waiting on his right side.

Long, lonely minutes seemed to tick by. *Does she need the lamp?* He heard the water tap, the door opened, and Karen was back in the room. She held her stockings and shoes. She saw his clothes on the floor.

"Well, you look comfortable." She turned the lamp's wick down, leaving a faint yellow glow in the room, and rested her hands on the mattress. "David, have you done this before?" she asked quietly. Nervously.

He took her hand and gently pulled her onto the bed.

\*\*\*\*

They lay in the dim glow of the lamp, sweaty skin beginning to cool in the night air, the bedclothes strewn about the mattress and floor. Enders listened to their collective breathing and the random sounds of the night creeping in from the bedroom window overlooking the open back porch.

Karen stretched her arms above her head and leaned into Enders. "I wish we could stay here all night."

He chuckled. "That would be a sight for my crew, come morning."

"You're working tomorrow?"

"Yes. Likely most Saturdays for the rest of the summer. JJJ made promises to some of the buyers they'd be in their cottages before the end of the summer. So that's more work for us, but more money too. And…you and I, at least, still have all these summer nights."

She touched his smooth scar. "You never did answer my question."

He moved her index finger away, propped himself

on an elbow, and looked into her face. "I'll tell you whatever you want to know. I won't lie to you. But I may not tell you what you want to know right then and there. I don't think you want to hear about other women when I'm supposed to be concentrating on you." Enders paused, a thoughtful look on his face. "Do you think an omission is a lie?" *I know what Ella would say.*

"Maybe. If it's an important detail. Why? Did you lie to me by omitting something?"

Enders rolled back onto the pillow. "No. Not to you. To your parents. That story about my having to parachute out of the plane."

"What could you have left out?"

"The man I killed before I jumped."

"I told you my machine was all shot to pieces. Renard was dead. I was working up the nerve to bail out. The German pilot who got us suddenly pulled along the right side of my plane. A big green Fokker Dreidecker—triple-winged—with black iron crosses painted on it. Like the Red Baron's plane. The pilot lifted his goggles, looked over at me, and cackled. Yeah. Cackled. That seems like the right word for what he did. Then he made a pistol shape with his fingers to tell me he was going to fall back and finish me off."

"He could have pulled alongside and saluted. Or waved. Left me to my fate. But no, the bastard wanted me to know he was going to kill me."

Enders took a deep breath. "Well, I was furious. There was no reason for it. No reason to be a…bastard about it. So I yanked my pistol from my coat—the one I showed you—and started firing like a guy with nothing to lose." He looked at Karen. "I hit him."

Enders realized he had his arm outstretched, and his

index finger and thumb mimicking a pistol. He let his arm flop back onto the mattress. "I hit him twice. He slumped over, dragging the stick over too. His plane rolled to the right—good thing, away from mine—and headed for the ground. I watched him crash; there was some satisfaction in that. Then I tucked the gun away and started worrying again about how to get out of my plane in one piece."

He stared at her dark profile. "That's what I omitted. I didn't want your mother to think she had a cold-blooded murderer sitting at her table."

"But it wasn't murder; it was war. Right?"

"Sometimes it was hard to tell the difference."

Later, Karen disappeared into the bathroom again. Enders lay there for a moment thinking about her, about birth control, and briefly, about a woman back in France. Grinning like a happy fool, he stared at the radium arms of his wristwatch and forced himself off the bed. He dressed, then spent several careful minutes returning the bed to its original, undisturbed state. He turned up the lamp and looked at the remade bed and glanced around the floor for any wayward objects.

She came back into the room. "I straightened the towels in the bath."

"Tidying up the scene of the crime?"

Karen looked around the small room. "I suppose it is a kind of crime, isn't it? Everyone says so."

"To hell with them."

"Certainly, the diaphragm is. That's why they're smuggled in."

"It's ridiculous now what's considered a crime." Enders stared past Karen and mumbled, "Maybe Lonergan's right."

"Who?"

He looked at her, amused at the idea of bringing Lonergan's declarations into the conversation. "A friend of mine in Milford. He wants to run off to Paris because he says there are too few liberties here and too many there."

"Oh, I think I'd like to meet him."

"Yeah, he said the same thing about you."

In the living room again, Enders placed the lamp back on the center table and cranked the wick down to smother the flame.

"We'll have to bring some oil too," said Karen.

"I have a flashlight." Ender turned to her and laughed. "I wasn't sure what to bring tonight. Now I know. Blanket. Sheet. Towels. Flashlight. A thermos of drinks?"

Karen dangled her small purse. "And this." She rocked the purse back and forth on its thin chain.

"Yeah, let's not forget that." Smiling, he leaned in and kissed her. Eventually, he took her hand and led her toward the door to the front porch.

He heard a motor and the squeaking of tires and springs on the rough sandy road. Headlights swung into the field. A car stopped behind their truck. He stepped back into the dark of the living room, pulling Karen with him.

"Someone from work?" she whispered.

"No." Enders peered out the window. It was late, and the few residents at White Sand were already to bed, their cottage lights long extinguished.

A car door opened and shut. Enders saw a match flare in the yard. A man cupped the match to light a cigarette.

"It's that summer deputy, Pierce. I saw him earlier tonight in Sound View."

"What's he doing here?"

"Up to no good. He tried to hit us up for protection money a while back. Now..." Enders stepped to the front door, eased it shut on its oiled hinges, and locked it. He moved back into the living room to stand by the fireplace with her. "Let's wait him out."

Pierce might have been impatient. Enders watched him drop his hardly finished cigarette and grind it into the sand. The deputy looked around the shadowy field. He pulled his hat down on an angle and walked toward the one-story model cottage.

"He's coming this way," said Karen.

They retreated into the dark hallway between the living room and the kitchen. Seconds later, they heard shoes scuff the wooden steps and the screen door open. Deputy Pierce was on the porch.

Karen squeezed Enders' right hand. The door lock clicked back and forth. Feet shuffled on the porch floor. The screen door opened and banged shut again.

"Is he gone?" she whispered.

"He's off the porch." Enders stepped quietly into the living room and looked out the window. He did not see the deputy. He went back into the hall, to the kitchen, and peered out the window above the sink. A shadow moved toward the two-story model. She bumped into him, and he turned to point to the two-story cottage.

"That's the other furnished model?"

"Yes."

"How does he know which are the furnished models?" she asked.

Enders looked at her shadowed face. "Good

187

question."

They watched the deputy turn away from the second cottage. He stopped near the cars, hands on hips, and looked around. He seemed to glare at the sliver of the late July moon as if demanding more light from it. Finally, he returned to his two-seat Dodge, got in, and drove away.

Karen took hold of Enders' arm and said, "Well, that was curious. And scary. Do you suppose he snoops around here all the time?"

"I wonder."

They stepped onto the front porch, and after Enders locked the door behind them, they walked back to the JJJ truck. He leaned against the door and hugged her. "A wonderful night, Karen. You're wonderful. Let's do this again."

"Yes."

"Tomorrow night?"

"Yes." She kissed him.

Enders let out an exaggerated sigh. "Tomorrow is going to be such a long day." He pointed to the other furnished cottage. "How about we try another place tomorrow?"

"Sure. I'd like to see it. Does it have the same décor?"

"Yeah, just more of it. Hey, do you have any framed paintings or sketches? Maybe I could replace the cheap stuff hanging in the model homes with some of your work. Real art. Stick a little card in the corner of the frame with your name and a price? You might sell some to the buyers traipsing through the cottages."

"Your boss won't mind? That is a nice idea. I have a few I could frame this week at Miss Florence's. One of the outbuildings has framing tools."

"Sure. Do it. I'll hang them up and we'll see what happens with the house hunters. They may like the idea of some local art for their new summer home."

Karen pushed herself almost nose to nose with Enders. "Will you be expecting a commission?"

"I've already got my piece of the action." He laughed as she pretended to slap him.

****

Enders stepped into the JJJ field office on Shore Road. It was early morning, and he could smell fresh-brewed coffee. Spencer sat at his desk, tieless with rolled shirtsleeves, reading the *New York Times.*

He raised an eyebrow at the intrusion and, seeing Enders, said, "Hey. Come in. Have a seat. Grab some coffee."

Enders went into the storeroom to the coffeepot. He needed another jolt. He had not slept well. The July Fourth fireworks launched from the Sound View beachfront last night had sounded to him more like a bombardment than a peaceful celebration.

The evening barrage had reminded him of the *Fusées Le Prieur*, the incendiary air-to-air rockets he had fired at German observation balloons. The rockets were dangerous—as likely to ignite his wings as they were to ignite the hydrogen that kept those gray-and-green sausages of the *Deutsche Luftstreitkräfte* aloft. You had to get close—close enough to draw machine-gun fire from the men in the observation baskets hanging under those bloated bags—but not so close you might crash into the balloon or the fireball that could erupt from an on-target rocket strike. After the war, he came to appreciate the subdued Bastille Day celebrations in

189

France, where few citizens had much enthusiasm for nighttime rockets and sudden detonations.

From behind him he heard Spencer say, "So, Mr. J is impressed. The model cottages. The aerial photography for the ads. The flyover to deliver his things."

Enders came back into the main room and eased himself onto a hard-back chair. "So I'm not fired."

"Not this week. No." Spencer folded away the newspaper. "You're doing good, flyboy. How's the rest of the week looking for White Sand?"

"No problems. Plenty of hands and supplies. We're trying to get the promised cottages built as quick as we can." Enders stretched out his long legs, and before he thought about where any follow-on questions might lead, he said, "I did see that summer deputy, Pierce, poking around the site a few nights back. Does he normally do that?"

"Well, the town pays him, so he's around to all the beaches, including Point O' Woods. We—the company—are not paying him any extra, but maybe he's popping into White Sand now and then because there's summer people living there now. Maybe it gives them a sense of security having a constable drive by. Though honestly, what's to be afraid of? Nobody locks anything around here."

Spencer tipped back in his chair, his coffee cup resting on his stomach. "How do you know he's around at night?"

Enders stiffened. *Yeah, dammit, how do I know that?* "Well…I drive through every now and again. Just to check on things."

"Hmm." He nodded more to himself than in

response to Enders. "I was over there the other day; you must have gone to the clerk's office. I see the artwork has improved in the models. 'Karen Bates, Old Lyme.' Nice stuff."

Enders felt himself squirm and smile at the same time. He raised his coffee cup to hide the grin struggling on his face. "Just helping the Old Lyme art community." He swallowed some coffee, too much, coughed, and said, "Thought it would be a nice touch. Local art."

"You getting a percentage?"

Now he was smiling like an idiot. "No. Just helping a friend."

"Yeah, that's a nice-looking friend. I saw her at Bridges' place a while back."

Finished toying with Enders, Spencer sat up and grabbed the newspaper. "You read the business and real estate sections?"

"From time to time."

"Well, there's some things to pay attention to as they may relate to JJJ. For example, Fairfield County, down your way. It's become a regular Gold Coast with summer homes and private beach clubs along that stretch. And the people summering there, they're not just sitting in the sand and sun. No, they're buying things. Boats, yachts, furniture, nautical stuff, groceries, dining out, buying autos *to get to* their cottages. It's a windfall for the state and the local businesses."

"I imagine so." He drained the rest of his coffee cup.

"Of course, with private property and private beach associations, well, that leaves the town beaches along the shore more crowded with the locals, the out-of-towners, and with the colored help of the people buying those cottages and yachts."

"Yes. Didn't we have this discussion a while back?"

"We did. This is an update. So the towns' people don't want to be crowded out of their own beaches by…others. Some of the towns are working to redefine what "public" means and restricting their seaside parking and who has access to the water. That should keep a lot of Connecticut lawyers busy."

"It's more segregation of the shoreline by wealth and race." Enders started rotating the empty coffee cup in his hands. He watched Spencer behind his desk.

"Like I said before, we didn't start this. Fenwick did. In Old Saybrook in the '80s, and the Hatchetts in the '90s. But now there's pending litigation. Maybe some town-by-town legislation to protect their beaches from outside traffic. The NAACP is making noises about suing some towns in Westchester and Fairfield for discrimination." He dropped the newspaper back on his desk.

"Jim Crow's come to the beach."

"Yep. And it's our job to work around him. We can't change how people behave. All we can do is build and move on. Leave the towns and associations to decide who's in, who's out."

Enders stood and stretched his back. He was surprised at the tension that had built up in his lower back and shoulders while listening to Spencer. He put his coffee cup on a side table and asked, "Anything else?"

"Yeah. Pond Point. You know it?"

"Sure."

"We just bought that stretch of beachfront. Gonna start building cottages there."

"It's a pretty narrow slice of land. There's nothing but marsh the other side of the road."

"We can work in a couple dozen. Be perfect for you. Practically in your backyard."

Enders stopped moving. Spencer's comment was a sudden worry. "I'm, ah, pretty settled here. You're not thinking of transferring me to Milford?"

Spencer held up his right palm. "Relax. No, you're doing great at White Sand. I know you're set here. Got a girl here. Plane nearby. I'm not suggesting anything. Just assumed you'd be interested in knowing about Pond Point since you're from there."

Enders wanted to exhale. Instead, he said, "Well, if you need me there, I probably could commute on the train."

"Relax. That's down the road. For now, you've got a site to work." He looked at his watch perched on the desk. "Best get to it. I'll stop by sometime Friday."

"Okay. Thanks for the coffee. And the legal update."

\*\*\*\*

Friday morning, Enders drove to the clerk's office. But he rolled by the office and up to Florence Griswold's property to see if Karen might be painting in the yard or the nearby fields. He saw her on the opposite side of the road from the "Holy House." She stood off to the side of the Lyme auto garage, at her easel, dressed in her paint-marked kimono. He pulled ahead of her and hopped out of the truck.

"Karen, hi." He leaned in to kiss her. He stepped back to study the painting that was emerging on her canvas. "The garage?"

"Something different. Don't you think?"

"Are you going to paint Fred Winsted too?"

"The owner? No, I don't think he's the modeling type. Did you know he was a pilot?"

"I did. He's the one who told me about the Jennys in Niantic."

She grabbed his upper arm with her free hand. "Guess what? Mr. Bridges bought my painting of his boat. He came by late yesterday. Forty dollars. I'm so excited."

Enders smiled with her. "Congratulations. Maybe Fred will buy this one."

"Hmm, maybe. he seems more the photography type. But who knows? Any buyers for the cottage paintings yet?"

"Not yet. May take a while. But my boss noticed your paintings."

"Oh." Karen brushed her lips with the back of her hand. "Did he say anything?"

Two cars roared down the dusty road at what seemed to be twenty miles an hour. "No. Well, he jerked me around a bit. I think he suspects we're using the cottages as…"

"A love nest?"

"Is that what it is?" asked Enders amused at the phrase.

"Den-of-iniquity? Sodom and Gomorrah?"

"I like 'love nest' better. Speaking of which, how about we do something different tonight? Instead of Sound View, I'll pick you up in the truck, and we'll drive to Niantic and fly to Long Island to scout the shoreline. There's plenty of daylight. We'll be back in time to…go to the love nest. How's that?"

"I like it." She reached up and kissed him. "But what are you looking for in Long Island?"

"A place to land. I thought sometime we could fly over and spend a night on the beach. There's not much around the Point but corn and potato fields, so no one will bother us. Tell your landlady you're going to visit friends."

"Yes. That's a wonderful idea. I like it. Very risqué. I'll bring my sketch pad."

"Do you think you'll have time to sketch?"

****

Enders dropped to a thousand feet as he approached Plum Island, a flat porkchop-shaped bit of land. He flew past sleepy Fort Terry, the island's 1898 artillery defense against the once-great Spanish fleet. He dropped lower as he crossed Plum Gut and flew by the coffeepot lighthouse that marked the channel. Enders shouted to Karen in the rear gunner's seat about the ferry dock. "I see it," she said.

He was over Orient Point, the sandy tip of the north fork of Long Island. The plane dropped to fifty feet. Enders began following the track of beach along the curve of the land until he came to a sharp point of half-submerged rocks and boulders on the shoreline. He banked the machine and came around for a second pass.

He shouted to her, "Looks good. Wide enough. Inland farmhouses. Nice and private." Enders came around again and shouted to Karen, "Hang on, I'm going to touch-and-go. Like a practice landing."

He powered down the engine and let the plane settle. The sandy beach seemed to rush at them. He felt the wheels and the tail skid impact at the same time—a three-point landing. He opened the throttle and pulled the stick back. They were off the beach again and gaining altitude.

"What was that hop?" she asked as he half-turned in her seat.

"Just testing the ground. Everything's fine. We'll head back now. Time to celebrate."

\*\*\*\*

They leaned back on the pillows piled against the bed frame and sipped gin and tonics from Enders' thermos. The electric light was off, but the waxing moon speckled the room with a pale light filtered through high thin clouds and wispy curtains.

"Do you think Deputy Nosy will come around tonight?" asked Karen.

"He didn't show last Saturday. Maybe it's a random mood that takes him."

They were in the ground-floor bedroom of the two-story model. The doors were locked, and the company truck was parked several lots away. It was early enough that many of the White Sand residents were still awake with their cottage lights on.

Karen slid closer to Enders. "Tell me about this flying picnic you're planning for next week?"

"Sure. Maybe on Saturday? It'll give me time Friday afternoon to pull supplies and gear together. We'll fly over Saturday afternoon. Set down, build a fire, and cook some dinner. Sleep...*en plein air*. Or maybe under the wing of the plane."

She put a finger to his chin and asked, "How's that imaginary detective of yours? Is he still snooping around for clues?"

Enders started laughing. "Nope. He's closed the case and happily retired."

"Good." She kissed him. "But I have some questions too. You never said anything about what you did after the war. You spent three years in Europe afterward. Where did you go? What did you do all the time? Were

196

you alone the whole time?"

*Here it comes. It was gonna happen sooner or later.* He tipped his glass up, finishing the remains of his drink. "That's too long a story to tell tonight. It's three years' worth of stories. I'll tell you what—next Saturday, on Long Island, we'll have plenty of time. We'll sit around the fire and I'll tell you whatever you want to know."

She whispered, "Does your story have a happy ending?"

"Of course it does. I came home fit as a fiddle…and found you."

**** 

The framework of a middle-class community of seasonal homes was emerging on the former potato fields of White Sand. Forty-by-one-hundred-foot lots lined up in cookie-cutter fashion along the four north-south roads that ran from the Shore Road to the Sound. Along the waterfront, cottages already were occupied by early buyers. Farther back from the water, two dozen summer homes scattered beside the dirt roads now were inhabited by the newest summer residents.

The JJJ building crew was as busy as Spencer and the New York office could keep them. Enders had hired a few high school kids who needed work or wanted to learn construction skills or both. In addition to the company crew, there were local independent contractors hired by property owners to build faster than JJJ could or build something different from the standard company models. Though the company had very fixed ideas about how different 'different' might be.

As the new property owners' deeds noted, "This conveyance is made, given and received on condition that neither the said grantee, nor his heirs, administrators or assigns will erect or permit to be erected upon each single lot herein conveyed any building other than a single detached dwelling house, constructed solely for occupancy and use by not more than one family. The plans of all buildings to be erected on the land must however be submitted in advance to the James Joyce Johnson Realty Company or other designee of the seller and their approval thereof in writing obtained before any work on said building shall start."

Spencer made regular visits to the site looking for any design or material deviations.

The cookie-cutter uniformity and lawyerly construction details tended to make Enders' work easier. A standard number of cement or cinder block footings would be sunk and poured. A common frame of joists would be laid on the footings. Framing would begin. The placement of septic tanks and the occasional well would be measured against distances from the emerging house and the surveyed road. Wiring, plumbing, and roofing started, and then the crew would be on to the next empty lot. Standing in the middle of a future road and watching the work, Enders had a half-formed, half-fanciful vision of assembly-line house building—a machine-like persistence that would not stop until the last weedy lot had a summer house sitting on it.

He looked up and down the narrow street. *Definitely gonna be a club-like atmosphere. Everyone's gonna know everyone else, whether they want to or not.* A horn beeped, and he turned to see Sammy maneuver a truckload of building materials around him. He waved, and Enders followed him to the current job site. Together, they unloaded the supplies and tossed rolls of tarpaper to two high schoolers perched on the hot plywood roof of a new cottage.

"Cut and tack, guys," said Sammy.

At the end of the day, he watched the crew fade away. The teenagers biked back into town. The clammers wandered back toward Griswold Point. Sammy took one of the trucks; the other guys piled into the second one heading for the field office and the train station. Enders sat on a rough stoop making notes in his notebook and glancing through a couple of new sales deeds. Finished, he wandered through the half-built cottage to put away the occasional stray tool.

He collected his things and led his bicycle to the Shore Road as he thought about what he still had to do this week. *Call Karen. Call Beaumont. Check the newspaper weather reports. Buy some food for the weekend. And a beach blanket. Borrow some utensils from Mrs. Kloss.*

Still plotting and planning, Enders rolled up to the Italian grocery for an early dinner. He ate a large plate of spaghetti supplemented with sun-dried tomatoes, capers, chopped bits of spinach, and olive oil. He washed it down with ice water and Coca-Cola. Outside again, he stood on the steps and watched the midweek foot and car traffic. It was unexpectedly busy. Relaxed people, tanned from the beach and dressed in casual clothes, strolled about with no more urgent purposes than Enders had this evening. He was supremely content. There was Karen. And a job he liked most of the time. And the plane he felt at home in again.

He rarely thought of the rum runner he had sunk; he had heard no talk or rumors of any such events anywhere along the shoreline. Often, he found it hard to believe it had happened—that it had been anything more than a passing dream, over in a sudden flash of imagined flame and smoke.

More of the pedestrian traffic was moving south now, toward the Casino or O'Conner's Dance Hall or Doyle's Pavilion. Enders decided to follow the crowd. He left his bike in front of the grocery and made his way to the big white casino building. Couples planning to dance entered through the large double doors at the front. He walked around to the right side of the building, to a small set of stairs that led directly into the speakeasy. He knocked. A panel opened in the door. Enders waved at the unseen guardian. The door opened, and he slipped in.

At the bar, he asked the youthful barkeep, "What's good tonight?"

"Beer. Local guy. Used to work at the Narragansett Brewery. Primo stuff." He pointed an inquiring finger at a stand of beer glasses.

Enders nodded. The man set a tall, cold glass of beer before him. He took an exploratory sip. "Yeah, that's good." *Bobby should be buying from this guy.* He leaned on the bar, chatting with the bartender and whoever else stopped to buy a drink. Enders finished a second beer and decided that was enough for the evening. He left by the same side door and went back up the street to his bike. Sitting on the grocery store steps next to his bike was Deputy Pierce.

Pierce had his star pinned to a light gray sports coat. He wore a straw boater and two-tone shoes dry and cracked from a lack of polish. As Enders approached, he stood up, blowing Turkish smoke from a sagging Chesterfield cigarette.

"Evenin', Deputy." Enders nodded at him and reached for his bicycle.

"I can smell the beer on you, mister. There's a law, you know."

"Oh, I thought Connecticut refused to ratify the Eighteenth."

"Don't matter. It's federal. Where you been?"

"No state's rights around here, huh?" He grinned, trying to lighten a mood that seemed destined to become something ugly.

"Some people got no respect for the law or us enforcin' the law. Guess you're one of them. And maybe that harpy you're going about with is too. You know, I could have her scooped up like that," said Pierce, snapping his fingers for emphasis.

Enders turned to fully face Pierce, furious at the mention of Karen. His eyes narrowed, and he took a sudden step toward the reedy peace officer. Pierce threw up his left arm to stop him as he fumbled under his coat for something on his belt.

Chapter 9

"Don't do anything stupid, kid."

Enders backed away. He glanced at the screen door of the grocery and its lighted interior. He searched the street. No one was watching them. *This clown isn't the sûreté or the gendarmerie. He's not even a New Haven beat cop. He's a creep with a tin star.*

Enders jerked his thumb toward the store and said, "How 'bout we step around back and settle this by me pounding you into the sand?"

Pierce kept a twitchy grip on whatever he had under his jacket. "I told ya, don't be stupid." Pierce backed up. "I got responsibilities. Ever hear of the American Plan?" The deputy sucked on his cigarette and rolled it from one corner of his mouth to the other. "Like as not. You don't pay anyone respect."

"What the hell are you talking about?"

"It's the law. I got the right to arrest any woman— any lewd, wanton, or lascivious woman—suspected of having the clap. If they don't, we let 'em go. If they do, they get held till they're clear of disease. The State Farm for Women has plenty of them. Probably room for one more chippy."

Enders drove past the women's prison farm on the way to Niantic. It was a real place. A real prison. He stepped toward the deputy again. "How about if I twist your fucking head off right here?"

Now Pierce had his gun out and pressed against the side of his leg. "Pay attention, mister. Pay me some respect and we won't have these problems." Pierce edged backward, turned away, and cut across the street.

Enders stood there. Almost snorting. Wanting something to smash. Wanting Pierce's scrawny neck in the vice of his calloused hands. Wanting to see the terror in the little man's eyes as he crushed his windpipe.

He snatched his bike and marched it to the top of Hartford Avenue. By the time he reached the Manor House, he was calm enough to smile and wish Mrs. Kloss a good evening. Upstairs, he lay on his bed thinking about Pierce. *Did he keep saying 'pay'? Did he mean money? Money for Karen's safety? And what the hell is the American Plan?*

He'd been away too long. Or not long enough. He couldn't ask Karen. Or Spencer. Lonergan. He would know. Lonergan got to his desk around nine. So he probably took the 8:20 out of Milford. He'd still be home at eight in the morning; Enders could catch him there. He rolled off the bed and looked out the back window. The night was still and warm. The tide was in; he could hear waves slapping the sand. He opened a dresser drawer and found the bottle of rum runner's whiskey with the charred label. Enders poured some whiskey into a water glass and dragged a straight-back chair to the rear window. He put his feet on the windowsill, sipped the Canadian whiskey, and wished it was morning.

****

Enders skipped breakfast and hurriedly snatched up Mrs. Kloss' foyer telephone. He listened to the operator making the connection, and in less than a minute, he had Brian Lonergan on the telephone.

"Brian. Hey, it's me. Quick question for you. What's the American Plan? Some kind of public health law?"

Lonergan said, "Well, good morning to you too. What's the problem? You got the clap and now you're in jail?

"No jokes; I don't have time now. Just tell me what you know and I'll explain later."

Lonergan was silent for a moment, as he likely considered the tone in Enders' voice. "Okay, during the war, the government was shocked—shocked, mind you—to discover a lot of soldiers and sailors had syphilis or gonorrhea or both. Like they were shocked to discover a lot of them were also functional morons. But that's another story. Anyway, the U.S. Attorney General encouraged the states to set up morals squads to round up suspicious women—only women—and test them. They get 'vagged,' and then…"

"Vagged?"

"Vaginal examination."

"What the hell…?" His two-handed grip on the telephone tightened.

"If they're clean, they're released. No apologies, no legal recourse. If they've got something, they're held until cured. No trial. No lawyer. That's it."

"Unbelievable." Enders looked around the foyer for a chair. Or something to punch.

"Far as I know, every state has one of these laws now. And places like Manhattan and D.C. I was still in California. I remember a Sacramento case where some woman—Hennessey, I think her name was—and her sister got grabbed by the local morals squad and taken to the hospital to be examined for any sex diseases. They didn't have any, of course. She had a husband and a kid. Anyway, the charges were dismissed, and that was that. She couldn't do anything about it. It's got a lot of women scared to walk around by themselves."

"I can't believe this is legal. Don't we have a search-and-seizure amendment?" Enders turned at the sounds of the breakfast table down the hall. He hoped he had not been too loud on the phone.

"It is. Officially, it's called the Chamberlain-Kahn Act. Lots of support from Republicans and Dems, and church groups, bluenoses, and such." Lonergan stopped talking for a moment. "You in trouble?"

"No. I just heard this last night. Listen, I gotta get to work. Thanks. I'll see you when I see you."

Enders hung up. He placed ten cents beside the phone. He rode to the field office imagining Deputy Pierce in the back seat of the Jenny as he rolled it upside down over the deep green Sound.

****

Saturday afternoon with the sun still high in the sky, they landed on the Long Island beach a mile behind Orient Point. The Jenny rolled to a quick stop in the soft sand. Enders hopped down and helped Karen out of the front seat.

"Oh, this is beautiful. The trip over was beautiful," she said, looking around the sweep of shore that had become their landing strip. Beyond the grassy dunes was a field of tall corn stalks, dry in the summer's heat and the stingy rainfall.

Enders smiled at her animated face and bright eyes. After a moment, he took her hand and asked, "Help me unload?" He stepped lightly on the wing and handed her boxes and baskets from the larger front seat. He tossed a bundle of blankets and sheets onto the sand and retrieved her overnight bag from the back cockpit.

Jumping down again, he said, "I'm going to push the plane around for tomorrow before she settles in the sand. Mind the wings as I swing around. I don't want to knock you over." He unzipped his field jacket and tossed it into the back cockpit. At the tail, he lifted the machine off its skid and pushed it around until it more or less pointed back in the direction from which it came.

"All right, that's all the heavy lifting for today. Swim? Before the sun goes down."

Karen, bag in hand, looked around the beach. "I don't see a changing room."

"I'll close my eyes."

"Liar," she said, laughing.

"You're suddenly bashful?"

She slipped around the plane. "This will do. No one but the fish to watch."

Enders spread a blanket against a dune as her clothes accumulated on the fuselage of the plane. When enough time had passed and enough clothes had been shed, Enders stripped to his shorts and hurried around the tail section. He found Karen standing in the ankle-deep water wearing a blue Jantzen bathing suit.

"Very nice. Let's hope the beach police don't come by with a measuring tape."

"Will you pay the ten-dollar fine?"

"Absolutely." He took her hand and they waded into deeper water.

\*\*\*\*

Karen sat on the blanket against the dunes, oil-sketching the plane on a small wooden board fixed to her *pochade* box. Enders moved around the quiet beach collecting stones and driftwood for a fire.

"If you'll stop moving, I'll paint you into the picture."

"Pretend I'm that antsy seagull you painted at Bridges'."

"It was more cooperative. Stand near the plane for a minute. I'll brush you in."

Enders submitted, leaning back against the fuselage, barefoot, his shirt open, his pants cuffed, and his hands knotted in his pockets. Karen was silent, quickly working on his lanky image against the yellow fuselage, the dark blue sky, and the green Connecticut shoreline in the distant background. She looked at her reluctant model. "I think I'll call this, 'The Pilot Vagabond.'"

"Good title. Tell me when I can move again. I want to start the fire and let it burn down to coals."

She looked up suddenly, insight shining in her eyes. "You were a vagabond once. Cooking over a fire."

"Hmm, perhaps. But yeah, I've had a few campfire meals."

"And you're going to tell me about all of it, right?"

"Only if you finish sketching."

She did, releasing Enders to start a fire of driftwood and branches collected from the edge of the cornfield. When the flames subsided, he set a steel grill across the stones encircling the fire and started their dinner. Karen put away her paint box and came up behind him. She knelt and leaned on his back, her arms around his neck.

"What are you making? Can I help?"

"*Paella*."

"That doesn't sound French."

"It's Spanish. Kind of the seafood version of 'hunter's pot.' Whatever's on hand goes in the pot."

"Were you in Spain?"

"I learned this in Marseille and Montpellier. But I was in Spain once. For a week or two. I don't remember why or who I went with. But I remember a little seaside town called Cadaques close to the border."

She tightened her grip on Enders and tried to shake him. "You're sounding more mysterious, not less. What's *my* imaginary detective supposed to infer from such scraps?"

Enders twisted around to face her. Almost eye to eye, he said, "I'm not mysterious. I'm the man who loves you." He kissed her until they both tipped slowly into the sand.

Karen pulled away. "Let me tell you something. I fell in love with you at lunch at the Lyme Inn. When you were telling me about being shot down. I might have told you then, but I'm sure you would have thought I was some silly schoolgirl with a weekend crush." She brushed his hair back with her fingers. "It's not a crush." She kissed him. "Can I help with dinner?"

"Ah. Yes. Dinner. Right." A little unnerved by his passionate declaration, Enders rolled up on his knees to feed more wood into the fire. He picked up a small wooden box packed with jars and the leaking remnants of ice.

"Couple of things I learned about this dish. First, a good wood fire; this will have to do. Second, a man should do the cooking. Why? It's a mystery. Third, it should be eaten *en plein air,* or whatever the Spanish equivalent is. Fourth, it should be eaten at midday, not dinnertime, but…here we are. And finally, the rice and the fish stock are important so, I bought from the Italians in Sound View."

"Well, that seems like a lot of rules for a campfire meal."

"Yes, but it all goes into one big pan, which makes things easy. Observe."

Enders went about chopping and sauteing onions and garlic, adding tomatoes, the stock, and the rice, and later mussels, tiny clams, shrimp, and a chopped-up flank of blackfish. He covered the pan and let the *paella* simmer while he retrieved a bottle of white wine he'd buried in the wet sand and set out some enamel plates and cups. Enders upended the wooden box for Karen to use as a table. Then he served their dinner.

"This is good. And the wine."

"Well, it's not your mother's table, but the view is hard to beat."

\*\*\*\*

The moon rose, and bright stars punctured the purple-black sky. They made love, sheltered between the dunes and the plane. Afterward, she said, "This is what we should do: become aerial vagabonds. Flying wherever we want, landing wherever we want. Roaming forever."

Enders added to the fantasy, saying, "We could get to California. Or south into Mexico, all the way to the Panama Canal."

He rolled onto his back and Karen leaned against him, one hand on his chest. "So, now, tell me about your own vagabonding. What were you doing in Europe these last years, mystery man? You owe me a story."

"Where to begin?"

"At the beginning, silly."

"How about at the end? The end of the war."

\*\*\*\*

It was strange. How a war ends. One day it's a mass of roaring machines and screaming men. The next it's not. Like turning an electrical switch on and off. One day in November, the Huns fell back and there was no one to bomb or strafe. We suddenly had nothing to do. It was the shock of no war after four years of total war. Everything stopped.

We were near a town called Chateau-Thierry, around sixty miles northeast of Paris. Since we had no one to fight, a bunch of us caught a lorry toward Paris, then a slow-moving train jammed with soldiers. We got into the city suburbs where the streets were packed with every resident and visitor—all smiling and waving the *tricolore*, everyone relieved to be alive and the war finally done. There was peace.

It would take a while for people to fully realize the enormity of the war's destruction, the huge numbers of dead and wounded. Most of northeast France was almost uninhabitable—a kind of wilderness of trenches and craters and churned-up earth and flattened towns. The unburied dead, including livestock. Booby-trapped buildings. Wreckage everywhere. But for a few days, everyone refused to think about it.

Days later, my squad and I got back to the forward aerodrome near Chateau-Thierry, which must have been a beautiful town before the German spring offensive and the Allied counterassault. There, in the rubble, my unit was formally discharged from the *Armée de l'Air.*

I was not.

I stayed on. Why? Well, I wasn't sure. But I knew I did not want to go back to the States. I didn't know what I'd do there, and I didn't want to join four million other Dough Boys looking for work and places to live. I was still a pilot, but in the absence of war, I had no mission. I was…adrift…for the first time in years. Like being in that parachute—floating randomly between the earth and the sky.

Fortunately for me, that drifting state didn't last too long. The Allies had entered western Germany in December, and the French reclaimed the Alsace-Lorraine region, which had been held by the Germans since the 1870s. A formal occupation of the Rhineland was being worked on in Paris. The French Army already had moved *Troupes colonials*—West African troops—into the Rhineland. It was a lot of territory to hold and, in the case of Alsace-Lorraine, rebuild. The best way to police the region was by air. So the *Armée de l'Air* started sending planes and pilots north to fly regular reconnaissance missions. They packed me off to a nearby American base to train on the Curtiss JN-4. Like the plane resting in the sand right there.

Once I could fly the Jenny, it was repainted in French colors. We had a big Graflex camera mounted beside the second seat. I took an observer/photographer up twice a day to survey and photograph the remaining infrastructure of Alsace-Lorraine and the military facilities abandoned by the Germans. Not unlike what I did in Old Lyme with you and Mr. Debrie. Later, we moved into the Rhineland. Flying up and down the Rhine River, deep inside Germany, and not a care in the world about being archied. It was almost relaxing. Until it wasn't.

One day, we were flying south of a city called Mannheim, crossing and recrossing the Rhine. We were flying pretty low. I noticed two men near the riverbank. As we got closer, I could see they had rifles. I guessed they were hunters. But they started shooting at the plane. I was suddenly back in combat. I yanked the plane away, came around again, dropping very low, crossing the river on a strafing run. The plane had no guns, but I was furious and determined to scare the hell out of these idiots. My observer was screaming at me from the back seat because we were practically scraping the ground and headed for the forest. The hunters saw me coming and bolted for the safety of the woods behind them. At the last second, I pulled up over the treetops and headed back to our base.

It was the last day I flew. I had survived the war; I didn't want to die in the peace, shot down by a couple of clowns popping rabbits in the brush. So I resigned. I took my pay and papers, got my last salute, and took off my worn uniform. I was a civilian again. An American again.

I didn't have any plans beyond getting out of the wreckage of northern France. So I headed south, traveling sometimes by train, sometimes on foot, wandering from village to village until I reached the coast.

I guess it was along the way south, alone, I noticed I wasn't sleeping well. I felt…nervous. Tense. Maybe I'd been like that for a long time, but in the middle of the war, day after day, surrounded by guys who were probably feeling the same way, I didn't notice or think much about it. It was the normal state of things: flying missions, trying to stay alive, waking up the next morning, and doing it again. Now, in the peace, in a part of France untouched by the war, I became more aware of myself. Aware I wasn't quite myself. Wine was cheap, so I started drinking more of it to sleep and to relax during the day.

I ran out of money. I took odd jobs. Construction. Hauling produce in and out of town markets. Occasionally, cleaning myself up enough to work in cafés frequented by Americans or Brits where my English was helpful to the owners. I slept in flophouses and sometimes on the beaches of small towns and fishing villages. I wandered all over the place. From Perpignan near Spain to Montpellier, up to Marseille and Nice, and dozens of little places in between.

Ah... I remember there were some bar fights. Brawls with fishermen and former soldiers. The *gendarmerie*—I spent a few nights in jail cells. That kind of living—if you can call it that—went on for a long, long time. Living rough. Sleeping rough. Eventually, I headed north again. I arrived in a town called Annecy. A beautiful little lake town, from which I was escorted out as an undesirable vagrant. Moving on, I reached Geneva. I followed the lake's shoreline, sleeping in the woods, fishing for dinners, and bathing in that cold blue lake. I got to the town of Lausanne, which was still in the French-speaking part of Switzerland.

When was that? Spring? Yeah. Nineteen-twenty-one. Wow. A lot of lost time. Christ. Anyway, I was in Lausanne, sleeping in the park. The police didn't much care for bums sleeping wherever the mood struck them. They picked me up and took me to a police station.

The desk sergeant searched my things before they put me in a cell. He unwrapped my old scarf and found my air medals and insignia. He seemed surprised to find such things.

"These are yours, *monsieur vagabond*?"

"Yes. I was a lieutenant with the *Armée de l'Air*."

"Not the *Escadrille de La Fayette?*"

"No. I stayed with my French unit. We were a tight, experienced, and successful group. Not like the Americans, with no planes and no experienced pilots."

He nodded to himself, still staring at my medals. "My brother was a pilot with the *Escadrille* 67 near Verdun.

"They flew the SPAD 7."

"Did you know my brother? Marcel Navarre."

"A *sous-lieutenant*. I had a few drinks with his squad. You look like him." Now I knew where he was going.

"He was shot down. We have no body."

"I'm sorry."

He folded up my medals again and repacked my things. "We have an empty cell. You can sleep there tonight. With the door unlocked. The toilet is over there. Have you eaten?"

I hesitated to answer, so he said, "Never mind. I'll get you something from the café around the corner."

"Thank you."

"In the morning, I will drive you out of town. There is a tight bend in the rail tracks before the river. The train must slow to a crawl. You can catch one of these trains back to France. Yes?"

"Yes, thanks. I'll do that."

The next morning, we had coffee in a nearby café. We talked about the air war and his brother. He drove me through town, following the railroad tracks. At one point, we passed an old villa, walled and whitewashed.

"That is the *Société des missions évangéliques de Paris* for French Switzerland. These church people work with the *Institut Pasteur* to aid lepers in Africa and

Indochina." He looked over at me and said, "So, perhaps your concerns are not so serious. The war is over; you are whole. So much else is not."

I didn't know what to say. A minute later, we came to the spot he mentioned. "This is the westbound track. It will take you to Lyon. A lovely city. Find a job. Stop tramping about, Lieutenant." He handed me five Swiss francs and said, "Go."

I waved, and he drove off.

Well, he was right; the train slowed to a crawl. I hopped aboard and settled in a boxcar. Ninety minutes later, I was in Lyon. There's a huge park there by the river—the *Parc de la Tête d'Or*. Despite Sergeant Navarre's suggestion, I spent two nights sleeping in the park and spending his money on street-vendor food. After that, I wasn't sure what to do or how to proceed. I'd been wandering around, doing nothing, for so long I couldn't seem to stop and then start…anew.

On my third day in town—just in the park, I hadn't moved much—I meandered down Rue Duquesne toward the Rhône. The river. Halfway there, I stopped at what looked like the château of some long-dead baron. A beautiful house, more like a castle, with a high wall and wrought-iron gates. The gates were open. Around the lawn and on a side patio, I saw men in pajamas and robes. Some of them had crutches. One or two were leaning on canes. It looked like a hospital, though no one looked terribly ill or war-damaged.

I was about to turn away when I heard a voice say, "It's a very nice facility. I wish there were more of them."

I looked around to find a woman standing there. She was…well…striking. With Teutonic blonde hair and

215

blue eyes that reminded me of alpine lakes. She was very well dressed and carried a thin leather portfolio. She seemed interested in me in the way one might be interested in an automobile whose driver seemed destined to crash into something. I gave her a little smile and reluctantly turned away.

"Were you in the war?" she asked.

"The *Armée de l'Air.*"

"A pilot?"

"Yes."

"Oh, that's interesting. But you're not French?"

*Interesting?* I told her I was an American and had been a pilot and lieutenant with the French since 1917.

"What have you been doing since the Armistice?"

I shrugged. "Not much. Sightseeing. I was headed to the river."

"Could you spend a little time answering some questions for me? It should not take much of your day. It would help my work." She gestured to the open gates. "The river is not going anywhere."

I looked in again and said, "This is a hospital?"

"Yes. I work here. I am Doctor Ella Allard. Please." She stepped inside.

I hesitated, but as she said, the river wasn't going anywhere. It would be there whenever I felt like leaving. I followed her in, saying, "You're not going to lock the gate behind me, are you?"

"There is no lock, Lieutenant."

"I was joking."

"This is a good sign," she replied without looking back at me.

We walked toward the patio. I noticed a man in pajamas sitting alone and staring at nothing. A few feet from him, another man sat in a bathrobe and slippers nervously glancing about the grounds as if he expected someone to come running up and hit him. We approached a side door. I stopped and said, "This is for the shell-shocked. I wasn't in the trenches; I'm not shocked or disturbed. Or a coward. I'm not a patient."

She turned and said, "Yes, I know. You said you were a pilot. The pilots are not shell-shocked. You were above all the fighting. Far up in the skies. That is what I want to know."

****

We went to her office, which was spacious and without the usual trappings of a medical office. Yes, there was a desk—which she sat behind—but also comfortable chairs, a sofa and coffee table, and what looked like expensive floor lamps, and bookcases with neat rows of recent fiction and history. Two hand woven rugs, Algerian maybe, covered portions of a parqueted floor. It was one of the nicest rooms I had ever been in. Settled behind her cherry desk, she asked me various questions about myself as she completed what I later discovered was a patient intake form. I was about to object to all the questions, but a staff member wheeled in a cart of coffee and afternoon pastries.

I was hungry. Starving, actually. But I took only a cup of coffee and sat back down. She had watched me and said, "Oh, please. I can see you need to eat. Eat! Just save me one of the red macaroons. It is probably Freudian, but I like them nonetheless."

So, I did eat, devastating a small tray of *choux à la crème, chouquettes,* and *canelés*. I left the macaroons. By then, she had come out from behind her desk to take an upholstered chair across from the coffee table. She took a red macaroon, examined it briefly, and nibbled at it.

She said, "In the war, a man is killed or bodily wounded. It is simple. But this business of war trauma is very confusing. The British called it 'shell shock' as far back as 1915. But it means two different things to them. One is organic injury or concussion from repeated blast forces. Literally, the brain is shaken within the skull. The other is a mental disorder arising from the terrors of relentless war. You must know in France we say *commotion cerebrale,* or *accidents nerveux.* The Germans refer to *kriegneurosen* and *krieghysterie.* Their patients are called *schüttlers*. Shakers."

"Anyone would shake who was on the receiving end of some of those shells. You could feel the blast waves of the big ones a thousand feet up. They would toss the plane around. Imagine being close to such blasts. Every day. Sometimes every minute."

"We have patients here who were that close. But again, do they suffer from organic damage or neurasthenia, a psychiatric disorder? It is important for the patient's prognosis to distinguish the one from the other. You know, perhaps, *les morts-vivants*, the French mentally wounded, receive no pensions unless they are interned. When they are interned, their wives receive only the equivalent of a widow's pension. The State considers them dead. Others, who are not in asylums, are left to wander. France is full of these physically unscathed but still wounded men."

True enough. I had seen them in small towns and on the roads. Quiet nights in cheap hostels were sometimes shattered by the screams of these men. Damaged men reliving the terror of the trenches, I supposed. Though some nights, I had to wonder if my own dreams of crashing or being on fire didn't scare me awake too. I wondered in those moments if I had been one of those screaming men in the night.

I stood and said, "Yes, I'm sure it's a problem. But I was never in the trenches. I can't help you. I'm not a doctor. And I'm certainly not a patient."

She rose from the chair and walked back to her desk. She picked up some magazines and came back to the coffee table. "The war is ended, and now we can catch up on important medical news from other countries. It seems the British are ahead of us in addressing these issues of shell shock. And especially of nervous pilots."

She handed me the magazines, which turned out to be old copies of a British medical journal called *The Lancet*. Several pages were marked with cardboard bookmarks, and I flipped to those pages to find articles about "predisposing factors of war psycho-neurosis," "repression of war experience," and "the psychology of soldiers' dreams."

I dropped the journals on the table and said, "I can't help you with this. These things are beyond me. I don't know all these medical words."

"But you are an educated man. Yes? You can read. You were a soldier and an officer for France. I have some training in this psychology, but I have no English. Read me the articles and I will tell you what they mean. I will be the doctor, you the translator. A partnership. Yes?"

She had grown up in Alsace, speaking French at home and German in school, but her English was poor. She said, "This British doctor, Rivers, William Rivers, at the…Craig…lock…hart—Oh, what is it with these British names—he has a "talking cure" and has worked with many pilots. I want to know what he knows about pilots and talking them out of repression and into recovery." She looked at me and said, "Please."

"Craiglockhart War Hospital," I said. "And what's this about nervous pilots?" *Was I in such a category? If so, what did it mean?*

"The British believe war pilots are medically different from the common soldier in the trenches. And what makes them different is the pilots' unique environment—high in the air—and employment—flying and fighting and dying in machines that did not exist a dozen years ago. I have been told the British Army Medical Corps believes flying—the cold and the hypoxia at high altitudes—affects bodily functions but also wears down the nerves that regulate the normal psychology."

I remember looking at my watch. It was getting late. Ella—I mean Dr. Allard—said, "I have kept you too long? So, stay. There is dinner and an empty room. Stay the night and we will translate these articles tomorrow. Do you have a more pressing engagement? No. Well, you should please follow me."

It must have been her German half—giving orders. I followed her to a narrow room where I left my things. We went to a large cafeteria, which was eerily quiet but for the sounds of shuffling slippered feet and unsharpened cutlery on plates. She led me through the serving line and deposited me at a side table of nurses and orderlies, telling them I was a former pilot and officer staying over to help her with some technical translations. I'm sure they knew otherwise, but they were polite and inquisitive and drew me into their conversations about the hospital, the patients, and the town at large.

I went back to my room and slept. Slept like the dead. Through the night and most of the following day. I woke to afternoon light seeping in through the room's glazed window and the sounds of people in the hallway. My left arm dangled off the bed, touching the cool linoleum floor. I got up, a little disoriented, and stepped into the hall. A nurse at a desk a few feet away directed me to a men's shower and toilet. I took a long hot shower, shaved, and dressed in my cleanest clothes. I felt good... or at least awake and aware. The nurse took me to Dr. Allard's office, telling me she was almost finished with "group" and I could wait there.

I wandered over to the bookshelves, touching the spines of volumes written in French and German. She had several French translations of books by the famous psychiatrist, Sigmund Freud. *Studies of Hysteria. The Interpretation of Dreams. The Psychopathology of Everyday Life.* One, in German, was entitled, *Drei Abhandlungen zur Sexualtheorie,* and judging from the obvious last word it might have been entertaining, but I didn't know enough German to make the effort.

Ella. Dr. Allard. No...Ella. She came in and, seeing me by her Freud books, said, "Ah, Freud. He did not like you Americans. Puritanical and prudish. Narrow-minded. Anti-intellectual. Always chasing after money and commercial things."

"Yes, that sounds like us."

"Please. Sit. It's late in the day. I wondered if you might be dead, so I had a nurse look in on you." She smiled.

"I didn't realize how tired I was. But now I'm awake. Would you like me to look at those British articles now? You'll have to help me with the long Latin medical words."

"It is late. Tomorrow. Instead, perhaps you can tell me about being with the *Armée de l'Air*. Was there a daily routine? Were you always in combat? What of your comrades? All French? Belgian?"

So, it began. Therapy disguised as conversation. I told her about my unit. I told her how we flew twice a day, weather depending, and not always fighting. But whatever the General Staff imagined an airplane could do, we did. Reconnaissance, artillery spotting, denying enemy planes the same observation missions, which meant dogfights with them. There were bombing runs and strafing the trenches, which meant plenty of archie at "low and slow" approaches to the trench lines. Attacking supply lines and trains. Near suicidal attacks on fixed, heavily defended observation balloons. Extracting the occasional spy from behind the German lines. All of these things would be done in daylight and again at night. Night was the worst.

We came back from missions—those of us who made it back—to regular meals at the base. Wine and warm beds. Occasional forays into the nearby towns. Drinking. Laughing. Though thinking back to those nights, maybe there was too much drinking among the pilots and observers. And maybe the laughter often seemed to border on hysteria. And there was, I supposed, good reason for hysteria. The near-misses in aerial combat. The crashes. Archie. Constant archie. Planes vaporized by direct hits from arcing shells. Watching all those burning planes on long lonely plunges back to earth. You could burn alive long before your plane impacted. Madness and chaos thousands of feet up, in the cold air. The headcount at the end of the day let us know how many had not made it back.

"You were exceptional?" she asked. "I am told the life expectancy of a pilot could be measured in days. Or just hours. Much, much less than an officer in the trenches."

That was true. But I had not been around for the Fokker Scourge in 1915 or the battles of Verdun and the Somme in 1916. I was there for Bloody April in '17, but most of the Allied losses were on the British side with their slow-moving BE.2s. Later, we had better planes and better weapons. And we had experience. So, we lived longer.

She asked, "Knowing the odds, why did you continue to fly?"

I thought it a silly question and told her, "If I didn't go, someone else would have had to. Maybe someone with less experience. Or luck. So I did what everyone else did. I climbed back in my plane and went up. And I always came back. One way or another."

I told her—after a lot of prying and persistence on her part—of my own shootdowns. About the planes I was responsible for bringing down with my guns. The men I had sent to their deaths. It was a lot more personal in the air. Not like lobbing shells from miles away at unseen men hiding in trench bunkers.

She wanted to know about flying in the cold, and what it was like to fly at thousands of feet with so little oxygen. Did I suffer from headaches, memory loss, or poor concentration, fatigue, troubled sleep, or anxiety? Well, we all did, though the headaches and memory things cleared up once you were back on the ground. Fatigue, anxiety, insomnia—everyone had them. It was more or less normal to be tired, and anxious after the last mission. And waiting for the next.

We got around to reading some papers from the British *Lancet*. She liked the so-called "case reports" buried in the articles, and finding a particularly interesting one about some poor devil of a former pilot, she would ask me about him. I began to suspect her English was better than she had let on.

"Would you identify with this man?" she asked. "Is he like you in some manner? The same symptoms, perhaps?" Asked if I thought an "artistic temperament," or reckless daring was necessary to a good pilot, I said, "If so, all of those *artistes sauvages* are dead now. I think it was the regular pilot you could count on to return to base at the end of the mission."

"You may be correct. Taking unnecessary risks often is a sign of war neurosis. So, is that you? Regular? Pedestrian?"

"I'm not sure I'd say 'pedestrian.' But steady, calm, dependable. Sure."

"But not apathetic or unimaginative or dull or wooden or slow?"

"No. I imagine they're all dead too."

"Yes, I suppose one must be clever in the aeroplane. The man on the ground is concerned only with two dimensions: left, right, back, and forward. The pilot must deal with three dimensions simultaneously, including and especially up and down."

She was quiet for a moment, glancing through some papers on her lap. Then she asked, "Would you describe yourself as a nihilist?"

I chuckled at the question. "I don't know what that is."

"In a nutshell, it is someone who believes life is

meaningless."

"Well, my life has plenty of meaning. At least to me. And my family and friends—their lives have meaning to me. And the guys I flew with—waiting, sometimes in the dark, the cold, the rain, for every last plane to drop back onto the field. So, no."

She looked at her papers again. "Perhaps I am extrapolating from reports of the British airmen who have been described as nihilistic and mutinous and prone to heavy drinking."

"If that's true, it may have had more to do with poor flight training and mediocre aircraft. They lost a lot of pilots. In combat, of course, but also in training. If they were mutinous or drunk or…nihilistic, you could likely fault their Army General Staff."

Ella seemed to believe wholeheartedly in William Rivers' talking cure for getting at repressed ideas and memories. So, we kept on talking. She asked if, being above most of the fighting, almost beyond the war, I had felt disconnected or removed from it. In a sense, superior to the men on the ground? I said, "No. Not when one bullet could send me straight down into the mix."

I told her about one day—a cloudy, windy day that discouraged flying—when I went into the little village behind our airfield for a meal and some wine. I ran into an American officer from Connecticut. We got to talking, and he offered me a quick tour of the trenches to our south. I'd only seen them from the air. Well, we entered a brown maze of mud and wood and sandbags. Everything was wet. These endless, winding trenches smelled. Smelled like a dump on a July afternoon. And the men, as dirty as anyone could get, all wore blank faces. I don't think I could have aroused an expression from anyone if I had appeared in a pink Easter Bunny costume. They seemed beyond the reach of any normal reactions.

Standing at one reinforced intersection of the trenches, I kicked up a brownish-white thing, which I took to be a stone. My guide glanced at it and said, "Looks like the lower end of a femur. You get to recognize bones around here better than a hometown doctor. If the surgeons have to dig shrapnel out of you after an attack, it's as likely to be bone as it is steel. The dead are just another hazard."

It was then I realized I was surrounded by the dead. Their bones. Their smell. Teeth and bits of uniform. This wasn't a trench. I was in a giant grave that had not yet been filled in. I wanted to claw my way out of that trench and run. Just run.

I was angry remembering this visit to the trenches. I told Ella she was wasting her time trying to distinguish the men with physical brain damage from the men who were emotionally traumatized by the war. I didn't see how anyone could recover from the wounds or the sheer horror of the ground war.

I dropped the journal I had been holding on the coffee table and said, "I'm tired of talking about me and the war and flying around above it. I shouldn't be here. I'm not really a patient." I waved my hand in the general direction of the first-floor patio where many actual patients sat or took in the grounds.

Ella sat there in her chair. Calm. Beautiful. She said, "Hmm, perhaps we could try the Kaufmann treatment."

"What's that?"

"Electro-shock."

"You're not serious?"

"Or perhaps the Max Nonne approach? But you must be naked to increase your vulnerability."

"Well, that sounds interesting. Do you undress first or do I?"

She laughed. And got me laughing. Or at least smiling. She got serious again and asked me about strafing men on the ground.

"You have not spoken of this, yet it was a common utility of the aeroplane. Am I correct?" She badgered me about this for so long I thought she might get up and poke at me with her finger. Finally, I told her, "I never liked doing it. Shooting men in the back as they ran for their lives. I tried to wait until a few of them would turn and raise their rifles. Then it seemed more like a fair fight, and I would open up with the Vickers guns."

I told her about the German pilot I shot with the pistol. She thought that was interesting, perhaps as an example of "single warrior combat" in an age of mechanized war and national armies.

"I did it out of rage, not some knightly or chivalrous nonsense," I told her.

She shook her head. "No, I think you did it out of necessity. Practicality. You couldn't jump with the parachute if he was waiting there to shoot you as you hung helplessly in the parachute's canopy."

That had not occurred to me. At least consciously. Maybe she was right.

One afternoon, she asked me why I was still in France. Why was I wandering around jobless, friendless, directionless? The war was over. Why was I still here? I guess that was the heart of the matter, and she went to work prying loose some answers.

Eventually, I told her I didn't want to go home to

endless questions about what it was like. The war. What I did. What I saw. Every question would force me to remember things that should have been buried and forgotten. And there would be the faces of people who had maimed sons, missing fathers, dead friends, and relatives who might be silently asking me, "Why are *you* alive?" As if being alive was a crime and I was the accused. So I avoided the Homefront stares and questions and just kind of wandered around thinking tomorrow might be better. Or at least different.

But things did not get better—I did not get better—until Ella lured me through the clinic gate.

Near the end of my stay, Ella said, "You have medals of valor from the *Armée de l'Air*. You survived three crashes. There is nothing wrong with being skilled at your job or being lucky in life. You are both skilled and lucky. Yes?"

"No. No, I don't suppose there is anything wrong in being both."

"Therefore, you should not feel guilty for being good and lucky. Yes?"

"I suppose." Though I didn't think I had felt guilty. Had I? Being alive seemed an odd thing to feel guilty about, yet it might be true of me. And perhaps others.

She told me the night nurses had stopped hearing any noises from my room. It was true; I slept better through the night, waking rested and not exhausted or dazed as before. One bright sunny day on the château's patio, she asked me to breathe in and exhale. I did. It seemed as if I emptied my lungs of years of high-altitude air, acrid cordite, and castor oil fumes, and took in the cool morning breeze coming off the Rhône.

"The war is over. You are alive and whole. If you

should dream of falling from the sky, remember the parachute. Remembrance without obsession or fear." she said. "You taught me about pilots and flying. Thank you. It will help with other patients. You should go home now. To family and friends. Your war is over."

Yes, the war was over. She had talked me out of dwelling on it. Still living in it. I had no reason to stay on at the château, taking up a bed and staff time, and of course, Ella's time. I left that morning.

Chapter 10

But I didn't go home. Having left Ella and her analytical questions—I think I referred to her methods as nagging—I guess I wanted to test my legs. And Lyon was an easy walk. I wanted to build my strength before I tackled that long trek back to America. I stayed in Lyon, finding work as an English-speaking waiter in a bar off a huge plaza called *Place Bellecour*. Easy work. A nice café. Polite British officials and tourists as customers. Some days off, I'd spend sitting in the *Théâtre Gallo Romain de Lyon-Fourvière*—an old Roman amphitheater—above the River *Saône*, sharing a baguette with the pigeons and admiring the city.

One day in the plaza, I stopped to listen to an outdoor orchestra playing. Walking on toward the other end of the *Place Bellecour,* I stopped a wayward soccer ball some kids were kicking back and forth. I joined their play for a minute, finally sending one shot over their heads. I was standing there, across from an outdoor café, when I noticed Ella. She was watching me. I strolled over to her table. She stood, surprised, and said, "You're still here. You look well. Relaxed."

"I am, thank you. Thought I would enjoy the peace of Lyon before catching a boat back to the States."

She was leaving the square, and I offered to walk with her for a bit. We walked and talked through the old streets. At her building, she looked up and down the narrow, cobbled lane and asked, "Would you come inside for a brandy, Lieutenant?"

Surprised, I said, "I would." I was also surprised she called me "Lieutenant," as if granting me a status or a class beyond that of the patient she had known. I followed her up an iron-and-marble staircase to a second-floor apartment. She showed me around, commenting on the old French furniture and the new German plumbing, and left me at the double doors to a small iron-railed balcony. Ella came back with two delicate balloon snifters.

I took the offered glass, raised it, and said, "To the walking, and flying, wounded." She smiled, and we both sipped the brandy. There must have been some kind of…transition. I don't remember exactly… The next I knew, we were in one of those hesitant, exploratory kisses. And then we were in bed.

That continued for a while. Staying with her. Wandering around Lyon together on Sundays or sometimes taking the train to Geneva for the day. Once or twice, I was tempted to ask if this affair was the Allard Method, a new patient therapy. But I thought better of it, letting it be what it was and not peering too deeply into what we were doing or why. Our time together felt…delicate. As delicate as those brandy snifters— press too hard and the thing shatters in your hand. So, I was content to let things be from day to day, week to week. I was content.

In the early fall, Ella met me at a café one morning. I had not seen her for a few days. She told me that we should stop seeing each other. That it would never last and we should part now before things became too complicated. That hurt. But she was right. She was older than I was. Certainly smarter. She was a doctor; I was a waiter. And a former patient. Ella said she had been thinking about returning to Alsace, to family and friends, and to personal things she needed to resolve. At that moment, she sounded like me. So, for the second time, she sent me on my way, but as a better man at each sendoff.

Soon after, I started for Paris with the idea of finding a booking agent to get me a cabin on a seaworthy freighter home. I settled in a cheap *pension* and began a poor man's tour of Paris. I had seen the city from a distance, high up in a plane. But from that vantage point, it had been more myth or Oz than an actual place. Now I had some time to make it real.

One day I was sitting in a café along the *Quai d'Orsay*—near the foreign ministry—drinking wine and watching pedestrians amble by. At the next table, a bunch of American reporters was hunched over some newspapers and government statements about the occupation and the reparations. They couldn't read French. I leaned toward their table and offered to help. I told them I was an American and a former pilot and officer with the French Army. Once they knew I had some skills and knowledge, they paid my lunch tab, and I translated the things they wanted for news stories to be wired home. That eventually became an almost regular-paying job. Sometimes I'd go with a couple of them to interviews with French officials and interpret for them. Other times, I'd sit in the wire service offices reading out official statements in English, surrounded by reporters with pencils and typewriters at the ready. Often, I'd go along with a reporter or writer-wannabe for what they called "man in the street" interviews: you know, ordinary people and their views on the armistice and German reparations.

It was interesting work and good pay. And amusing company. The international meetings, like the Reparations Commission, for example, were fun to watch but dull to have to pay close attention to. Lots of elderly officials in morning coats and top hats, and not a few with black canes and bright sashes. There were monocled generals weighted down with gaudy decorations. Lots of *frou-frou*. Young lawyers and junior diplomats sitting on the periphery of palatial chambers ready to spring to the principals' table with whatever piece of paper was needed at any given moment. Everyone so polite and formal you'd almost forget only a few years earlier they'd all been trying to kill each other.

The Paris translating work got me enough money to book passage on a ship bound for New York. So…I came home. At last.

****

Their fire had burned to warm ash and pale orange cinders. Karen, who had remained silent through Ender's long journey from the European air war to Long Island's placid seashore, snuggled closer to him. She pulled him tight. After a while, she said, "That's quite a story. I have so many questions. I should have been writing them down."

Enders chuckled. "You don't have to ask them all tonight. Save a few for the morning. Or Thanksgiving."

"I'm glad you met that doctor."

"Me too."

"Did you love her?"

*Of course, that would be her first question.* He

glanced at the dying fire. "Yes. I suppose I did. But that's over. She's back in Alsace. Married now."

"How do you know?"

"I wrote to her from Paris. Before I left. She wrote back wishing me luck and saying she was going home to marry a man—another doctor—whom she said would make a 'reliable husband.' Her words, a reliable husband. Not someone she said she loved. Just reliable."

"As in pedestrian?"

"I'd like to think so."

****

Enders woke as the morning sun began to warm the sand on which they had been sleeping. Quietly, he started a fire and used the last of their fresh water to make a pot of coffee. Then he slipped back under the sheet to rekindle another fire. Later, he coaxed Karen to her feet, and they stepped hand-in-hand into the cool morning tide.

They sat before the low-burning fire, sipping the hot coffee and working their way through stale donuts. They hardly spoke. There was little need for words. They seemed to be waiting for the rest of the world to wake up. Eventually, it did. Gulls appeared overhead. A trawler passed through Plum Gut. A farmhouse bell rang in the distance. It broke the morning's peace.

She put her mug aside and asked, "That doctor in Lyon. Was she French or German?"

"French. Her family was French, and they spoke French at home. At school and out in public, you spoke German. I guess Alsace-Lorraine was a bilingual place. Whether you wanted it to be or not.

"My family is German. You wouldn't know it from the name. We were Bach, not Bates. My father changed

234

it when the war started."

Enders had heard such stories. He nodded at her. "Yeah, I read a lot of people had to do that. German, Jewish, or anything too foreign sounding suddenly became Smith or Jones. Everyone desperate to anglicize their names. No more German studies in school. Sauerkraut becomes Liberty Cabbage. It's all nonsense." He stretched a hand toward her. "Bates, Bach, I like you all the same."

"My parents still speak very good German. I know some too."

Enders moved closer to her. "Ah, a spy for the Kaiser at Miss Porter's? What secrets did you learn there?"

They flew home before the morning ended, lifting off from the damp sand of Orient Point and climbing high above the placid Sound. Enders, in the front seat, took them to ten thousand feet above Niantic and cut the engine. In the sudden silence, he turned his head to tell Karen, "This is what the birds hear and see." He put the plane in a wide spiral, letting drag and gravity pull them back to Earth. Karen leaned to the right and the left, watching the town and the river grow soundlessly closer. The silent shadow of the plane flitted over busy streets and moored boats, causing people to look up as the muted Jenny drifted by. With a light grip on the stick, Enders could feel the wind buffet the rudder. He could hear the flex and creak of the fuselage as the plane banked in its lazy spiral.

"Do we still need the engine?"

"We do." Almost reluctantly, Enders restarted the engine. He pushed on the stick. They rolled away to the east, over the Niantic River, and came in for an easy landing at Beaumont's field. He had not enjoyed flying like this since a day in France when he had taken a plane up to test an engine repair and stayed away for so long he had been on the verge of being declared lost. He smiled at the memory.

****

Enders stood in the middle of the White Sand property, a lonely potato plant at his feet. Leafy elm and chestnut trees blocked his view of the ocean, but he could hear large waves—driven by a storm near Bermuda—breaking on the shoreline. The wind was up. Sheets of tarpaper tried to take flight in the blustery air.

One of the local summer hires in a worn undershirt and a Boston Braves cap asked, "Think it'll rain?"

"Maybe. That's okay; there's plenty of interior work to keep us busy." He grinned at the kid and walked back to the truck to sit on its tailgate and think about the week's progress. They had finished enclosing several cottages, and the new owners hurriedly moved in to enjoy the remains of the summer. Other cottages were being framed and enclosed as still others were emerging from their primordial pilings.

Enders dropped his fedora in the truck bed and peeled off his work shirt. It was late in the week; the crew had been working hard and fast. He looked forward to the coming weekend, and that set his mind to thinking of Karen.

Then he remembered Deputy Pierce.

*What to do about this guy? He's got a gun and a badge, and even if he's bent, he's still the law. Crooked laws. Crooked coppers. He's a reverse kidnapper. He's handed me a ransom note threatening to grab up Karen on some obscene little morals suspicion. What the hell kind of law is that? And how does anyone have the nerve to use the word "moral" to describe it?*

He worked past his anger and anxiety. At the end of the day, he pedaled back up the road to the Manor House, dodging the increasing summer traffic of automobiles, farmers' oxcarts, and Gypsy horses. He showered and ate an early dinner with Mr. and Mrs. Kloss and their six renter guests. Afterward, in his room again, he paced around the bed. *Pierce. Pierce.*

Enders yanked open a dresser drawer, looking for loose change, but spied the bottle of Canadian whiskey given to him by the Poverty Island clammers. He looked at the label with its charred edges from the boat fire. He closed the drawer and left the house to walk to Sound View.

*Did gossip ever get anyone killed?*
                                 ****

He went to the casino first. In the backroom speakeasy, he bought a cold beer and leaned on the bar to chat with the bartender, a pale, angular man who spent no time on the beach. Enders had never seen him anywhere but in the casino speakeasy. He was a denizen of the night, and Enders assumed someone had to be, in a place like the speakeasy. He bought another beer and asked the man, "Hey, that summer deputy ever come in here?"

"Pierce? Nah. Keeps his distance."

"Hmm. Yeah. Seen him wandering around Hartford Ave. Likes to talk to people. I heard him once hinting he might have helped burn a rum runner."

The bartender looked at Enders. "Burned?"

"Could have been part of some police raid. Last month. You know, a boat loaded with booze burned to the waterline. Could have been local cops getting rid of the illegal liquor. And a fast boat. Or maybe cops unhappy with their cut? Who knows?"

The bartender bent toward him. "There was rumor of a sunk runner off Saybrook. Supposedly, some of their stuff washed ashore. They say quality Canadian."

"So, maybe Pierce knew. Lotta people are involved in smuggling these days. Buying, selling, bribing, looking the other way." He smiled and raised his glass. "And I'm glad there are. Cheers."

Enders left the casino. He went to Doyle's and then to O'Conner's, each time buying a beer or two and chatting with the bartenders about rumors of a sunken rum runner and the possibility Deputy Pierce had known something about it.

It was late now. He'd had six beers—some of them of questionable quality—and he had to work in the morning. Enders walked back to the Kloss farm. He was not proud of what he had done. But Pierce had left him no choice. The weaselly little deputy had pulled a gun on him. Worse, he had threatened to have Karen violated by public health officials and tossed into the women's prison farm in East Lyme. The threat was serious, and according to Lonergan, such threats were all too common across the country. Spreading a rumor about Pierce seemed like the least he could do to throw him off his game.

*Okay, I'm lighting a little fire under this guy. Let's see how he likes the heat.*

\*\*\*\*

Enders stopped the truck across from Florence Griswold's mansion. Karen sat on the stoop on the other side of the street. She was clutching a folder of papers and talking with a gray-haired man dressed in casual summer clothes. He looked like another artist. As Enders crossed the street, the man raised his straw hat to Karen, turned up the walkway, and disappeared through the mansion's front entrance.

"Hi. Who was that?" Enders sat beside her in a pose Dr. Allard might have described as "marking his territory."

"William Robinson. He's an impressionist. One of the founders of the Old Lyme Art Academy. He bought a house here last summer."

He brushed her rouged cheek with his lips and pointed at the folder. "What's all this? Homework?"

"Information about the Paris Society of American Painters. Some articles on classes at the *Académie Julian*. And the American Art Association of Paris at *Rue Notre Dame de…*"

"*Rue Notre-Dame-des-Champs*. Near the *Boulevard Montparnasse*."

"You know it?"

"I've been by it a few times."

"Oh, good. I won't get lost."

Enders shook his head and laughed. "This Robinson guy planting ideas in your head?"

"William said being in Paris was a wonderful experience. He won an Honorable Mention at the Paris Expo years ago. Now he's helping me with my atmospherics and brush strokes. I like him. He's like me: loyal to a painting style being eclipsed by cubism, surrealism, expressionism, dada."

"Dada?"

She laughed. "Don't ask. I'm sure you'd hate it."

Enders stood and pulled her to her feet. He inclined

his head toward the parked truck. "Unless you'd like to paint it, how 'bout we hop in and drive over to Saybrook for dinner? I'm starving."

"Is this a dinner date?"

"It is, missy. The Pease House, if we can get in. A clam shack if we can't." Enders smiled at his use of "missy."

"I brought this." Karen dangled her small purse before him like a hypnotist dangling a shiny pocket watch.

"Money? I'll pay," he said, playing dumb.

"Noooo."

"Lipstick? Change?"

"I'm beginning to worry you were right about being an idiot."

Enders laughed, caught her arms, and whispered to her. "Is it dessert?"

"Yes." Then she blushed.

\*\*\*\*

"Pull it tight, but not too tight. Shouldn't sag over time," said the elderly electrician.

Enders pulled on the black-wrapped wire with one hand and tacked a length of it in place with a staple gun. The electrician stripped the end of the wire, connected it to the gray metal fuse box, and screwed in another copper-and-ceramic fuse.

"Lights in an hour," said the man in a tone that hinted at something miraculous.

"Great," said Enders, who suspected the man had been around at the lighting of Edison's first bulb and whose scarred fingertips suggested he might have learned his trade through trial and error.

He glanced out the empty frame of a window to see

a JJJ construction truck pulling into the middle of the sandy property. Jesse Martin from the Point O' Woods development was at the wheel. Enders stepped outside to see what he wanted.

"Hey. You lost or here to poach my guys and supplies?"

"I'll do any poaching after hours. I stopped by to say some NAACP boys in suits and ties were nosing around the site this morning. Even took some photographs with a Kodak. One of them was a lawyer asking questions about the property deeds and the private club clauses."

*They'll be coming here. Probably right in the middle of a sales pitch.* Enders nodded and said, "Yeah, Spencer mentioned some lawsuits in Fairfield County. He around today?"

Jesse shook his head. "Saybrook office. I called there soon as those boys left. Spence said be polite and remind them they're on private property. We don't want to be in the newspapers about who's moving in and who's not."

Enders exhaled and looked around the property as if searching for an escape. "Yeah, I don't want to be quoted trying to untangle private property from right and wrong and who can buy that private property. Where's a court and a judge when you need one?"

Jesse slapped the outside of the truck door and grinned like he was skipping school. "Okay, just so you know. Drivin' into Saybrook. Need anything?"

"No, I think we're set here." He raised a hand as a goodbye wave, and Jesse drove off, bouncing along the sandy track toward the Shore Road.

****

They showed up in the late afternoon, three men in

a shiny blue Buick D-45 with whitewall tires, brown spokes, and a black fold-down top. They pulled alongside Enders, who, with a pencil in one hand and a notebook in the other, must have looked like someone in charge. The man in the back seat stepped out, saying, "Hello. I'm Marvin J. Woods, legal representative of the Northeast Chapter of the NAACP. May I have a moment of your time?" He removed his boater and put on a pair of wire-rimmed glasses.

Mr. Woods stuck out his hand and Enders stepped forward to shake it. "Dave Enders, site foreman. What can I do for you?"

"Perhaps answer some questions about the property?" said Mr. Woods.

"Well, it's all in public records. The town clerk can show you every word and every sold deed you might want to see."

"Yes, thank you. Now, this is JJJ's White Sand development…"

Before he could reply, the driver, a thick man in a collarless striped shirt, said, "White Sand. That says it all right there."

"It's the color of the sand here," Enders told him.

"Color of the people laying on that sand, too."

His companion in the front seat said, "Till the summer's end, when lot of them are as brown as us."

Mr. Woods waved his colleagues into silence.

"We are concerned so much of the coastline in this state is being purchased for private gain. And for exclusion by other residents, both along the coast and inland. The way things are going, Connecticut soon may feel like a landlocked state without, for all practical purposes, a coast."

The driver stepped out of the car and stretched his arms and back. His front-seat companion got out and aimed a small camera at the ongoing construction a few yards away. Enders did not try to stop him.

"Well, it's an issue of private property and commercial investment. Perhaps the state will step in at some point."

"It's more an issue of exclusion by race, by religion, by ethnicity, is it not, Mr. Enders?" Woods looked around the building site and asked, "How many cottages will you build here?"

"Hundred-eighty-seven lots."

"Any of those for black folk?"

Enders glanced at his dirty boots. He looked back at Woods. "Seems unlikely, Mr. Woods."

"You're Jim Crowin' the beach." The driver climbed back behind the steering wheel. "And this is the North."

"Bill, please," said Woods to his colleague.

"Think there's any point in our trying to talk to a Mr. John Spencer or the company president, Mr. Johnson?"

"I doubt you'll get in to see Mr. Johnson. I can't see him."

"And you, Mr. Enders, what do you think is going to happen to all this once-open coastline?"

Knowing it was a feeble response, he said, "Well, there's the state beach at Hammonasset."

"But a narrow spit of land for all of Connecticut's citizens? Surely, that is not a serious solution."

Enders looked across the street line to a completed cottage. "Then I guess some people will enjoy the beach and some won't. Just like always."

"The past doesn't always have to guide the future.

We're fighting for change. And you, Mr. Enders?"

"Changing the world…? I tried that. In France." He released an almost silent sigh. "I was thinking I could always leave the country."

"Would that we all had some other place to run to." Woods glanced around the site again and said, "Thank you for your time." He extended his hand again and Enders shook it.

Enders stepped closer to the car as Woods climbed into the back seat. The driver looked up at him and pointed a thick finger at his neck. "You in the war or just clumsy?"

Enders stuck his pencil behind his ear. "I could be both, I suppose." He did not try to smile at his own joke.

"I recognize the mark. I was 369th Infantry. Attached to the French Army."

"Harlem Hellfighters. Seen you around."

"Where?"

Enders pointed up. "From a couple of thousand feet up. With the *Armée de l'Air*."

"Pilot. And officer." Bill, the driver, looked around the property again. "Looks like you done fell to earth, mister pilot." With that, he started the engine and turned the car in a tight circle around Enders.

****

"Oh, stop right here. Pull over. I've been meaning to tell you." Karen twisted around in the truck seat to look back at the intersection of McCurdy Road and Johnny Cake Hill Road. "This is so scandalous. Everyone's talking. There was some shooting here the other night. Cars roaring down the road, waking everyone in the neighborhood."

Enders looked around the dirt and gravel street,

seeing nothing more scandalous than the trees and the creek. "What's going on?"

"That creepy deputy—"

"What happened?" His voice sounded louder than he intended. He looked out the side window as if the view might impart some information he didn't want to hear from Karen.

"Did you know he lived up there? The town paid his rent on a carriage house behind that old colonial mansion there."

Enders pivoted in his seat to look at the house visible through the foliage. "I didn't know where he lived." He turned back to her. "Is he dead? Someone shot him?"

"Well, there's the mystery. Some people heard cars late Wednesday night. And shouting. There were shots. Gunshots. Then the cars again. One neighbor said later they heard another car drive away. Very fast."

Enders was silent, looking around at the few surrounding houses hiding along the creek bed, and he wondered if he had got Pierce killed. By rumor. By a fictitious story about an actual event for which he was entirely responsible.

"I came down here this afternoon with Bill Robinson and Matilda Browne, but we didn't see anything. Just a state police auto and two Hartford vice cops. Pierce's jalopy is gone."

"So maybe he got away. Hid somewhere—the marsh—when the shooting started. Then ran to his car. He could be safe back in Middletown right now."

Karen looked at Enders. "Are you cheering for him? You sound almost…relieved."

"Ah, no. No. I was not any fan of that guy. Like you said, he was a creep. And crooked." He looked at her again. "But you don't want people to think the town is dangerous. Full of mobsters and murderers. Let's hope it's some personal thing and not the start of a bootlegger war."

He put the truck in gear and drove toward Shore Road. "How about some dancing tonight? I feel…electrified. I need to move."

"Speaking of moving, aren't you supposed to show me how to drive sometime?"

Enders put his hand on her leg. "One crime—I mean, one crisis at a time."

****

Spencer anchored his elbows on his desk and stared at the property deeds. "Nice lot. POW. Why here?"

Enders hunched forward in his chair and looked at Spencer. "The Point O' Woods train station is convenient. This particular lot is just up from the bridge on a slight rise. You can see the water without having to worry about it being washed away during some hurricane."

"You don't trust Jesse's construction?" Spencer smiled from the other side of the desk.

"I don't trust Mother Nature. Things happen."

Spencer nodded. "Good choice." He slid the deed across the desk. "Sure you want to do this? All that hard-earned money we've been paying you…"

Enders produced a pen and began signing his name to the deed. "Don't talk me out of it. I've already laid awake nights considering the costs. And the time. All that stuff." He pushed the deed back to Spencer. From his shirt pocket, Enders withdrew a folded bank check and placed it on the desk too.

"Kid, it's like you're working for free now. Most of

246

the money we've been paying you, you just handed it back. With more to come."

"I'm hoping it all works out down the road."

"Yeah, that's the real estate game. Lotta hope." He dropped the deed into his wire basket. He pocketed the check.

"Any of the Woods crew got a beef with you?" Spencer flipped open his cigar box and rooted around for one of his slender Cubans.

Enders sat back in his chair, still holding his pen. "No. Why?"

"These are the guys who are gonna be building your house. You don't want the roof to blow off the first time it storms. Or a fire to break out when you turn on an electric light."

Enders smiled and shook his head. "No, we're copacetic. No problems."

Spencer grunted and puffed out a pale swirl of smoke as the tobacco began to burn. "Be around for the eight o'clock tomorrow?"

"Sure." Enders took that to mean his meeting in the field office was over. He reached for his hat and knapsack resting on the floor.

"Any trouble with the NAACP lawyer?"

"No. Had a polite conversation and they left."

"Okay." Spencer clamped down on his pencil-thin cigar and searched his desk for a notepad. He found it, held it out at arm's length to read, and said, "Management's gonna do a fall mailing so we'll probably want more aerial photos. You and that guy in Saybrook—"

"Debrie."

"—can do a couple more flyovers?"

"Sure. We might want to wait until early November. All the leaves will be down and we'll get better pictures of the property sizes and what's been built to date."

Spencer scribbled a note to himself and looked back at Enders. "Okay, flyboy." He put his cigar aside and said, "So, you're planning a future for yourself. Any local artists in that future?"

Enders' grin might have said it all. But he said, "Maybe. Right now, I'm thinking it would give my mother something to do since my sister passed. You know, furnish the cottage. Collect the rent next summer. Get her out of the Milford house and away from painful memories for a bit. Just taking the train out here would be—what's the word—therapeutic?"

Spencer nodded. "Yeah. Anyway, it's good you're planning ahead. Business is booming. You are too. Keep it up."

Enders waved and banged out the screen door to his bike. Pedaling along the side of the road, he thought about Beaumont's little aerial refrain to him, *Think down here, act up there*. He was doing both on the ground now, and his level of thought and action would have surprised Beaumont, and Spencer, and especially Karen.

****

Saturday, August 12, Enders and Karen followed a loud and dusty parade of cars and horses, marching adults, a blaring school band, and a throng of wild-eyed children through the hot streets of Sound View and Hawks Nest. The human contents of the parade eventually spilled onto the hot sand of the beach where swimming contests, three-legged races, and a beautiful baby contest were being organized.

"So, what do you think of Beach Day?" Karen's face

was hidden by her floppy straw hat.

Enders searched around the crowded, noisy shore. "The paper said there was going to be a bathing suit beauty contest too. They might need more judges."

She punched him in the arm.

"Ouch." He touched his bicep. "Hey, I'm trying to show a little civic pride, you know, wanting to participate in the community activities."

"There's the beach clean-up tomorrow morning." She looked out from under her hat and grinned at his tanned and happy face.

A gaggle of children ran past them spilling paper cones of flavored ice and kicking up more sand than a pack of hounds chasing a rabbit. "We'll get run down and buried here. How about we grab some sodas and dogs and head toward the Kloss farm?"

"Isn't it all rocks in the water?"

"Past that. To Saltworks Point. It's a sandy bottom. I swam there a few times after work."

****

Enders laid out their towels and sat on the smooth mass of rock to drip dry after a swim off the Point. She lay beside him, rolling her shoulders and trying to find a comfortable spot. After a few seconds, she said, "Sand is softer."

Enders smiled at her complaint. "Yes, but it's a minefield of rocks back there. At least here, we're sitting on one giant slab. Step off and we're in water with a sand bottom." He tossed his knapsack behind him and leaned back to use it as a pillow.

Karen, on her back, groped blindly for his hand and held onto it. "How are things at work?"

"Good. Busy." Enders had his eyes closed against

the high sun. He could hear band music blaring from Sound View.

"Any buyers asking about my paintings?"

"Sorry. No nibbles this week." He turned his head toward her. "You know, we might be in violation of the property deeds. Selling paintings on the property might fall under the commercial restrictions of JJJ's standard beach association language."

She glanced at him. "I thought those deeds restricted the kinds of people who could buy."

"Ha. You'd be surprised what's in those deed restrictions. Stuff about fences, hedges, tents, the angle of the roof, garages, whether it's a cold-water cottage or a year-round house. On and on with little details. So, there's also a clause covering dangerous or offensive trades and businesses, including stables, pigsties, slaughterhouses, forges, steam engines, hospitals, and factories."

"Offensive trades? Are you comparing my paintings to a pigsty or a stable?" She squeezed his hand as hard as she could without hurting herself or shaking off her grin.

He started laughing. "Not at all, my dear. And I promise to redouble my sales pitches to all the house hunters I meet next week."

"Thank you." She threw a smile in his direction.

"But don't you sometimes paint cows and sheep? That might fall under the livestock exclusion."

\*\*\*\*

Enders walked back along Main Street from the company's office to Saybrook Junction train station. He had taken the train since the company trucks were collecting lumber and building supplies in Niantic. Ahead, a local train idled on the southbound track. He saw several policemen emerge from the train's carriages. Two more were standing in the parking lot talking with three men in suits. He cut through the station house. On the platform, he stopped a passing conductor.

"Hi. What's with all the coppers on the train?"

"Lepers."

It was the last thing Enders expected to hear. "Lepers? As in the disease? Leprosy? Like in the Bible?"

"Crazy as that might seem, son, yes. From Massachusetts. Seems there was a special hospital on an island up that way. Governor closed it and had all the leper patients shipped to a new government hospital in Louisiana."

He had a sudden image of the disfigured creatures in the H.G. Wells story, *The Island of Dr. Moreau.* "Lepers on an island?"

"Story was in the Boston papers and the *Times.* Good riddance, I say." The conductor adjusted his cap and crossed the tracks to the idling train.

Enders called after him. "So, why the cops?"

"Couple of them escaped off the train the other day."

*How hard could it be to find lepers around here?* Enders stepped back from the edge of the platform as the northbound New London local rolled into the station.

\*\*\*\*

Enders got off the train in Old Lyme and went back to the library where he had left his bicycle. He pedaled up Lyme Street to the Griswold mansion, looking for Karen. He found her by the old rowboat dock. She had set her things a little beyond the dock and was painting the three old boats as they floated on the slack current of the Lieutenant River.

"Hi." He stepped behind her, glanced around the

river foliage for other artists, and kissed the back of her neck.

"I thought you were working."

"I am. Just hopped off the train from Saybrook. So tomorrow, I can drop you at Hawks Nest if you still want to paint Rainbow Row."

"Thank you. I do like that line of painted cottages across the beach. And the early morning sun could be interesting."

"All right, I'll leave you to it. I've got a couple of miles to pedal. See you tomorrow." He kissed her neck again and walked to the top of the riverbank. Enders turned and watched her paint for a moment. *Wish I could sit here a while*. He went back to the mansion and retrieved his bike.

Riding past the library again he swerved to the left, up Library Lane, and stopped. "Well, I'm here. Might as well go in," he mumbled to the front lawn of the building. Inside, he asked the librarian for any Massachusetts newspaper that might have recent stories about the island lepers being shipped to Louisiana.

"Oh, yes." She slipped on a pair of bifocal glasses and went around to the newspaper racks. In a minute, she returned with two recent issues of *The Boston Globe.*

"Here you are, Mr. Enders. I must say, this is not your usual reading material. Which reminds me, you have two books due back very soon."

"Yes, sorry. My nighttime reading has…slowed. You know, too many summer distractions. *I'm sleeping with a beautiful woman up the street*. I'll try to drop them off this weekend," he said, smiling.

"Of course." She drifted back to the front desk.

Enders sat at a long table with banker's lamps and a

single neck-high shelf of reference books. There was a below-the-fold story about three dozen leprosy patients living on an island called Penikese, not far from Martha's Vineyard. A small map was printed on the following page. As soon as a new federal leprosarium was completed in Louisiana, Governor Cox had the island's inhabitants put on a southbound train. With the island deserted, he ordered its empty buildings fumigated and dynamited.

The second *Globe* article described the patients in Massachusetts—all of whom were foreign-born—noting one or two patients over the years had disappeared or escaped from the island. Three more had now jumped the Louisiana-bound train somewhere between New Bedford, Massachusetts, and Stamford, Connecticut. The piece also compared the brand-new federal leprosy center in Louisiana to the government's first Leprosy Investigation Station in the Hawaii islands territory, which had been holding lepers since the mid-nineteenth century.

Enders sat back and folded the newspapers. *Wow. Who knew? Must be tough living on a small New England island. Tough winters. Penikese Island. Not so far from here. I could make it there and back without refueling. Course, there's nothing to see now.*

Chapter 11

Even from the top of the street, the normal Friday night crowds at Sound View looked different. There was less movement, less communal noise, and more ordered congestion. People stood on either side of the sand-packed street as three large automobiles and a black container truck occupied the center.

A shrill police whistle stopped Enders and Karen near the Italian grocery. A spicy aroma of tomato and garlic seeped through the store's screen door. The crowd noise dropped to a low muttering of whispered voices. A gramophone eked out its last notes as beach residents leaned out their upstairs windows to watch. Uniformed policemen strode through the doorways of Doyle's and O'Connor's, with several manacled men in tow. Farther down the street, a similar scene was playing out in front of the casino.

As they got closer to the crowds, Enders could see the words Police Patrol painted on the side of the truck. "It's a raid," he told her unnecessarily. Though for a split second, he had imagined it had something to do with the lepers from the train.

They joined the crowd on the street and Enders asked no one in particular, "What's going on?"

A seersuckered man in a sloughing newsboy's cap turned to them with a grim look on his tanned face. "Hartford Vice. They're grabbing all the owners for gambling and liquor."

Another man said, "They're padlocking the joints. No songs or suds tonight, my friends."

The police helped the casino owner onto the steps of the wagon. The owner turned to the crowd and yelled, "Somebody call Tom Dorset." He bent down to the policeman, then yelled to the crowd, "City Hall station." He disappeared into the dark wagon.

The police packed up their prisoners and climbed into their cars. The crowd got braver. Men loosened their ties and started booing. As the police convoy pulled away, the crowd of summer residents and thirsty weekenders jeered and shouted at the back of the paddy wagon as it disappeared up the shadowy street.

Karen leaned into Enders. "Well, that was entertaining. What should we do next?"

He looked at the darkened fronts of Doyle's and O'Connor's. "No dancing, no music. And I don't have a truck tonight, so getting over to Saybrook will be by train, if you want to go."

She looked around the crowd and whispered, "Do you have your flask?"

"Yeah."

She inclined her head back toward the grocery. "We could grab some food and sodas and walk the beach to White Sand."

Enders gave her an overly serious look. "Miss Bates, I like you more and more every day."

****

The construction crew worked through the day, pausing only for a brief lunch and trips to whichever finished but unoccupied cottage had a working toilet. Enders was as busy as the others, not noticing the pace of their efforts until late in the day, when one of the high schoolers asked about the time. Quitting time had arrived. After announcing this important fact to the crew, the men put aside their tools and assembled their belongings for the journey home.

Enders grabbed his thermos, shook it for evidence of any surviving bits of ice, and hearing none, put it aside and picked up his notebook. He looked around the property, which consisted of a jumble of new cottages, missing surveyor stakes, half-buried curbstones, cement pilings, stacks of lumber, rolls of tarpaper, assembled floor joists, and narrow-backed brick chimneys standing defiantly against the late afternoon sky.

*It's a mess, but I understand the whole mess. Guess that means I know what I'm doing.* He wandered to a nearby property stake lying in the sand and replanted it in its designated spot.

Behind him, someone cleared his throat and said, "Boss."

Enders spun around, surprised by the unexpected sound.

The Portuguese worker from Griswold Point stood there in his damp shirt, broad-brimmed hat and sweat-stained leather gloves.

"Vasco."

"Boss. I have problem. Must go."

"It's quitting time." Enders raised a hand toward the Point. This was the longest conversation he had ever had with the man, and now, out of amusement and curiosity, he wondered how long he might keep it going. Enders waited for a second and was surprised to hear the man say, "You are good man. I see you speak to *italianos e africanos*. And the rich womans. Same voice."

*What the hell…? Same voice? Same way?*

"I go to Stonington. Portuguese church. Portuguese *barcos*…boats.

"Okay…? This weekend?"

"Not return," Vasco looked across the jumbled lots.

"You're quitting? Why? We need you."

"You are good man." Vasco squinted in the afternoon light.

"You said that. Are you asking me now or telling me?"

"Praying."

*Praying?* The man was distressed, in his words and his nervous motions. Enders stepped closer, spread his arms wide, and grinned at his enigmatic employee. "Vasco, just tell me what you want."

"I leave Penikese year ago. Go back to New Bedford. Many Portuguese. Easy to stay. Then Penikese close. Everyone on south train to Louisi… Now… ah… *polícia* at trains. On roads. They search for other people. Patients."

Later, when he thought about Vasco, Enders was secretly pleased with himself for not having backed away from the man.

In an instant, Enders connected the names, Penikese and Louisiana.

"You're… You have leprosy?"

"They say. Maybe they wrong."

"But you were a patient on the island. On Penikese."

"*Sim*. Many years. Then I hide on supply boat. Go back to New Bedford. Now here."

Enders was silent, thinking about what to do and pushing down a flicker of primal fear at the word "leprosy," a word that embodied rot, horror, contagion, and biblical admonitions. He knew he could just call the police and be done with the matter. And with the man before him. Instead, he stood there scratching at his hair and shifting his weight from foot to foot. He looked at Vasco again.

That Enders was still there, and silent, maybe gave Vasco some courage. Or hope. He shook off his gloves and held up his hands. "See. *Nada*. Nothing *terrível*." He tilted his head back and pulled at the jawline skin, which was hidden by his beard. "Small marks. Little wounds. *Seco*. Dry. Dry." He held the backs of his hands out to Enders again.

Enders swallowed and timidly leaned in to look at the man's hands. There were a few purple splotches on his hands and wrists. His fingers seemed bent and overly thick, but the man worked with his hands. Worked hard with them. To Enders, he seemed healthy, as healthy as the rest of the crew. There was no gangrenous odor. No dangling limbs or digits waiting to fall off. No hideous sores that were the mark of the unclean, the living dead.

Enders stepped back and sat on a stack of shingles. He tried to remember if he had touched anything Vasco's bare hands had handled. No. He'd never seen his hands until just now. Did they ever share food or water? No, he was certain. He looked at Vasco and asked, "What do you want me to do?"

Vasco stooped to pick up his leather gloves. Squatting in the sand, he said, "Help me go to Ston…"

"Stonington, yes."

"Many Portuguese there…to help. Portuguese church."

"You can't take the train. Can't hitch on the road."

"*Polícia*."

"Well, I can't take a company truck that far for that long." Enders glanced at the Ford sitting under a tree. He looked back at the small dark man before him. He thought about the nights he had spent in the cells of small French towns and the police who urged him out of town or off the beach. "All right. Let me think about getting to Stonington. How… Just come to work tomorrow. Maybe I'll have an idea. Maybe."

Enders stood and stretched his tight back.

"Thank you, boss." Vasco pulled his gloves back on.

"I won't rat you out. Come to work like normal and… We'll see."

Vasco nodded and hurried away. Enders watched him disappear around a cottage and walked to the truck. *Trigger-happy bootleggers, bent deputies, raided speakeasies, now lepers. How can so much be going on in a summertime town of nine hundred people? I'm going to have a long, long list of things—omissions—to confess to Karen someday. Oh yeah, and the cottage I just bought.*

He stopped with his foot on the running board. *What would Ella say about all these held-back omissions?* Enders wasn't sure, but he smiled at the idea of her having to ask and drag answers out of him. He stopped himself again to wonder what she would ask about him helping Vasco, a public health fugitive: "Do you identify with this man? Or is this an act of rebellion against the social order? Or simple kindness? The difference matters, yes?" He jumped into the truck and started the engine before the spirit of Ella could pry any answers from him.

\*\*\*\*

Enders arrived at the job site early. He lazily

followed the sunny street to the beachfront and looked around. Several little boys already had staked out their section of the sand with towels and toys and two black, bouncy inner tubes. The odors of coffee and bacon wafted from a nearby cottage. Bridges' cottage was empty; they would not be back until the Labor Day weekend. He looked beyond their house toward Griswold Point. He saw three men trudging through the beach grass toward the job site. Vasco was one of them.

Enders had lain awake last night thinking about Vasco. He wondered what life had been like on that barren little island, connected to the world by only an occasional supply boat. It was only five miles from the mainland; did anyone try to swim the distance? Islands had always made good prisons. Water was an effective barrier to potential intruders. On the edge of sleep, he realized water also could be the best escape route.

The three men approached Enders and waved or mumbled good mornings to him. He returned their morning salutes and stepped up beside Vasco as he walked past. "After work," Enders told him in a low voice. He slowed his pace to let the men pull ahead of him.

****

To Enders, the day seemed to stretch beyond the usual quitting time. He wondered if Vasco felt the same slowing of the clock. In the heat of the late afternoon, the men happily put aside their tools and scattered to homes and entertainments at Sound View. Enders sat on the tailgate of one of the trucks and tried not to think too much about what he was planning to do.

Vasco emerged from a framed cottage, looked around the construction grounds, and shuffled over to

Enders.

"Boss." He waited.

"All right. I thought about the plane…"

"Aeroplane?"

"Yeah. Fly you there in minutes. But first, we'd have to drive to the airfield, then find a place to land. Problem is landing planes attract attention. Someone might see you and me in Niantic or Stonington. So, I have another idea. Can you sail?"

"I am Portuguese."

Enders smiled at the answer. "Okay, I guess that means yes." He nodded his head toward the beach. "You know the catboat down the road here?"

"I can sail," said the man, his face becoming livelier than Enders had ever seen it.

"No one is at the cottage this week. There's a small outboard motor out back. Take it. You might need it. Check the gas."

"But you. What about…?"

Enders held up his palm. "Leave tonight when no one is around to see you take the boat." He reached into the knapsack beside him and withdrew his wartime compass. He tossed it to Vasco. "You may need this at night. Or in a fog. Helped me a couple of times in the war."

Vasco pried the cover open with a gloved hand, and moved the compass around a bit, watching the magnetic needle. He closed the lid and said, "Yes."

"It's twenty miles as the crow flies."

"More like the seagull."

"Yeah." Enders nodded. "Yeah, the wind will decide the real miles. But it should be an easy sail. There's sure to be a town dock. Leave the boat there. In two days—that should be time enough—I'll have to take the train there and sail the boat back."

"Yes. Dock. Two days. I do this. No problem."

*No problem! I can think of plenty.* "Okay." He hopped off the truck and pointed to a corked glass jug in the truck bed. "Take that for water. The envelope under it, that's the last of your pay." He grabbed his knapsack and tossed it into the cabin. He turned back to Vasco.

"There's a piece of paper in the envelope too. It mentions a treatment at the University of Hawaii. You know, the islands way out in the Pacific Ocean. The Ball Method or the Dean Method; there's some confusion about what it's called. I read it in the newspapers. Some day you can find a Portuguese priest or doctor who can write to the University. Ask about treatment."

Vasco clutched the envelope and nodded his head.

"Well, good luck. You were a steady worker here. I'll tell the crew you had to leave. Family business or something."

"If I become caught, I tell them I steal boat. You know *nada*." Vasco waved a gloved hand and walked away.

"Smooth sail." Enders reclined against his truck and worried about all the little things that might go wrong. But he had plotted this course and now he had to wait to see how it all played out. Again, he gave a quick thought to the ignorance or surprise he might have to feign to Bridges. The police. Spencer. The lies he might have to tell. More "omissions." Temporary omissions to Karen.

\*\*\*\*

In the morning, Enders rode his bike to the White Sand waterfront. The Bridges' cottage was unoccupied. The little Johnson outboard was missing from its backyard mount. He stepped out onto the beach. The boat was gone. The tide had washed away any drag marks and footprints. Looking out over the water, he saw no early morning sails.

*Guess he launched.* He got his bike and pedaled back to the morning's work site.

The crew drifted in, and they began their day by shedding lunch pails and shirts and strapping on tool belts and leather knee pads. The two Griswold clammers approached Enders, tools in hand.

"Gentlemen. What's up?"

"Vasco headed off," said the taller man.

"Yeah, he told me yesterday. Some family thing back in New Bedford. Too bad. He was a steady worker. No complaints from him."

"Gonna hire someone in his stead?" asked the other man.

"Like to. Know anyone looking for late-season work?"

The two men looked at each and shrugged in unison. "We'll ask around," said Davidson. "Funny guy, that Vasco. Never did like the sun, so what's he doin' livin' at the shore?"

****

The White Sand crew worked through the rest of the week. A man short. The high schoolers would be gone just before the Labor Day weekend. The annual salt hay harvest would eat up any stray hands wanting work in Old Lyme. Lot sales might fall off in two or three weeks; they might not pick up again until the end-of-the-year JJJ mailing to potential buyers got some of them thinking about the summer of 1923.

Enders knew these things, and they were helpful

distractions from thoughts of the missing Deputy Pierce and Vasco's late-night escape in a hot catboat. Spencer came by several times with buyers, showing them the beach and the models and singing the benefits of a private beach club. Mrs. Spencer appeared one day, intent on adding more knickknacks to the model cottages. He had followed her through both structures, worried she might find stray evidence of his and Karen's late-night presence in the bedrooms.

Friday evening, he drove into Old Lyme to pick up Karen. She was waiting on the corner of Library Lane. He pulled the truck over in a cloud of dust, which continued drifting along the street for several yards. She slid onto the seat wearing a mauve flapper's dress and a gray cloche hat. She leaned over and kissed him.

"I have to work this weekend."

Enders turned to face her. "I know. The art show. Do what you have to do. I'll be busy most of the weekend too. But I'll be thinking about you." He smiled at her as he spun the truck around, heading back toward Sound View.

She placed her left hand on his leg. He glanced at her and covered her hand with his right hand.

"The gallery next week. I have two paintings on display. The show committee relegated the rest to the library. But I'm so happy. Two in the gallery."

"That's wonderful. Congratulations."

"You're coming next week?"

"Wouldn't miss it. Have I seen these two paintings? The ones in the gallery."

"One, you haven't. It's a big square canvas of the ocean and the sky with a huge white cloud mass in the center. That doesn't sound very interesting, perhaps, but

I think the overall image is striking. I was thinking of Joseph Turner's marine paintings while I worked on it. Turner was a British painter who influenced impressionism and even abstract art. As a matter of fact, for some of his more abstract canvases, you need to read the painting's caption to get a sense of what it is you're looking at."

"Well, I hope someone buys it." He smiled at her delighted face. "What's the other one? *The Pilot Vagabond*?"

She laughed. "No, that one is in the library. But it's for sale too."

"A picture of me in an art show? It'll never sell."

She tilted her head as she looked at him. "I may have to lower the asking price."

****

They parked near the Hotel Harvey, a three-story wooden structure, which looked flimsy even by the standards of seasonal buildings. The sand-packed avenue already was crowded, and they stopped to watch people coming and going from the Pavilion and the Dance Hall.

"Looks like things are back to normal. Raid or no raid," said Karen.

"People want to dance, drink, have fun. It's just too hard for the coppers to hold back that kind of desire."

She took his hand. "Well, I desire to dance." She led him toward the Pavilion.

They danced. Enders mixed cocktails from his flask. They had a quick dinner in the Pavilion's noisy restaurant. Then they strolled to the beach, to the cooler, quieter air.

He looked at his watch. "It's getting late. We should go."

"Go where?"

Enders could see the mischievous look on her face. "Home. Don't you turn into a pumpkin or something at midnight? Or does Mrs. Foley just lock you out? Then I'd have to sneak you into the Manor House."

"Oh, that would be fun. But how would we get out in the morning?"

"How about we give Mrs. Foley and Mrs. Kloss a break and just head over to White Sand?"

On the drive to the beach club, she asked, "What do you suppose happened to the nosy Deputy Pierce? It's nice he's not snooping around at night, but I wonder what happened to him?"

"Maybe the bootleggers ran him off. I'll bet he's hiding back in—where was he from—Middletown?"

"Maybe," said Karen. "I guess the town stopped paying him since he disappeared. I'd hate to think he might be dead."

*Not if you knew what I know about him.* "Probably sitting at home counting his bootleg bucks." *I hope.*

Later, they walked to the water in their bare feet. A quarter moon and the occasional light of a cottage window lit their path. At the water's edge, they stopped to view the near and distant lighthouses as they flashed their nocturnal warnings.

Karen looked around the beach. "The boat's gone. The one I painted." She turned back to Enders. "Did Mr. Bridges take it somewhere?"

*Damn.* For a second, he thought to play dumb. "I lent it to someone. That's why I won't be around this weekend. I have to go over to Stonington and sail it back. Why? Did you want to paint it again?" He leaned in to kiss her and hopefully end her questions.

"No. Stonington, isn't that almost to Rhode Island? Does Mr. Bridges know?"

Enders could sense he had to provide more truth than a vague, *I lent it to someone*. He gave her a distracting kiss and said, "I lent it to one of my crew. One of the guys out on Poverty Island. He needed to get to Stonington, so I lent him the boat. The police were looking for him. He couldn't take the train or hitch on the roads. They have a still out there, so maybe it was about moonshining. I didn't ask. He was a good guy. A good worker. I thought I could help him out." *I'm a decent guy. I am.*

She leaned into him. "Well, look who's the rebel now. Do you need help sailing it back? Maybe…"

"No, I'm fine. It's an easy sail. I should be back sometime Sunday."

She kissed him. "Don't drown or get shipwrecked. I'd miss you so very much."

Enders gave her a reassuring smile. "I'll be fine. I know what I'm doing."

****

Enders woke early. He dressed and packed his old rucksack with a light jacket, his thermos, his wartime binoculars, a small Ray-O-Vac flashlight, and an old map of Connecticut. He did not have a proper nautical chart. But the roadmap named the contours and islands of the coastline and that would give him a sense of where he was along the shore. Enders ate breakfast downstairs with the last of the summer renters. He told Mrs. Kloss he would be away for the weekend. Out in the foyer, he found a May issue of *The Saturday Evening Post* lying on the telephone table. Enders stuck it in his pack. *Campfire reading or campfire tinder.* He shouldered his pack and went to the Sound View station.

The train was on time. He sat on the shoreside of the rail car, catching the morning light and kinetoscopic flashes of the Sound through the trees and cornfields. Point O' Woods zipped by, and then he was crossing the narrow bridge over the Four Mile River. The bay looked calm. A light breeze ruffled the cattails. He had the same sense of easy wind and water as the train pulled away from Niantic Bay.

He thought about Vasco. Did he make it? Was the boat okay and waiting at the town dock? What if it wasn't? What would he do? And what lie might he have to tell Mr. Bridges? He had no answers, and after a while, he stopped worrying. He would know soon enough.

Enders had been tempted to use the plane. He had done clandestine landings in France. Twice he had flown behind German lines to drop off and pick up French spies. The missions happened in broad daylight. Even then, it was tricky business to avoid detection and to find a designated landing spot; the pre-war maps showed villages, brooks, and hilltop landmarks, but all had been obliterated by years of artillery bombardments. And if the Germans had caught him, he would have been shot as a spy or as one aiding a spy. The consequences of being spotted around Stonington with Vasco, while not fatal, still would be bad. And bad news for Beaumont and the JJJ company. Enders might be arrested; he would lose the plane and his job.

The train crept inland and through downtown New London to cross the broad Thames River crowded with ferries, skiffs, freighters, lobster boats, and Coast Guard cutters. The rail track curved toward the Sound again, skimming the western shoreline of Mystic Harbor before stopping in the little seaport. From his open window, Enders could smell seaweed, fish, and the taint of marine diesel engines. The train continued its looping swings inland and back toward the shoreline until it rolled to a stop above the town of Stonington.

Enders hopped down from the car and walked toward the harbor. He wandered onto Water Street, which was lined with small shops, smaller cafés, and narrow two-story homes. He cut down a side street and through a boatyard. Ahead was the town dock. He wanted to run its length searching for the catboat. But he told himself to walk slowly. *Don't stand out. Don't do something memorable for the locals. Just find the boat and go.*

Then he saw it, across the way, on the end of the floating dock set aside for small boats. He scurried to it and dropped his pack in the sailboat. The main sail was neatly furled and tied. The outboard was tilted out of the water. Bridges' catboat was tied loose and rode quietly against two old car tires. *Excellent work, Vasco. Wherever you are.*

Enders went back to Water Street, where he found a well-stocked grocery with electric refrigeration and a deli case. He bought some donuts and apples and had the owner make two thick ham-and-cheese sandwiches to go. Back at the boat, he placed his food in the pack and stowed it under the forward decking. As he pushed the pack forward, out of the way and into the driest place on the boat, he spotted his compass. Enders picked it up and opened the cover.

"Thank you, Vasco. Hope I don't need it, but you never know." He slipped the compass into his pants pocket. Enders stood clutching the boom and made a quick assessment of the boat's lines and sheets and deck tackle. Satisfied, he went to the outboard motor, pushed it back into the water, and unscrewed the gas cap. "Still full." *I guess Vasco is a real sailor.*

Enders removed the sail ties and checked the halyards. A light wind was blowing across the harbor. He was sure he could push off the dock and hoist the sail before he hit the opposite shore some fifteen hundred feet away. A few rowboats were about, but otherwise, the harbor was not busy. The commercial fishermen and lobster boats already had put to sea. He untied the boat, jumped in, and used the paddle to clear the dock. As soon as he was away, he dropped the daggerboard and hauled up the gaff-rigged sail. It began to fill with the light morning air. Enders pushed the boom to starboard and straightened the tiller. The sail puffed out over the boom. He was on his way. Clear of the docks and moorings, he hauled in the main sheet and adjusted the peak halyard. The catboat slipped between the harbor breakwater and the rocky edge of Wamphassuc Point.

Now he pointed the boat south and west into the open Sound. Enders settled on the narrow windward seat, leaning against the gunwale, his sneakered feet pressed against the opposite seat. He kept a light hand on the long wooden tiller. From his perch, he glanced under the forward deck to see his pack, the anchor, a canvas-and-cork life belt, the tin bailer, and the rolled-up canvas sail cover.

"All right. This is almost as good as flying. Almost. Now if the wind holds…" He tied off the tiller while he opened his road map. "Well, that's a good omen." His present course would take him by Enders Island. Then he could remain on a southerly course to pass by the long curve of Ram Island. On that heading, he should be able to clear Groton Point before having to head in closer to shore.

After an hour, and both donuts, the wind was building and shifting more to the south. Enders looked across Fishers Island to the very tip of Montauk Point in New York. There was a dark gray smear on the horizon.

\*\*\*\*

The green water of the Sound was decorated with dancing white caps, the choppy waves pushing and pulling the catboat along a wobbly course. The wind began to gust and shift around as if trying to find a comfortable tempo and direction.

He kept a firm grip on the tiller as he watched the sail and the receding Connecticut shoreline. The sun vanished. A darker line of clouds appeared above the faint smudge of Long Island. Enders knew he was between the mouth of the Thames River and the western end of Fishers Island. If the wind would cooperate, he still might keep a straight course back to White Sand. Or at least to Sound View. He looked back toward the tip of Long Island. The dark line of clouds was blowing across the Sound toward him.

*Goddamn. That's rain.* A gust of wet air pushed the boat over, almost burying the gunwale. He threw his weight in the opposite direction to right it. He stared up the high wooden mast. *Too much sail. Too much risk.* He brought the boat around, pointing directly into the wind. The sail luffed madly as he scrambled forward to untie the halyards. He dropped the sail a few feet, re-cleated the halyards, and scrambled along the boom to reef the sail. *Sloppy ties, but they'll hold.*

He stepped back to the mast and hoisted the sail

271

again. He hurried astern, grabbed the tiller, and pointed the boat northward again. The boat ran before the wind. Enders considered the shortened sail as it filled with air. *Maybe still too much sail.* He kept a grip on the tiller and the mainsheet, wanting to be ready for the moody, unpredictable wind gusts.

*Gets any worse, I'll have to drop the sail and run the engine.*

The cloud mass now overtook the pitching catboat and began dumping a torrent of cool rain. He tilted his face to the falling rain. "Vasco, you better not get caught. Dammit. This is more trouble than I bargained for."

He eased the main sheet and moved the tiller back and forth, hunting for a less violent course. But the choppy whitecaps had devolved into crowded rollers of fast-moving water. He rode up one watery hill only to fall into the trough and then climb to the top of the next rolling wave. Looking around the dark waters, he could see no other boats—at least none as small as his.

"This is nuts." He shifted course, heading more directly toward the Connecticut shore. Where exactly, it did not matter. Land was land. Land was safety. The sail was off the starboard side; the boat was on a broad reach. Enders crouched low in the boat to see under the boom, which was blocking his view of the land ahead. His hand slipped off the tiller. A wave pushed the unguided boat around. The boom flew back across the boat. It hit Enders as he scrambled to grab the tiller handle.

He went over the side.

Chapter 12

The blow from the heavy wooden boom felt like a prize fighter's punch. He was in the water, trying to breathe again. He felt the boat pulling away. His left hand slid along the slippery varnished gunwale. Wet fingers caught the quarter knee at the stern. He tightened his grip on the slick wooden corner. With his right hand, he groped blindly for the top of the rudder. The sail was snapping aimlessly in the wind as the boom swung back over the boat. Almost broadside to the waves, Enders felt the boat on the verge of rolling over and sinking. He threw his weight on the boat and hauled himself back in and crawled along the bottom boards to the mast. On his back, he struggled to un-cleat the tight, wet halyards.

*I'm not gonna die in a boat a mile from shore. I refuse.*

The boom and the gaff came crashing down, with the sail fluttering between them. Enders pulled and kicked the boom into the boat. Then he dragged the shorter gaff aboard and pulled in the madly flapping sail and stuffed it between the heavy wooden boom and gaff. Once he had crawled over the tangle of lines and sail and pushed the outboard into the water, he grabbed the flywheel knob on top of the motor and started spinning it around and around. "Start. Right now, goddammit."

The outboard motor coughed to life. He reached over the stern, into the water, to release the rudder pins, pulled the wooden rudder free, and tossed it onto the nautical mess in the center of the boat. He pushed the outboard around and headed for the shore.

The heavy rain and the growing darkness made it hard to see. The morning's neat demarcation of land and sea and sky had vanished, replaced by a formless blur of black and gray colors.

Enders was soaked to the skin. He discovered he was panting like an exhausted distance runner. He forced himself to breathe normally. He pushed wet hair off his forehead and stared at the distant coast, which was little more than a dark line against a dark sky on a dark day. There was water sloshing around in the bottom of the boat. He didn't care. Only the closing shore mattered. He was still running before the wind; the following sea pushed him along, dumping water over the transom as an occasional wave overtook him.

He got closer to the shoreline. A flat peninsula emerged from the gloom off to the right. *Could be Black Point.*

Protecting its flank was a cluster of bare rock islands, almost submerged rocks, and larger islands sprouting scrub and gull nests. Behind the rocks and islands should be Giants Neck. If so, to his left would be the rocky outcrop of Point O' Woods. JJJ's beach developments surrounded him, and if he stayed on course, he would run up on a sand-bottomed stretch of shore near the shuttered Menhaden factory.

*Anywhere there's solid shore to sit and wait out the weather.*

Ahead, a large black rock sprouting a beard of green seaweed and brown barnacles emerged in the trough of two waves. Enders pushed the engine handle over and pivoted the boat around the rock before it disappeared again under another wave.

Now he was close. He could see the windswept beach and its assortment of driftwood and shells thrown onto the curving bowl of sand and shore grass. He was cold. And mad. *Almost drowned on a fool's errand. And I'm still not home. What the hell am I doing?*

Enders could almost feel the land. He bent forward and yanked up the daggerboard. He held the engine straight on for a few more seconds, then shut it off. He pulled the lower unit out of the water with the propeller still spinning. The bow of the catboat scraped against a sandy bottom.

Enders jumped out, tripped, and fell into the shallows. He staggered upright, trudged to the bow, and pulled the boat higher on the shore. An enormous wave helped him move the boat. He sat back in the wet sand, his head bowed, his breath rasping in the gusting wind.

After a while, he got up and pulled the anchor and line out from under the bow deck. He used the anchor to dig a hole in the mushy sand, dropped it in, and covered it again with his hands. In the boat, he found some spare rope to tie down the flapping mess of sail so the wind would not blow it loose and tear it to shreds. He grabbed his pack and the canvas sail cover and stumbled up the beach.

In the distance, he saw the outline of an abandoned building. The fish parts fertilizer factory. He was in the right spot—not too far from Point O' Woods. The old factory might offer a solid roof from the rain, but Enders remembered Spencer saying the place had "a stink beyond description." That would not help his mood.

Beyond the crashing line of waves, he found an

enormous tree trunk stripped of its bark by the sea and bleached by the sun. He climbed over the massive trunk and rolled himself in the boat canvas. Sheltered from the wind and rain, he was asleep in seconds.

****

Enders opened his eyes to a close-up view of green canvas pressing against his face. He was hot. And wet. He felt like a steamed clam. Throwing off the canvas, he sat up, blinking in the bright wash of morning light. He searched behind the driftwood barrier—the boat was still there.

He flopped back against the tree trunk and looked at Sunday morning's blue sky. "This feels like my fourth crash."

Enders considered yesterday's sail and decided he was still alive, not from any great seamanship but from dumb luck. He thought about Karen and where she was today. The South Lyme train station was not far off; he could find her quickly enough by land. But he still had to travel by sea. There was a boat to return. There was a fiction to maintain.

Enders felt his hunger and took one of the Stonington sandwiches from his damp pack. He devoured it, and half of the second one. He drank the remaining fresh water from his thermos. More alive now, Ender considered the boat sitting safely above the tide.

He stood and kicked off his wet, sandy sneakers. He rolled up his damp pant legs and took off his sticky shirt. At the boat, he refolded the twisted sail, tied the flapping halyards, and untangled the main sheet. He bailed water from the boat. That took a while. Enders dug up the anchor, washed the sand off it, and stowed it under the decking, and then stowed the rest of his damp gear and clothes.

He dragged the bow of the boat around and pushed and pulled it into the foamy water. Large rolling waves were still coming ashore, but the wind was light, and the sky had been washed clean of all but a high, tenuous string of translucent clouds. He wiggled the boat into deeper water, jumped in, and started the motor. He wanted to clear any of the semi-submerged rocks before resetting the sail.

Enders chugged into deeper water, pointed the bow into the wind, and shut off the engine. In a quick minute, he had the sail up, the daggerboard down, and the rudder pinned astern. He took a length of rope from under the stern seat and looped one end around his waist. He fixed the other end to a stern cleat and yanked it hard.

"Should have done this yesterday." He wondered what Karen would have thought if he'd fallen overboard and drowned. "She'd never know…" He thought about her for a long part of the morning.

Steering a course between two large, barren islands of brown rock called the North and South Brothers, he aimed for the old Victorian mansions on Hatchetts Point. By late afternoon, he had sailed past Sound View and Hawk's Nest. Both beaches were crowded with summer guests eager for one more sunny day at the shore. The wind was light but steady, and without having to make too many course changes, Enders set his sights on the line of White Sand cottages that backed against the newly named Seaside Lane. He angled in on a steady wind, raising the daggerboard at the last moment and driving the boat up on the yielding white sand. He released the main sheet and slumped back against the stern of the boat. "Oh, good Christ, let's not do that again. Ever."

Later, he made himself get out of the boat and put
everything in order. He set up the boom crutch and
folded and tied the sail along the length of the boom and
gaff. He tied off the sheets and halyards and coiled up
loose lines. Then he laid the sail cover over the boom,
stretching it from mast to stern. He carried the outboard
back to its stand behind the Bridges' cottage. He
reminded himself to replace the gasoline he had used.

His shirt was dry, and he slipped it over his
sunburned back. He ignored the buttons. Enders stared at
his watch. It had stopped. He could see water under the
crystal. He got his pack and hiked through the
construction area to Shore Road. Barefoot, he trudged
along the paved road to the Manor House, taking his time
and thinking of nothing more than an early bedtime.

****

He was tired before he got to work on Monday. He
had tried to call Karen as soon as he got back to the
Manor House, and again that morning, but she was not
at her landlady's house either time. At lunchtime, he took
a company truck into Old Lyme to look for her. Driving
by the library, he saw the double doors were open and
people were bringing in easels and wooden stands. Up
the road, the gallery doors also were open. Two men
carried framed paintings through the gallery doorway.
Enders pulled over and hopped out. Inside, he found
Karen in a back room having tea with two other women.
She saw him and jumped up with a smile. She took his
hand and led him back to the main gallery.

"Where have you been? I was so worried. All that
stormy rain on Saturday. I wondered…"

He hugged her. Harder and longer than he should

have in such a public place. He didn't care. "It's okay. I got wet. I tried to call you last night and this morning."

Two men came through with a long table covered with small paintings and sketches. Enders and Karen stepped out of their way.

He searched around the main gallery, noticing the mounted paintings on the walls and smaller works of art presented on easels scattered about the room. "Almost ready for the show? Where are yours?"

"I thought I'd start bringing mine over tomorrow. And to the library on Wednesday."

"Good. Looking forward to seeing them." The gallery was empty now, and he gave her a quick kiss. "I have to get back to the job, but how about dinner tonight? I was thinking the Morton House in Niantic?"

She gave him a sly look. "The hotel part or the restaurant part?"

Enders released an exaggerated sigh. "I wish it could be both." Out of habit, he looked at his watch but found only a naked wrist of untanned skin. "Gotta go. How 'bout I pick you up at six-thirty for a seven o'clock dinner?"

"Don't be late." He heard the smile in her voice. She gave him a peck on the cheek.

Outside, he got in the truck and drove the few yards to the Lyme Auto Service garage opposite the Griswold mansion. He borrowed a tin gas can from Fred Winsted and used it to buy half a gallon of gas for the Bridges' outboard motor. They likely would be back on Friday night for the Labor Day weekend.

****

Showered and wearing a suit and tie, Enders drove back to Old Lyme to get Karen. He pulled onto the gravel lane beside her landlady's house. Before he stopped the motor, she emerged from the house, wearing a light blue dress with flutter sleeves. He had never seen it before and wondered briefly how many outfits she owned.

When she opened the passenger door and climbed in, he said, "You're dressed too nicely for this old truck. I wish I had a fancy sedan to drive you around in."

"Just as long as the cab is free of wet paint and rusty nails." She used her shoe to nudge his pack along the floor beside her seat.

"Sorry, I forgot to take that out."

She lifted the wrinkled issue of the *Saturday Evening Post* from the open neck of his pack. Enders backed out to the road saying, "Weekend reading material, but I never got a chance to read a page." He turned back onto Lyme Street as Karen leafed through the still-damp magazine.

She stopped to read something. "Oh, listen to this, Mr. Pilot." She read aloud,

*"I know that I shall meet my fate*

*"Somewhere among the clouds above…"*

"Yeats. I heard that poem last year in Europe."

She read more to herself and said, "I like this phrase. '…this tumult in the clouds.' I guess it was a tumult, from what you've said. There's a whole series of war poems here."

He turned onto Shore Road, heading to Niantic. She flipped through several pages and read aloud, "Reported Missing." She read silently for a moment. Karen glanced at Enders, whose grip on the steering wheel had tightened at the title.

"Oh, this is lovely." She read aloud,

*"I laugh! I laugh!—For you will come again—*

*"This heart would never beat if you were dead.*
*"The world's..."*

Enders stared through the windshield as he reached over and covered the magazine with his hand. He gently pushed it onto her lap. "Don't read…"

She stared at him. "David…?"

He glanced at her before staring back at the road and the occasional car passing by. "I almost died this weekend. Drowned, almost… Knocked right out of the damn boat. Like some fool kid." He stopped the truck and turned to look at her. "And later, I thought if I had died, you'd never have known what I was doing. What I was planning for you. For us. I would have left you wondering. Maybe wondering who I was…"

Karen opened her mouth to say something, but all either of them heard was a loud horn as a car swerved around Ender's idled truck. The driver screamed at them as he disappeared up the road.

Enders shook off his sudden angst. "Wonderful. I'm going to kill both of us now." He drove a little farther up the road and pulled over. He got out and hurried around the truck bed to open her door and help her out, to stand on the roadside. He looked around—almost amused at the location he had selected. "Between the fish market and the Black Hall marsh. It's not ideal, but at least we won't get run over here."

"Tell me what happened." She slipped her arms around his waist. Her face bore a serious, almost anxious look.

"In a minute. First, I want to tell you about all these little pieces, little plans, I thought should fit together—fall into place." He held up his hands and moved his fingers like he was assembling an invisible, intricate device. "But I realized the first part, the first plan, was the only one that mattered. Everything else lived, or died, depending on the first part."

"David…"

He could see she was confused and losing patience with his halting monologue. He swallowed and asked, "Will you marry me?"

She was silent and immobile for a second and then hugged him so tightly his sunbaked back hurt. Her face was buried in his shoulder. Enders hugged her back and finally whispered, "You have to say something. Say 'yes.' Please." He heard a muffled 'yes.' She looked at his expectant face.

They both smiled. Then they laughed. He remembered to kiss her.

"I don't have a ring right now…"

"That's all right…"

He put an index finger to her lips. "…but next spring, I'll have two second-class tickets on the *SS Paris* bound for Le Havre and the boat-train to Paris. The ship's supposed to be very *Art Nouveau*. Whatever that means."

"Paris. We're really going? How…" She threw herself at him again.

"I also bought a cottage lot from JJJ. At Point O' Woods. Which is another reason I don't have a ring for you." Smiling, he said, "You might even have to pay for your own dinner tonight."

Karen looked puzzled. "I don't understand. If we're going to Paris, why did you buy a cottage?"

"For spending money. Get it finished by the spring. Rent it for the summer. I figured after property taxes and the mortgage there might be enough left to keep us from breaking our teeth on week-old baguettes and having to pan-fry scrawny pigeons from the Luxembourg Gardens. And we'll have to come home someday. To something. Some place to live. At least in the summer when the plumbing works."

She turned him around and pressed him back against the truck cab. "All this sneaky plotting and tiptoeing around. You should have just said something earlier."

"Earlier? You mean I should have proposed at lunch that first day?" He laughed at the idea.

"I would have said yes." She sounded like she would have. "Are there any other plots or plans you want to tell me about?"

"You're right. I should have said something before now. Before it was almost too late." He tilted his head against the cab. "Other plots. Uh, gossip here and there. Minor details. Let's save something for the honeymoon or the voyage. It's a week across the Atlantic. Plenty of time to chat, Mrs. Enders." *Then I'll tell you about Pierce and the women's prison threat and getting shot at and sinking a rum runner. And Vasco, the possible leper. Yes, I've had a busy summer. Even when you weren't around.*

They stood on the side of the road talking, laughing, kissing, and hugging until too many passing drivers slowed to honk or wave at their roadside spectacle. He pulled out his old pocket watch. "We've missed our reservation. And damn this country; there's no champagne to celebrate with anyway."

"What happened to your army watch?"

"Drowned on Saturday. I'll find another one in France next year."

"Tell me what happened to *you* on Saturday. How

did you almost drown?"

He looked out at the road. "Over dinner. Don't I tell you about all my crashes over a meal? Come on, we'll catch a later dinner." He helped her into the truck and got them back on the road to Niantic. Along the way, she suddenly asked, "But what will you do there? In France. You won't have a job."

"I'll find something. Construction. Some translation/interpretation work again. Or something could turn with the Paris Aerodrome." He searched her face. "You paint. I'll find work. It'll be okay."

"How do you know?"

"Well, I don't. But I think we should try. Together."

"How long can we stay?"

"The one-way tickets are two hundred and sixteen dollars. We'll need money for the return. I guess we'll stay until we're on the verge of becoming vagabonds."

"We'd better leave before it comes to that." They were both silent for a moment, each thinking about the adventures ahead—marriage, a voyage, and Paris. Karen leaned against Enders and asked, "Are you going to ask my parents for my hand?"

His face took on a serious expression. "I'm trying to imagine telling your parents I have no money and no job and I'm taking their only daughter to a war-torn country for an unknown length of time." He looked at her and said, "I can see asking them only if we're standing dockside and the final boarding horn has just blown."

Karen laughed. "You're going to have to find the courage. And soon. I want to tell everyone I'm getting married and moving to Paris. Oh, there's so much planning. A wedding... Paris! I'm so excited. When can we go back to dinner at my parents?"

Enders looked at the woman beside him. He could not remember having seen anyone so utterly happy. She seemed to be surrounded by some joyous aura now expanding to envelop him too. He could feel himself grinning like the village idiot and didn't care. He smiled at the idea of another dinner with her parents.

But then he considered the reaction of his own family. What would they think of his returning to France a year after he had come home? It would be hard news for his mother. Suddenly there would be a daughter-in-law, which he then would whisk away to France, leaving his mother's house seeming emptier than it was now.

The rational thing to do would be to stay in the States, keep the well-paying job he enjoyed, and urge Karen to continue painting at the Old Lyme art colony. But he did not like the feel of the country. It seemed moody. Raw. Volatile. Sitting beside him was a woman who wanted to do one small thing in her life, and Enders could help her do it. He knew France, he knew Paris, he knew the language. He could be her guide. And she could be his.

He looked off to the right to a stand of pines. Beyond the trees was a marsh that led down to the barren beach he had washed up on two days ago. Karen hugged his arm and then picked up the abused copy of the *Saturday Evening Post*. She turned through the pages until she found her earlier spot. She was quiet for a minute. Enders glanced at her as she read. Her head was bent over the magazine, one hand pressing the wrinkled page flat, or maybe feeling the words of the *Reported Missing* poem she was reading. Finally, she read aloud,

"*Of these familiar things I have no dread*
"*Being so very sure you are not dead.*"

\*\*\*\*

Enders had begun the week in a shaky state caused by his hard and dangerous sail back from Stonington. Now he was reanimated and with a perceptible measure of energy and humor. Jesse noticed it within moments of driving onto the White Sand job site. Leaning out the truck window, he grinned at Enders and whispered, "You get laid recently?"

"I'll never tell. Not without a drink or two. What are you doing here?"

Jesse nodded his head in the direction of the truck bed. "Being generous with my time. Got your nail kegs and wire." He surveyed the area, now crowded with framed cottages, occupied cottages, automobiles, kids, workers, and vacationers. "Lookin' busy. Almost as busy as the POW."

Enders turned around and took in the same scenery. "Yeah, we've done a lot. People are buying and moving in."

"You wonderin' when we're gonna start building yours?"

"I imagine you'll have to wait till the vacationers clear out and see what kind of off-season crew you're left with."

"Righto," said Jesse.

"Don't wait too long to start." Enders waved a couple of his guys over. "Gotta unload," he announced as he pulled two coils of insulated copper wiring from the truck. Jesse relaxed in the cab as they unloaded.

In the late afternoon, after two more Hartford buyers had come through and left with sales deeds, two black Ford sedans rolled onto the site. Enders looked out the windowless frame of a cottage. *That looks like police.*

He turned to McMurphy, the Poverty Island clammer. "Hey, I think the cops are here." The man looked out the open doorframe. "Yep."

Two uniformed officers climbed out of their respective cars, followed by two men in loose suits and new hats. They stood for a moment looking around the job site.

"If there's anything over to the Point or Poverty you want to hide, a still maybe, better go now. Head out the back and circle around. Then run." McMurphy nodded and put down his saw.

Enders, watching the police, said, "If not…" But McMurphy had already slipped through the back doorway. "One problem taken care of." Enders stepped outside and walked to the waiting police.

"Gentlemen, how can I help you?" He tilted his fedora back and tried to look both innocent and curious.

Another man stepped out of the second car. Hatless, bald, and sucking on a pipe, he rushed forward and said between clenched teeth, "I'm Doctor Franklin Brannon, Connecticut Department of Health. We're looking for a patient?"

Enders glanced around the site and shrugged. He opened his mouth to say something more, but one of the suit-and-tie policemen said, "A dangerous patient. He's got leprosy and needs to be in a hospital."

The public health doctor added, "It's contagious. Maybe you heard a couple of these patients illegally left a train bound for a new care facility in Louisiana?"

Endres nodded. "Yeah, it was in the paper. But look around. This is a construction site. Hard work. Heavy lifting. Everyone's healthy here. No one's losing any fingers or toes unless they're careless with a saw or something."

Enders looked back at the men and their cars. A puff of smoke emerged from the back seat of the second car. Someone was sitting back there.

Chapter 13

The other plainclothes cop asked, "Any new hires here? Or anyone quit recently?"

Enders shook his head as he watched the second car. "No. Haven't hired anyone new. As for people who left…just a couple of local school kids getting ready for the fall, and one guy who returned to his family in New Bedford." *One truth, one lie. So far, I'm even.*

"Mind if we look around?"

Enders waved an open hand, and the two uniformed policemen started off in different directions. The doctor strode back to the second car and leaned through the open window. The two plainclothes police introduced themselves as Detectives Franks and Peterson. They made small talk about bootleggers and the recent raid at Sound View. The public health doctor returned. He pulled a piece of paper from his suit coat, glanced at it, and asked Enders, "This New Bedford man, what was his name?"

"Vasco Silva."

He searched his paper again and said to his colleagues, "Well, there was no Vasco or Silva on the train, but there was a Vasco Carvalho—Portuguese—who escaped Penikese three years ago." The doctor looked at Enders. "Penikese. An island hospital in Massachusetts."

"Yeah, I read about it." *I hope the crew knows*

*enough to play dumb.*

Enders saw the uniforms coming back toward the group. They looked indifferent, which he thought was a good sign. No one had said anything interesting to them.

Detective Peterson asked, "Why'd this Silva guy quit?"

Enders shrugged again and said, "Family thing back in Bedford. I didn't want him to go, but I guess he needed to." He tipped his chin toward the second car. "You got a shy officer or maybe a prisoner back there?"

Franks said, "Kind of an advisor. Knows the area and the local people."

"Summer deputy?"

Both detectives grinned. "Yeah. He had to pack up and leave real quick one night. Guess there's some serious moonshiners and bootleggers around here. We may have to come back with a vice squad and kick someone's ass. Can't have people thinking they can run the law out of town."

Enders didn't say anything. The doctor folded his hit list and tucked it back in his jacket. He extracted his pipe from his front teeth. "You know this is a public health issue. You don't want to get caught aiding and abetting a fugitive. He's an alien, too, so immigration issues may be in play. You know, hiding illegals is…well, it's illegal."

He stared at the doctor for a silent moment. "You a doctor or a lawyer?"

"Mister, we've been *advised* you are a known lawbreaker regarding Prohibition. And you might be as likely to break other laws, even public health laws, when it suits you. So I suggest you…"

Enders pushed past the doctor to stare at the second

car. He turned back to the plainclothes cops. "Why don't we drag your advisor outta that car and see what he has to say about me to my face?"

Detective Franks put up his hand as if he was stopping traffic at an intersection. "All right. I think we're done here. Doc, that's it." He eyed Enders for a second and dropped his hand. "Thanks, Bud. We'll be on our way. Nice beach place you're buildin' here." The five men returned to their cars.

*Pierce. Now I know he's not dead. Which means he's still a threat.*

Enders watched the cars disappear in a cloud of dust and summer haze. He was more than satisfied Pierce was unwilling to get out of the car. Even in broad daylight. Surrounded by other cops.

Early Friday evening, he drove into town. He parked near Karen's rental house and strolled into the library. A banner hung above the open doors to announce the annual art show. The normally silent building hummed with the whispers of guests and townspeople sipping lemonade and examining the art colony's latest works. Canvases and painted boards were mounted on pedestals and little collapsible stands. To the right of the librarian's desk, he saw a scattered display of framed aerial photographs of the local shoreline. Debrie, the Saybrook photographer, stood off to the side. Enders wandered toward him.

"Mr. Debrie. Beautiful shots. You know how to make that camera work." Enders shook his sweaty hand.

"Thank you." Debrie glanced around the main room like he was expecting to find an angry bill collector. "I've never done one of these shows before. I hope someone buys something."

"Me too."

Debrie relaxed long enough to flash a brief smile. "Your ten percent, yes."

"How's the Leica?"

"Wonderful. Beautiful camera. Thanks for selling it to me."

"It's better off in your hands." Enders clapped him on the shoulder and headed across the room in search of Karen's paintings.

He found a small canvas watercolor of the auto garage across the street from the Griswold mansion. He remembered the day he saw her working on it. Enders stepped back to get a better sense of the entire painted scene. Then he leaned in, lingering over the gray lettering of her name in the bottom right corner. *Karen Bates. She should keep her name. Short and sweet.*

Moving around the room, he nodded to a few familiar faces, including the young librarian. Near a front window, he found Karen's painting of the tree at the end of the Griswold field. The one she was painting the day they met. When she'd complained about her heavy hand on the brush. He stared at it again. *I hope no one buys it. We should keep it.*

Around the corner, he found a couple of people staring at a small board painting of the Jenny on the beach. He heard one of the onlookers mutter the title, *The Pilot Vagabond.*

Enders couldn't help himself. He went to the group of onlookers and said, "I'm the pilot." They all looked at him in unison.

One of the women pushed her glasses farther down her nose and asked, "Really?"

"Yes, indeed. That's my plane, a Jenny JN-4, on

Orient Point."

The woman noted his pressed suit and bright tie, and his neatly parted hair. "Well, you don't look like a vagabond."

"I think the artist was trying to suggest…not poverty, but the freedom to wander. To pick up and go. Anytime. Anywhere. It's—" Enders was ready to laugh at his *ad hoc* artistic critique—"it's an expression of freedom. Don't you think?"

"That makes sense," said the middle-aged man in the group. He glanced at the program in his hand and looked at the painting again.

"Then buy it. Hang it in your office as a reminder of that freedom." Enders smiled at them and said he needed to get to the gallery. He moved away, amused with himself, but then he wondered if he had helped or hurt the chances of a sale.

Leaving the library, Enders drove past the gallery, which was crowded with parked cars and people milling around the front lawn. He pulled the truck into a field beside the service station and walked back to the gallery.

A small band of musicians gathered under an oak tree to the right of the entrance. Refreshment tables were set to the left. Enders ignored the tables, wishing for a gin and tonic. He picked up a program at the door. It listed the artists, their presented works, and the asking prices. Inside, guests and artists crowded the main gallery. The afternoon sunlight was angling through the skylights. He spotted Florence Griswold surrounded by a gaggle of her resident painters and some wealthy-looking local women. He wondered if she had been to the library yet to see Debrie's aerial photographs. Wandering into the back gallery, he spotted Karen talking with two women. He did not approach her, knowing that for her this was not a party but business. He slipped back into the main gallery to let her find him when she was ready.

Enders began a systematic survey of the left and right wings of the main gallery. Moving clockwise around the walls, he stopped at paintings of local scenes he recognized from around town. He stopped at other paintings by artists Karen had mentioned to him. Most of these latter paintings were not for sale, having been donated to the gallery when it opened its doors last summer.

He stopped before an impressionist painting of a young woman standing in front of an easel and wearing a floppy straw hat. It reminded him of Karen. He bent down to read the title card. *Poor Little Bloticelli*. He felt a hand on his shoulder and turned to find Karen beside him.

"Hi. Big crowd here. How's it going?"

"Good. I'm having fun. Meeting people. Praying someone buys something."

"I saw you in the back room but didn't want to intrude." He pointed to the painting on the wall in front of them. "I stopped to admire this. I thought you might have been the model."

"That's an old painting by Willard Metcalf. One of Miss Florence's early boarders. Bloticelli. It's a joke and an insult. Fifteen or twenty years ago, most of the artists here were men, and they looked down, way down, on female artists and students. Metcalf called them 'blots on the landscape.' So, he borrowed a Renaissance painter's name, Botticelli, and changed it to Bloticelli for this painting."

"Well, I still like the colors and brightness of it. And it reminds me of you."

"Oh, it's a beautiful work. I just don't want to be viewed as a blot or a blight or anything condescending."

Patrons and guests were crowding into the wing. They moved away from *Poor Little Bloticelli*.

"What are you going to do tonight? You know I need to stay here?"

"Well, first I'll miss you. Terribly. Then I'll probably grab a beer or two in Sound View. I'll try to come by tomorrow at lunchtime. But I may be too dusty to come in here." Enders looked around the crowded gallery. "I'd kiss you, but…" Instead, he took her hand and started praising her work loudly in French, occasionally gesturing at various paintings. He leaned in and dramatically planted *la bise* on both of her cheeks. He hurried away, slapping the program against his leg as he went.

****

Saturday, he left the lunchtime job site and drove back into town. One hand on the steering wheel, the other clutching half a sandwich, he slowed the truck just before the Black Hall bridge. He laughed to himself, thinking this bit of roadside was a ridiculous place to have proposed to Karen. *Still, she said yes, and I guess that's all that matters.*

On Lyme Street, Enders stopped in front of Rowland's store and swallowed the last bit of his lunch. He stepped out of the car and jogged across the street to the pharmacy. At the entrance, he stopped to stare at a familiar-looking car. Inside, the pharmacist was talking with Mr. Woods, the NAACP lawyer. Woods swiveled around on his soda fountain stool at the sound of Enders' boots on the wooden floor.

"Ah, Mr. Enders. White Sand. How are you?"

"Mr. Woods. In town for the art show?"

"Sadly, no. I am continuing our investigations of beachfront developments."

Enders glanced around the store and asked, "Where's your Hellfighter driver?"

"He's gone down to the river." Woods pointed toward the back of the store.

He looked at James, the pharmacist. "Well, I'm just in to buy some toiletries and the newspaper."

Woods reached into his coat pocket and extracted a folded piece of paper. "If you have a moment, this might be of interest to you." He unfolded the paper, placing it flat on the counter.

Enders stepped up to the polished stone counter to find a map of the Connecticut coastline. Black dots covered large parts of the coast from the New York line to New London.

"These dots represent closed beach clubs and associations. As you can see, the shore is darkened with a smear of these dots."

Enders bent over the map, silently counting off the developments he recognized. Groton, Black Point, Giant Neck, Point O' Woods, White Sand, Cornfield Point, Saybrook Manor, Grove Beach. Also marked were Fenwick, Edge Lea, Hawk's Nest, and the growing Old Colony development, but these were not JJJ projects. There were several dots on Long Island and near the New York-Connecticut line he did not recognize. He put a finger on the town of Milford—his hometown—and said, "Pond Point Beach. You missed this one. The company just bought this property. And here, next to the

Old Colony beach. The Kloss dairy farm. The company has an eye out for that bit of land too."

Woods looked at Enders and smiled. "Oh. Thank you for the intelligence. It's hard to keep track of the pace of acquisition." He took a pen from his coat pocket, unscrewed the cap, and inked in a black dot in the Milford area of the map. Then he picked up the map and held it at arm's length as if admiring a work of art.

"Not a pretty picture, if I do say." He turned back to Enders and to James.

Enders felt like he was being baited. He wanted his toothpaste and newspaper, and to be on his way. He looked up at the wall clock behind the high pharmacy counter. "Well, it might mean more people along the coast. At least in the summer. And I suppose that's good business for everyone." He glanced at Mr. James again. "You know the old Yankee saying, 'A rising tide lifts all boats.'"

Woods nodded. "Those that have boats. And are near enough to water to employ them."

"Touché." *Here I am debating with a lawyer when I should be talking with my girl. My fiancée.* Enders put out his hand and said, "Best of luck, Mr. Woods."

"Thank you. You too."

Enders stopped. He stabbed an index finger on Woods' map, pressing it between Point O' Woods and Black Point. "There's a sandy stretch of beach here. Pretty much abandoned. I know; I washed up there the other day."

Woods looked at Enders but did not say anything.

Enders removed his finger and said, "It might make for a fine state beach. Relieve some of the pressure on Hammonasset and the surrounding town beaches. It's long enough and wide enough for a good-sized state beach. You might try petitioning the legislature before someone comes along and buys it for private property.

"Well, that is an interesting idea. And there are no active buyers?" asked Woods.

"None that I know of. Do you have something I can write on?"

Woods removed a business envelope from his coat and handed it and the fountain pen to Enders, who quickly scribbled a name and telephone number on the back of the envelope.

"That's a friend of mine. Brian Lonergan. He's a reporter at the *New Haven Register*. You might ask him to write some stories about the need for another public beach. Get the public juiced about more beaches. Maybe he knows some state legislators you could approach. Of course, you'll probably have to buy him a drink. Maybe two. Tell him I sent you."

Woods looked at the name and tucked away the envelope. "Thank you. I think this would be helpful. Perhaps the start of a public campaign." He looked at Enders again. "Washed up on the beach, you did?"

"Stormy weather a while back. You know, any port in a storm."

Enders waved and hurried back up the aisle to grab toothpaste, a bar of soap, Beeman's chewing gum, a jar of Riker's Deodor, and yesterday's morning edition of the *New London Day*. James followed Enders to the front of the store to ring him up.

Outside, he headed back to the truck, but a voice stopped him. Turning, he saw Mr. Woods' driver, the Harlem Hellfighters veteran, coming around the corner of the building.

"Well, well, Mr. Pilot. Shoppin' in a colored man's pharmacy."

*Again. I'm never gonna get out of here.* "It's all the same products. All the same cash." Enders sounded defensive.

"Is it now?" He looked up the street toward the art show. "Whitest town I'd ever been to." He glanced back at the pharmacy's front door. "Poor Mr. James. He's but a tiny ink spot on the white page of this town."

"Very poetic. I'm sure he'd move if he felt unwelcome."

Bill, the driver, stepped closer. "You know, down South, they lynch a man still wearing his army or navy uniform. Can't be a war vet. Sure can't be a man. Try, and ya dangle from a tree."

The uninvited image of an American soldier hanging by his neck held Enders for a moment. Finally, he said, "Stay out of the South. It's a foreign country."

"Ain't that the truth." Bill pulled a small copper flask from his jacket pocket and unscrewed the cap. He raised it and quietly said, "*Vive la France.*" He took a mouthful from the flask and handed it to Enders, not out of friendship or comradery but as a challenge.

Enders shifted his package to his left arm and took the flask. He raised it a few inches in his hand and looking past Bill, said, "The dead and the missing," and drank a mouthful of what turned out to be very smooth whiskey. He handed it back. Bill capped it and tucked it in his coat pocket.

Enders pointed up the street. "I'm late for the art show."

Bill put his hands in his pockets and rocked back on his heels. "See ya around, Mr. Pilot."

Enders got back in his truck feeling both depressed and angry by his encounter with Woods' driver. The whiskey didn't help. "Everyone's got problems." He tapped the steering wheel with each slowly uttered syllable. "The whole country's got problems."

Enders drove under a banner near Library Lane, which announced the art show. He had to park just beyond the Griswold Mansion and walk back to the gallery. The front lawn and the street were crowded with people again, many of them looking like long-term vacationers in casual clothes and tanned faces.

At the refreshment tables, Enders plunked down a nickel for a lemonade. He passed on the cucumber sandwiches and stood off to the side, finishing his lemonade in one long gulp. He wondered if his sudden thirst was from his earlier sandwich or his encounters with Woods and his driver. He left his glass on a tray and stepped inside to look for Karen.

She came up behind him and hooked an arm around his right arm. "Good afternoon, Mr. Enders."

Surprised, he turned, smiling. "Mrs. Enders, how are things?"

"Mrs. Enders? Are we already married?" She led him into the back gallery. "I sold two paintings. I'm so excited." She pressed against his arm.

He stopped walking. "That's great. Was one of them *The Pilot Vagabond*?"

"Yes. Why? Did you…"

"When I was at the library show yesterday, I talked up the painting to a group of…onlookers, patrons, whatever, and told them I was the model. The pilot."

"Hmm, maybe I should use you as a model more often."

"Okay, but no nudes." They both laughed, drawing the attention of some of the gallery occupants. "I mean, what would my mother think?"

She put her hand to her mouth to suppress another laugh. "Can you stay a while?"

"No. I need to get back. Stuff to build. Money to make. Paris tickets to buy."

"We're still going to Milford and my parents next weekend?"

Enders exhaled and looked at the skylights. "Yeah. It feels like a suicide mission. But yes, we'll go and get it over with. Two sets of parents. Two meals. Endless questions. Probably a lot of warnings and advice I don't want to hear."

"That's the spirit." She leaned in to kiss his unshaven cheek. "Think of it as the gauntlet to the honeymoon."

"An actual gauntlet would be less painful.

Late in the day, he drove to the JJJ office above Sound View. A Model-T touring car was parked haphazardly in front of the small blue building. Enders heard voices as he pulled open the screen door and stepped inside. Two men in summer suits and loose ties sat before Spencer's desk as he signed two documents. He spun the papers around on his desktop and offered his fountain pen to the nearest man.

"Am I interrupting?" Enders took off his hat and plumped down in another chair against the opposite wall.

"Nah. Just signing a couple of sales deeds." Spencer sat back with a satisfied look on his golf-tan face. "Glad you came by. Got something to show you in a minute."

One of the men gave Enders a casual wave and went back to the papers in front of him. The two men finished signing their documents and pushed them across the desk to Spencer. Spencer straightened the thin stack of signed deeds and stood behind his deck. He stretched out his hand to the men and said, "Congratulations."

They shook hands and Spencer turned to Enders, who was slouched comfortably in his chair. "Dave Enders, meet two new property owners at Point O' Woods and White Sand. John and Paul O'Conner."

Enders crossed the room in a single step to shake their hands. One of them—he wasn't sure which man was which—said, "We're brothers. From Wethersfield and Rocky Hill. We own a couple of paint stores up that way."

"Well, I didn't think you were married." Everyone chuckled. "So, a cottage at each beach. Are we building…?"

"Yeah. Dave here, he's the building foreman at White Sand. He'll get your place up and running soon as possible."

One of the brothers said, "We're close…" He glanced at his smiling brother and said, "…but we don't wanna be too close. Two families, two cottages, two beaches." The other brother said, "You guys build. We'll do the touchup. We got a couple of *Eye-talian* boys to do the painting and staining. That's not a problem with the deed restrictions. Right?"

Spencer shook his head. "No problem."

"That's why we like these restrictive clubs. Okay to bring in the help; you just don't want them living next door. Down here, these summer homes, I don't have to worry about my daughter or some future grandkid selling the place to a tribe of Hebs. Or worse." He smiled at everyone.

Spencer nodded. "You're locked in. The beach associations have the final say on future rentals and sales."

"The other brother said, "Righto. Well, I guess we'll drive down from time to time and see how things are progressing."

Spencer stepped around his desk and reached the screen door. He pushed it open. "We're working year-round."

The smiling brothers marched out, and after a moment, Enders heard two car doors snap shut. An engine coughed, then hummed, and the brothers drove off. He turned to Spencer. "Well, they seem…close."

Spencer waved a dismissive hand as he walked back to his chair. "Lace curtain Irish."

Enders took a seat in front of the desk. "I need some more guys for the fall."

"I know. You and POW and Black Point. I'm having 'hire' signs planted in Saybrook, Lyme, and Niantic. Probably get a few farmers after the harvests, too." He reached into his top desk drawer and retrieved several pieces of elongated tinted paper.

"Look at these. Rough edits for new brochures. Fall mailing." He spun the sheets around for Enders to see.

Enders leaned in to examine the same artsy, exaggerated peninsula of Black Point that was mounted on the back wall of the office. Large houses on the oceanfront side, and the cities of Hartford and New London in the truncated distance. His plane—now he was thinking of the drawn biplane as his—hovered in the sky above. The back page of the brochure displayed a series of aerial photographs of the area, including Niantic Bay, and summer homes under construction. He read some of the captions. "There is gold in the Connecticut coast." "Cottages of six and seven rooms with complete bath, fireplace, and electricity can be built for under $3,000. Smaller cottages cost less in proportion to size." "Black Point is built up as a uniformly restricted, carefully planned seashore resort."

Spencer rolled out several other mockups. The White Sand brochure showed off two of the photographs Enders and Debrie had taken from the plane. One caption declared the 187 lots were selling fast. Another advertised summer cottages for $1200 and the "all-year houses" for $2000.

"Looks good, huh? We're working on something similar for Cornfield Point and Point O' Woods. Photos from the plane look great. Show off the whole beachfront at both sites. Good work on your part."

Still staring at the mockups, Enders nodded his head. "I just flew the plane."

"Well, plan to do it again later in the year." He sat back in his chair, his hands folded together across his stomach. "You just drop in, or something on your mind? With you, I almost hate to ask."

He sat back down. "Nothing serious. Just wanted to say I'm getting married sometime this fall…"

Spencer laughed. "That artist girl. Ha. Congrats, kid." He jerked forward in his chair and opened the bottom desk drawer. Enders heard the clinking of glasses. A bottle appeared. Spencer poured two shots of Canadian whiskey. "At least it wasn't another waitress from the Pease House."

He stood and handed a shot glass to Enders. "Cheers." They touched glasses and swallowed the illegal whiskey.

"I still have to ask her parents."

"Once more unto the breach, dear friend…" Spencer sat and opened the desk's middle drawer.

"I don't think the Bard had that kind of battle in mind." He stood watching Spencer write out a company check.

He tore the check loose from its mooring in the accounts book and handed it to Enders. "Here's a little bonus for good work, for the wedding, and for not bothering me too much about all this deed restriction stuff. I want to hear moralizing, I'll go to church."

"Thank you. For the check. And the whiskey."

"Good luck with the parents, flyboy. That's always an unpredictable front."

**\*\*\*\***

If Mr. and Mrs. Bates were an unpredictable front in a campaign to marry, then his own parents had been an entirely predictable battle. He and Karen had arrived on a Saturday afternoon to a nervous Mrs. Meredith Enders, who earlier in the week had thrown herself into a frenzy of cleaning, cooking, and dressing in preparation for meeting Karen. She had been thrilled to hear about their marriage plans. And then she cried openly at the idea of them leaving for France in the spring. For Enders, her reaction—the reaction he expected—had felt like a knife in his chest. He had made one woman happy and one woman sad. It did not feel remotely even.

His father had sat at the head of the table, drumming his fingers on the white linen cloth of the seldom used dining room table. "It's a foolish thing. Running off again to a foreign land with no money. No job. And a wife to boot. But you're gonna do what you want. Always did."

Enders had an image of himself jumping up to shout the Old Man down, then storming out of the house with his bride-to-be in tow. Instead, he smiled and shook his head. "I'm good at what I do…" He turned to look at Karen sitting beside him as he echoed the words of Ella Allard. "…and I've been lucky in life. Things will work themselves out."

"And what is it you do?" his exasperated father asked as he stared at his balled-up hands.

"I build houses. I fly planes. And speaking of building, you want some business advice?" He felt Karen's hand on his forearm.

"From you?"

"No. From an employee of the JJJ company. We just bought the beachfront property at Pond Point. So start cutting joists. Buy a stock of cement and block, and shingles and tarpaper. And plenty of drywall. Get a jump on the competition. At least thirty summer homes can fit in there. You'll have plenty of business supplying the local contractors."

He looked at Karen again and gave her a reassuring smile. He turned back to his father. "Maybe we'll be back in time to help with the building."

**\*\*\*\***

She stood on the train platform, her overnight bag in one hand, Enders' hand in the other. She tilted her head to feel the morning sun on her face. "That went well, don't you think? I mean, your mother is at least happy to help decorate the cottage. And take care of the renters."

He took a deep breath and exhaled. "Yeah. I guess it went as well as it could." He turned to her. "Now, on to the second gauntlet. Your mother. I think your father will be easy, but your mother… She scares me a little."

Karen started laughing. "Don't you have some kind of war medal for bravery?"

"Yeah, but that was easy. Germans with machine guns. I had a chance against them."

He spotted a newsboy at the far end of the platform. "Be right back. I'm going to get the morning paper." He squeezed her hand and walked away.

By the station door, he gave the freckle-faced kid a nickel and folded the paper under his arm. The northbound train rolled in and squealed to a stop. A conductor appeared on the platform, followed by a handful of passengers. Enders started back to Karen. Behind him, someone said, "Excuse me." He turned to find a young woman holding a small boy.

"Excuse me," she said. "Aren't you the soldier…? You were on the train this spring. I told you about my husband…"

He smiled at her. "Yes, I remember." He pointed at the child. "No stroller today?"

"He's walking. Sort of." She let the child slide down her side to the platform where the little boy stood on tentative feet. She stepped closer to Enders. "Thank you. That talking cure. It's helping. He meets with two other men a few times a month. They talk among themselves. About the war, I guess. He's more at ease now. He's sleeping without nightmares."

"Well, I'm glad to hear that."

"Thank you." She stepped closer and stretched to kiss Enders on his cheek. She scooped up the tottering child and looked at Enders again. "Thank you." She turned away and headed for the station door.

He walked back to Karen, who had watched the encounter. "I hope there's a better story there than the one I'm imagining. Pretty woman. Young child. Kissing you."

Enders pulled her close. He looked back as the woman and child disappeared into the station house. "Just the wife of another wounded soldier."

Epilogue

The summer sun found its way through the thick green canopy of the chestnut trees, leaving random spots of light on the smooth cobblestones. Water gurgled from a nearby fountain. A tram bell clanged twice out of the boulevard. Flocks of pigeons attempted to land in the cobblestone shade only to be driven into the air again by gangs of children running between the carousel and the café. A burst of pressurized steam from the espresso machine jarred the pleasure of the moment.

Enders folded the morning edition of *Le Monde* and set it on the glass-topped table. He dropped a pencil back into the battered rucksack at his feet. A waiter in black-and-white appeared at his side and set a tiny cup of coffee and a warm croissant on the tabletop. Enders nodded *Merci* and dropped a cube of brown sugar into the coffee. He stirred the black frothy drink with a toy-size spoon.

Off to his left, he watched three women standing in front of the *Palais du Luxembourg.* They had set up easels and canvases, and from time to time they would stop painting to look at each other's progress. One of them wore a floppy straw hat, a pale cotton kimono adorned with paint splatters, and unpolished black-and-white oxfords. He watched her for so long and so intently a psychic connection must have been established. She turned and he waved to her. She waved her paintbrush at him. *The happiest woman in Paris.*

Enders finished his coffee. He picked up his newspaper again, but a loud voice announcing *Salut* and *Bonjour* to several tables of young women farther back caused him to end his reading. He dropped the paper and waited.

A hand swung another wrought-iron chair to Enders' table, and Brian Lonergan plopped into it. He had a pained smile on his face as he squinted around the park. "It's too early for this much light."

Enders glanced at his wristwatch. "It's ten o'clock. What time did you get back to the apartment?"

Lonergan rubbed his stubbled face with both hands and then brushed his wrinkled pants. "I think the sun was coming up." He saw a waiter glide by. Lonergan raised his hand and shouted, "*Café au lait*." He glanced back at the seated girls behind them. "Cute girls all around this park. From the Sorbonne?"

Lonergan's rendition of the name sounded like "sore bones."

"I'm not looking. I'm married. Remember?"

"Yeah. You know, for a newlywed couple, you're awfully quiet at night. And I appreciate that. Me being a lonely, sex-starved bachelor sleeping—alone—on your sofa."

"I'll be sure to mention that to Karen."

"God, don't you dare. She'll have me on the street in a heartbeat." Lonergan got serious and said, "I hate intruding. This is your honeymoon. More or less. And I appreciate you taking me in. I had visions of knocking on your door here and finding the two of you living in some windowless, one-room flop. With me then begging for a rug on the floor."

The waiter arrived with Lonergan's coffee. Enders ordered another espresso and two more croissants.

Enders laughed at the image. "That might have been the case. But, you know, during my interrogation by Mrs.

Bates last fall, I jokingly told her Paris was very inexpensive, the *hôtel select*, as an example, over on *Place de la Sorbonne,* was only thirty-five cents a day. Well, she was horrified at the idea of her daughter staying in such a cheap place. She must have been thinking Manhattan hotels and prices." He looked Lonergan in the eye and said, "She gave Karen a lot of money before we left. I haven't asked how much."

Lonergan finished his coffee just as the croissants arrived still warm from the oven. "Well, someday I'll have to thank Mrs. Bates for the sofa space. In the meantime, maybe I should register with that hotel."

"It's not as bad as it sounds. But Brian, you may have the place to yourself most of next month. Karen wants to get her application into *Académie Julian* and then head to Giverny to paint. Apparently, Monet worked there. But I might be back and forth, depending on what I hear from *Le Bourget.*"

"The air traffic thing?"

"*Contrôleur de trafic aérien.*" Enders popped a piece of croissant into his mouth. "They started in '19 with a guy in a lawn chair in a field, with two red flags to wave in the planes. Now, with scheduled London flights, it's indoors. With maps, weather charts, timetables, a telegraph, and some fancy radio equipment. They're supposed to call tomorrow. I'd like to be able to contribute a little more cash to this adventure of ours. Ours. Karen and me." He threw a brief smile at Lonergan.

"Gotcha. Well, good luck whenever you hear. Me, I'm gonna clean up and go back and grovel some more at the *Herald* and the *Tribune.*" Lonergan squinted at the *Grand Bassin*. "Think you'll have a job when you go back to the States?"

"Yeah. It's gonna take years to fill all those cottage lots." Enders brushed crumbs from his fingertips and stared for a moment at his empty expresso cup. "How's that freelance stuff you were so excited about the other day?"

Lonergan brightened and sat up. "Great. As I said, I thought I was cursed, being on that tramp steamer over here. But it was full of deportees. Undesirable aliens and labor agitators with funny names. You always read about people coming through Ellis Island to start over in America. Now Ellis is a prison for the people the government doesn't want. They're deported *from* Ellis. Kind of ironic. I got some great material talking to them. How they reacted to deportation. Where they're going now. Plans for getting back to the U.S. again."

"Heartwarming stories, no doubt."

"Stories that should be told. I've got some other ideas too." Lonergan began pulling apart his croissant with his fingertips. "I read in the *Trib* there are race riots in Germany between the local Krauts and the French colonial troops. That could be good material, too. I could write something comparing the situation to Negro Union soldiers in the Civil War. Did we have colored troops during Reconstruction? You know, in the South?"

Enders tipped back in the café chair to watch Karen and her two colleagues. "No idea."

Almost to himself, Lonergan said, "Wonder how I can find out?" He looked at Enders again. "Hey, you're getting back in the flying game. How 'bout we get a plane, and you fly me to the Rhineland someday for a little on-the-spot reporting? German riots. West African soldiers. Interracial dating. And maybe some stories on efforts to find still-missing soldiers?"

Enders hooted at the idea. "Are you nuts? You want me to fly you into an almost-war zone. We'd be lucky not being shot at by the Huns. They still have guns, bub."

"Sore losers," said Lonergan.

"I have a lovely young wife I want to spend time with. Day and night. Especially night."

He turned a serious face to his friend. "You know, I came here years ago as a wide-eyed boy looking for adventure. Feeling Tom Swift-like in a fancy French flying machine, but—I'll admit—not as clever as Tom. I wound up in a gigantic war that eventually turned me into a wreck. What the British docs call a 'nervous pilot.' I was resuscitated—or maybe resurrected is a better word—by a chance encounter with an angel disguised as a doctor. She sent home a whole man. And just in time to meet the woman I really needed and wanted. Now I'm back here. Full circle. I feel a bit like that wide-eyed boy again. Largely because of that angel over there disguised as a painter from Miss Porter's." Enders nodded his head toward Karen across the park.

"As I said at Bobby's, 'from small things…'" Lonergan leaned back and looked at his friend. "So that's your long-winded way of saying no Rhineland recon?"

"I'm grounded."

Lonergan licked his fingertips. "Isn't that what you told your mother last year?"

# Books and Sources

Barker, P. (1991). *Regeneration.* Penguin Group (USA) LLC.

Burton, K. (2003). *Images of America. Old Lyme, Lyme and Hadlyme.* Arcadia Publishing.

Clark, N.A. (2006). *Poverty Island.* Old Lyme Historical Society, Inc.

Ely, S.H. and Plimpton, E.B. (1991). *The Lieutenant River.* Old Lyme Historical Society, Inc.

Griswold, W. (2014). *Griswold Point.* The History Press.

Hamilton-Paterson, J. (2016). *Marked for Death: The First War in the Air.* Pegasus Books.

Heming, A. (2022). *Miss Florence and the Artists of Old Lyme.* Old Lyme Historical Society, Inc.

Hochschild, A. (2022). *American Midnight.* Mariner Books, N.Y.

Kahrl, A.W. (2018). *Free the Beaches: The Story of Ned Coll and the Battle for America's Most Exclusive Shoreline.* Yale University Press.

Krause, L.B. (1976). "Residential Associations in the Coastal Area." Connecticut Department of Environmental Protection, Coastal Area Management Program.

https://www.govinfo.gov/content/pkg/ CZIC-kfc4058-k73-1976/html/CZIC-kfc4058-k73-1976.htm

Kyvig, D.E. (2204). *Daily Life in the United States, 1920-1940.* Ivan R. Dee (Chicago).

Lampos, J. and Pearson, M. (2021). *Rum Runners, Governors, Beachcombers & Socialists.* Old Lyme Historical Society, Inc.

Lee, A.G. (1968). *No Parachute.* Jarrolds Publishers (London) Ltd.

Lewis, C. (1936). *Sagittarius Rising*. Penguin Group (USA) LLC.

Maynard B.J. and Levy T. (2010). *Postcard History Series: Old Saybrook*. Arcadia Publishing.

Miller, N. (2003). *New World Coming*. Da Capo Press.

Sargent, D.C. (1972). *Hatchetts Point*. [S.l. : s.n.]

Wakeman, C. (2011). *The Charm of the Place*. Old Lyme Historical Society, Inc.

Weatherly, M. (2005). *Living in 1920s America*. Greenhaven Press.

## A word about the author...

Edward McSweegan is a writer in Rhode Island.

~*~

*The Cottage Industry* is a work of fiction. All incidents and dialogue and all characters are products of the author's imagination and are not to be construed as real. Where any historical persons or institutions may appear, the situations, incidents, and dialogue concerning those persons and institutions are entirely fictional and are not intended to depict actual events or to change the fictional nature of the work. In all other respects, any resemblance to persons living or dead is entirely coincidental. Quoted language regarding owner restrictions and related matters was taken from property deeds, many of which are available in the archives of the Old Lyme Town Hall. Every effort has been made to contact all copyright holders. The publishers will be pleased to amend in future editions any errors or omissions brought to their attention.